CITY OF ORANGE

ALSO BY DAVID YOON

Version Zero

YOUNG ADULT

Frankly in Love
Super Fake Love Song

CITY OF ORANGE

DAVID YOON

G. P. PUTNAM'S SONS
NEW YORK

PUTNAM
— EST. 1838 —

G. P. Putnam's Sons
Publishers Since 1838
An imprint of Penguin Random House LLC
penguinrandomhouse.com

Hardcover ISBN: 9780593422168
Ebook ISBN: 9780593422175
International edition ISBN: 9780593542071

Printed in the United States of America
1st Printing

Interior art: Flock of crows © Gwoeii/Shutterstock.com

BOOK DESIGN BY KRISTIN DEL ROSARIO

To Nicola,
for making me sit the hell down and write

And you could have it all, my empire of dirt.

—TRENT REZNOR

CONTENTS

CITY OF ORANGE

CALIFORNIA, AD 2010

PART I

THE
SURVIVOR

ONE

HE AWAKES WITH HIS EYES CLOSED.

He senses light all around him and is reluctant to expose his sight to the brightness. His head pulses with pain. He lies on his back, half-sunken in the earth. The back of his head feels crushed. It can be slowly leaking blood for all he knows, hot and thick like dark oil sinking into the sand.

Sand. This is sand, he thinks. He makes a fist with his right hand, idly plays with it. Warm and fine. Glue it to card stock and you get sandpaper. Fire it up and you get glass. Mix it with limestone and you can sculpt buildings and bridges out of it.

You can build a whole civilization.

His eyes slit open to a blinding sun. It takes a second for him to comprehend. There's a blue sky, a white sun in it. There's a concrete wall floating above him, enormous and massive and silent.

Wait. Not a wall. He grits his teeth, lifts his head an inch. The pain changes shape in that moment. His head drips with it. His eyes steady.

It's some kind of bridge. Concrete, bleached white in the sun, spanning a wide trench carved from the same colorless material. An inverted trapezoidal channel. River? Riverbed? Lying asleep in a bed, but a river?

Oh please let his head not be bleeding. He settles it back down again into its divot, as if sand can stop the flow.

He sweeps his right hand back and forth. Now with the left hand. This is called something. Except in snow. Snow angels? When he was little, he and a bunch of other kids had swept out angels in frosty winter mountains somewhere. He remembered he had to go super bad, but he was so fascinated by the snow that he'd held it, not like the others who tried to write their names in steaming yellow. It'd been a field trip for city children unfamiliar with cold weather. Junior high school, holy shit. What letter did the name of the school start with?

A? B? C? D?

Elemeno-pee?

And his name? This particular individual lying here in the sand. Maybe dying here in the sand.

He tests the dead batteries of his memory. He can remember a few fundamentals without much effort: These are called fingers, this is sand, this is his head. This is Earth, he is male, he lives in a place called California, USA, planet Earth, the Milky Way, the Universe, da dada dada. But anything beyond those basic facts remains out of view.

That's the sun up there.

There is the sky.

Here is a blank river of concrete a hundred meters wide.

Nothing else.

TWO

WHEN HE DOES STAND, IT'S LIKE HOISTING A CORPSE WITH PUPPET strings.

First he props up his torso with his elbows. Then he pushes off the sand. That alone is an excruciating project. Next his legs, folding up, then his arms extending so that he can now sit upright. Another moment, eyes squeezed shut with pain, before rising to a full standing position.

His mind is a flickering television screen, a storm of digital static occasionally breaking to reveal things he can't see coming. He wishes he could turn it off. He touches the back of his head. Why am I touching the back of my head? he wonders. To find a power button?

No, to check for signs of trauma. Someone taught him this once, called it *survival first aid*. Hit your head, run through the steps, find out if you are a survivor. First: is there blood?

With dread, he notices his hair feels wet.

He doesn't want to look at his hand.

So he observes his surroundings instead. *Ob-zurvz. Sir-roundings.* This is a good test, like a startup sequence. He tries recalling larger words, and more blip into existence.

Embankment. Aqueduct. Desertification.

The concrete channel looks as if it's been scrubbed white by an epoch of sandstorms.

He brings his hand to his eyes finally. Sweat, not blood. This gives him a slight burst of energy, enough to move on to the next steps. He touches his eyes—neither bulging nor sunken—and prods his skull. Takes a big breath in through the nose, whistles it back out. Hinges his jaw open and shut.

He seems fine. That's a funny word for this situation, *fine*.

He turns his head ninety degrees left, then back right. Nothing snaps, his spinal cord doesn't twist itself apart. *Fine.*

So what is this?

The channel has a twenty-foot-wide groove carved into its center, about a foot deep, evenly filled with sand. It's in this sand he lay. Footsteps lead away from the indentation of his body and vanish where they reach the clean concrete. Probably belong to the people who killed him. Tried to kill him, anyway. Came goddamn close enough.

Annihilation. Desolation. Apocalypse.

Only a few colors here, like the gods had to make do with just five crayons. The powdery blue of the sky. White everywhere. Rectangles and triangles of warm gray, and a thin burnt edge of hard scrub above. He'll have to go see what was up there at some point. But not now. Not now, no way. One thing at a time was hard enough.

He instead shuffles into the blue darkness under the bridge, and makes his way toward the inclined edge of the riverbank.

His hand cools as soon as it touches the shade, instantly turning his life's goal into getting the rest of his body within it. He reaches the edge and lies down again with his toes pointing downhill. Something about raising the head, to keep it above his beating heart. *Elevation.*

His name is Aaron. Alan. No, none of those. Starts with an A. Amazon. Asshole?

He used to live somewhere. Used to work at someplace, doing something.

Super not helpful.

Work is the thing people used to do for money. Money is the stuff you once needed to buy things like shoes. He likes the shoes on his feet, even if the right foot's a little tight. He can't remember buying them. It's like staring down at someone else's sneakers.

He touches his hair. Straight. He plucks a strand and sees it is black, a dark line in this pale new world. Be interesting to see what his face looks like.

In any case, he is undeniably alive, even if the world isn't anymore.

What caused the collapse again?

He can't recall any details. All he knows is that every last bit of it—societies and schools and money—has been done with. Wiped away, like his memory.

He imagines vandals roaming the silenced cities full of broken glass, car doors left hanging open. But no bodies. A very strange, very clean apocalypse. Only simple violence is left, scattered muggings and assault, a smaller version of the mass atrocities humanity used to commit.

Everyone's gone somewhere else now, to do something someplace.

He knows life is fragile and ends without ceremony. The gazelle watches her calf get torn apart by the lions as she flees with the rest of the herd. What thoughts run through her head at such a moment? *Why, God, must you take my only son?*

Maybe gazelles aren't that eloquent. Maybe they spend their days too perplexed to even make it beyond your basic *What?*

Maybe, at a certain level, *What?* is as good as it gets for humans, too, especially these days. *What?* probably ranks as the number one most popular thought among all people left everywhere.

It's what he's thinking right now, anyway.

The mass vanishing of humanity must've been something else. Something spectacular, humankind's greatest and most lasting achievement.

He'd heard a theory once. As a last resort, humanity could've migrated en masse into space if the world got too polluted. Maybe that's what happened. He and a few other unfortunates had been left behind, unable to afford fare. The sudden vacuum left by a departing civilization turned money and authority into empty symbols, and then turned ordinary people into thieves.

Money, the stuff you bought shoes with. He'd never had enough of it.

He laughs a little at this, then sits amazed at himself for doing so.

He'll never really know what happened in the end. Why should he? Does the gazelle? His eyes close again. The throbbing in his head grows.

Shouldn't sleep exposed like this. Above him the incline meets the bottom edge of the bridge to form a crawl space flanked at regular intervals by supporting columns. A dark wedge. Dying there would be better. It'd be quiet. At least a little more dignified.

He rolls over and the pain rolls, too, lighting up his skull, then his shoulder blade, then his hip. He took some kind of hit. Hits. Did he at least put up a fight? He checks his eyes again, his jaw, his bones, nothing broken, no signs of—what's the word—*con-cuss-shun*. He can manage crawling on all fours, which he does with a decent cadence. The dark wedge grows closer.

The crawl space is larger than he expected, tall enough to sit upright in, and contains nothing. Just blankness. Support columns form two walls to either side, the featureless underside of the bridge above him, replacing the sky. A monolithic support wall before him. The slope leading down to the cool rivers of sand at the far bottom. Everything clean. A grayscale world.

He'll figure out what happened to the world in good time, if he lives long enough. He'll start with his pants pockets. Left pocket, nothing. Right pocket, candy.

He squints. Not candy—headache medicine, right there in his hands like a little gift. Welcome to your new home!

He laughs at this, too.

THREE

HE TRIES UNSCREWING THE LID OF THE TUBE, WHICH IS WRAPPED IN plastic.

FOR YOUR PROTECTION

He finds the twin perforations running down its side, tears off a fluttering strip, and in his mind flashes the image of a bathroom sink somewhere.

He removes the plastic and turns the lid to no avail. *Tic tic tic.*

Right. There's a trick to this.

He pushes down with an open palm and twists again. Off pops the lid. Once again he sees the bathroom sink for a moment, just long enough to see its two faucets, one for hot, one for cold, both feeding one central tube pointed down toward a small drain set into the porcelain. He used to begin by unscrewing the cold dial. Knob. Then he would gradually introduce hot water to the right temperature by unscrewing the other tap.

That's the *how* of warm water. He recalls, without even trying to recall, that above the taps lived a family of cartoon animals stuck to the tile, each holding toothbrushes. One, two, three. Three toothbrushes. He knows they had names, but he doesn't care to think about that right now. What does it matter? For now, all he knows is he used to love this silly trio so much, especially the one that was littler than his or hers.

One, two, three.

Him, wife, child.

Stop.

He finds himself standing before a colossal shelf of ice suspended off a cliff's edge, filled with faces and objects and moments all held frozen within. The slightest movement could start an avalanche.

He'd had a family. Something bad had happened in the world. To them, too?

Must've.

Why else was he here, alone? Every single member of the surviving human race must have experienced similar loss, on a million personal levels adding up to a global horror. Now here he is, all the time in the world, hour upon hour to ruminate upon the unfair hand of the universe. The pain festering in his heart until it drives him to madness.

Unless.

What if they aren't dead? What if his last words to them were *I'll be right back with supplies?* and they're still somewhere waiting?

No way they survived. Why else would he be here and not with them?

Didn't he just ask that question already?

Best not to go down this path right now.

This path is a big circle leading to crazytown and back.

At some point, though, he'll eventually have to crawl up and out of this channel and see what there is to see.

And get sniped in the head, sure. His final dumb thought: *What?*

He shakes his head once, hard. He regards the tube of pills as if it's an evil talisman, a thing that could draw out memories by touch. EXTREME STRENGTH, reads the label, and right away he can see it on the shelf next to dozens of other medicines in a pharmacy bathed in fluorescent light. He looks away to shut out the awful familiar vision.

Don't despair. There's no point. They have to be dead. Hopefully just that and not something worse.

But he can always imagine something worse, can't he?

The pills are the color of new chalk, each stamped with P12 in tiny letters. These letters don't trigger any recollections, but they do provide a vague sense of legitimacy. So he swallows two pills dry, pours the rest of the pills into his pocket, and lets the tube roll down the bank where it—and all of its markings—falls out of his sight. His mind grows blank, and it's the blankness that provides him focus. The past only becomes the past when you turn your back and keep it turned. And that's what he knows he should do.

His head still throbs with pain, but pain he can respect. It at least keeps him distracted from remembering things—an unintended, if brutal, gift from the vandals. Maybe they'd even left the headache pills on purpose as a kind of troll move. So that he'll survive long enough to die an even slower death of starvation and struggle.

Sheer vanity right there, that kind of conspiracy thinking.

He remembers neutron bombs. In theory, they can destroy humans without damaging property. A white flash atomizing people into little puffs of oily mist. A simple wipe-down, and you're ready to resell. He chuckles again.

Whoever the hell I am, he thinks, I am one cynical motherhumper.

Humanity had to end at some point. It was inevitable given our natures, and given the way of nature in general. Certain motherhumpers even more cynical than him had probably even looked forward to it. Hoarders of gold bars and guns, preppers building underground bunkers full of canned food.

Humanity's just two groups now: predators and prey, with the weak being left to die out in the sun. Just like me! he thinks.

He laughs again, even though it hurts.

But I'm *not* dead, he thinks. I'm here. Is that a good thing, or a bad thing?

The attackers had left no clues about that.

Or about what happened with his family, or where they might be.

Stop with all that.

He used to know this dude. Someone important, a friend. Brian? Bacon? Waving a cigarette too close to his drink with a flapping manner. Liked to wear fatigues all day, everywhere, like he was about to go on patrol.

Get ready for when the big shit hits the great ceiling fan in the sky and everything comes raining stink-ass down, this friend would say. Hell with money, it's barter and trade at that point. Like instant. That's why you keep gold stashed in your undies at all times. The guy you used to be won't matter for shit. Instant, like I said. You sure you don't smoke anymore?

He understood his friend's outrageous fantasy. Clean slate, no more bullshit, live off the land, trade goats for leather and blablabla. The past? What past? The future? Shut your face hole. Living in present tense, like when we were little kids—but now in adult bodies that could fight and screw and venture and look the world right in the eye.

A glass of water would be wonderful, he suddenly thinks. There's my first real goal. A nice glass of water.

This all can't have been from zombies. That is stupid. Same with traveling packs of warriors in improvised battle cars speeding across a salt flat.

Because that's from an *old movie*. Which one? He jogs his head, but his memory offers nothing now.

He struggles to work out the *how* of apocalypse. Was it genocide, finally reaching the suburbs in a uniquely American take on ethnic cleansing? Cannibalism? Depends on how much time has passed between the collapse and the blow to the back of his head, and if people really tasted like pork like he'd read. How long, he wonders with growing amazement, has he been living on the run, foraging, scanning the horizon for threats, kicking dirt over his scat, squatting in abandoned houses, before today? Has he been unable to return to home? Is there a home left to return to?

With that, he now finds himself remembering the late-night conversations.

Conversations with *her*.

She liked to talk about God and armageddon and death and life and whatever else. Lying on a hardwood floor, the coolest part of the old dormitory in summertime, a cheapy-cheap plastic oscillating fan keeping hypnotic time. They had just met and were cramming for finals. He for history and she for biology. It was so early on that they had no idea that they were now in a real friendship, let alone the start of something bigger.

What if the story of the Bible wasn't just a story, she said, but turned out to be true?

Like some kind of user manual, he chuffed.

One day Judgment Day comes, she said. And everyone's like, oh crap, I should've at least skipped to the end of that book!

I couldn't make it past all the begats, he said.

Would you satisfy the applicant requirements?

Applicant requirements, he said.

I'm saying would God beam you up, she said.

She had a habit of using books as pillows, and slid one under her braids now. For some reason he is allowed to remember the braids she had back then. But his mind won't allow him to see her face in any detail. It is like many generic faces in one, and therefore no face at all. And that is strangely okay by him.

I'm asking you if you believe in God, she had said that hot, still night.

Not very much, he said. But I do think there's something out there. It can't be nothing.

I think it's very much the opposite, she said. God is everything. It's bigger and way more complex than mister generic White dude with white hair wearing fuggin' white pontificals. We're way too small to begin to comprehend what the term *god* even signifies.

My God, that way she used to talk. Like a string of inevitabilities clicking into neat rows.

Sugar is probably diamonds to ants, he said. Rainbows are invisible to dogs.

Speaking of invisible! she said, and flopped a book down onto his face. I just finished this. It's a crazy story about a German woman who's trapped in a forest because one day a transparent wall force-field thing appears all around her. Every animal and person outside the wall is frozen solid forever. She tries to escape, can't, and spends months teaching herself how to take care of a small farm with a cow and dog and other animals.

Rugged American individualism, he said.

Aha, except it's German fatalism, she said. Or something. The wall never gets explained, there's no real conclusion, just this one weird violent event and then the end.

Like a murder?

I think it's about accepting the actual really real reality of your situation, whether you like it or not, she said, ignoring his question because, he would later learn, her mind could run on an express rail.

I guarantee you'll hate it at first, she said. But then you'll love it.

Then I guess I'll love it, he said.

The entirety of this conversation flashes in his mind over nine brilliant seconds as he lies on the concrete with his eyelids closed, letting the headache pills do their work.

He borrowed that German book from her, read it in a single sitting, pausing here and there to admire her light perfect underlining. As perplexing as the story was—the main character seemed remarkably okay with forgetting about her missing friends and family—there was a selfish, indulgent allure to wallowing alone without any accountability to anyone. It was a portrait of a strange alternate reality that slowly became the main reality.

He never once imagined what he would do if that story turned out to be true.

FOUR

DUSK. THE THROBBING IN HIS HEAD HAS CALMED A LITTLE. GOOD. HE takes more pills, dry.

She'd taken him to the store where she found that book about the German woman and her invisible wall. It was a used bookstore specializing in science fiction. *Speculative fiction*, as she called it.

A fancy way of saying *I wonder what'll happen in the future*, he said.

She chuckled at that, and led him deeper into the musty den of books by running an unpainted fingernail along the bowed spines. She chewed her nails, he noticed.

Outside the bookstore the early-morning fog had muffled the streets into silence but for the quiet chatter of patrons meeting fireside at an outdoor café. What would later become their café, he knew. A string of white lights, coffee cups, a creamer jug sitting in ice.

He watches as each detail chains itself to the next to form a fast-growing lattice of unbidden memories. He wants to see more but at the same time does not want to see more. He knows why he can picture the face of his friend, but never that of her. Because memories of her—and of his child—will lead only to pain. He even knows what this whole situation is called, *dysmorphic amnesia* or *disinterested amnesia* or some such, and he knows in a way it's been protecting him for who knows how long until now.

But now he's *remembering*, and he'd rather not.

So he flings open his eyes—when did he close them?—to make everything go away.

He emerges from the crawl space to a purple sky already glinting with stars. No more light pollution pushing back against the empty black of the universe.

Is there an invisible wall? Is there not?

Is there, in other words, a chance his girls are alive somewhere? Do they even want to see him? Or has he made some big mistake that exiled him here?

A shooting star scratches out a brief white line high above, promising him nothing.

He heard that human beings can survive without food for a while. A week? Two weeks? Maybe. Food isn't the problem. Water's a different story, though. He can drink his own pee, but that is disgusting with the added bonus of being unsustainable. How many times can the same hot little volume of liquid cycle through his alimentary canal over and over again?

Anyway. Another day or so without water, he might not wake up from his next nap.

Not a totally terrible way to go. They used to say things like *He died peacefully in his sleep*, didn't they?

Night is falling fast. In the growing darkness he risks a few steps up the concrete slope. He feels an irritating rock in his right shoe but doesn't dare stop to shake it out. He peeks above the top of the channel for a moment before ducking back down.

He had seen the tops of shrubs. He pops up again for another look. To his right stands a wire fence, and beyond it a charred landscape marked by empty roads. Driveways leading to nothing. No houses, no signs of life.

To his left, the wide concrete river channel terminates into a trio of mountainside drains; to his right it stretches past another bridge, identical to the first, equally massive in scale, and then out of sight, a vast arc cutting across the desert basin and surrounded by hills. Across it he can see a high, infinitely long cinder-block wall and the tiled peaks of houses. A streetlamp glows orange. Most likely solar. It will glow for years unattended until its battery expires and leaves this ruined housing tract in permanent darkness.

Sudden movement by the streetlamp. He cowers by the bridge's edge to peer in the dark. It's a sagging vinyl banner sign, bleached blue with age and shifting in the torpid air. He can make out the words:

COME TO FABULOUS
Resort-style Living • New Homes
Arroyo Plato Villa Estates

Faded photos of a couple toasting, a family on bicycles, seniors frozen in a noble yoga pose. Deck chairs on the goddamn *Titanic*, he thinks. You drank in moderation? Doesn't matter, 'cause you're dead. You stayed flexible in your old age? You're stiff as jerky now, grandpa.

You turkey jerkies are all way past dead!

He wants to howl with laughter, just to hear himself, but has to look away quick because he can feel things dislodging in his mind, threatening to avalanche.

He retreats back to his crawl space and lies down. For hours he listens, waiting.

Then he has a series of dreams.

Mushroom clouds blossom, strobing the sky before casting a cloud ring of destruction.

A plague rages across the world, propelled by conspiracy theories. Armed survivors withdraw into enclaves, where new macabre nursery rhymes are sung.

Aliens arrive and systematically harvest our bodies for cheap energy.

And so on.

And oh—here are those improvised war cars again, streaking toward each other across an endless salt flat.

But now the cars become just normal cars, and now they idle on a wet highway clogged with traffic. The salt flat darkens in color and sprouts a vast field of gray city skyscrapers. The world is full and alive again. Man, no one has any idea yet. Even as the cars collide with a glittering pop, no one really believes they're swiftly approaching their end. All they can think is Holy crap, I'm in a crash, just hold on and get through it.

FIVE

HE MUST HAVE SLID SOMETIME IN THE NIGHT; HIS CLOTHES ARE HIKED up around him. It's chilly and he had left his ankles exposed. He sits up with effort and resets his sleeves and pant legs with slow, pained movements. These could be the last gestures my body performs, he thinks. Giving myself a slo-mo wedgie.

He hugs himself tight to warm up. I smell bad, he thinks.

Once, long ago, in a museum on a school field trip he saw an ancient human jaw. It was chocolate brown and marked with a specimen number by the archaeologists who had unearthed it. THIS JAW, read the plaque, IS AMONG THE OLDEST EVIDENCE OF HUMAN EXISTENCE FROM THOUSANDS OF YEARS AGO. Humans lived in the something region during the whatever period, hunted and gathered in the nude, didn't live very long. They hadn't figured out how to forge metal or order pizza through an app. In the geologic time frame of things, they'd just only yesterday figured out how to stand fully upright.

He'd wondered: What obvious mysteries have we modern humans not figured out yet? How to fly?

How to stop abusing one another?

THIS PROTO-MAN, the plaque concluded, MOST LIKELY DIED FROM AN EXCRUCIATING TOOTHACHE CAUSED BY A CAVITY. A moment of death millennia ago, all the way to a line of present-day middle schoolers gawking before a glass case, separated by a final thought: *This dang tooth is killing me.*

Details like toothaches, he realized, were crucial.

Back in the shelter, he notices he has three pills remaining. He takes one.

He had no dreams last night, which is a relief. There are things, really bad things, that happened before he arrived in this place. Stuff he'd really rather not know about. In fact, it'd be easier just to stop moving altogether and sleep and never wake up. Bring this stretch of consciousness to an end like so many have done before him. If he gets impatient he can even throw himself off the bridge. (She always said he could be impatient.) But with his luck he'd hit the ground just right—meaning just wrong—and instead of dying he'd wind up with a broken leg or be paralyzed. Then he'd have both time *and* pain.

Which would be a problem. The body doesn't give up without a fight. His head still throbs and whines, less now from the injury and more from thirst. His lips peel off little paper feathers. His tongue leather, his throat a sticky tube that closes whenever he tries to swallow. He imagines the headache pill simply trapped inside it, pointlessly massaged back and forth by peristalsis. No moisture left even to dissolve it.

Death, he concludes, would probably really hurt. Surviving would hurt less.

You win, God, he thinks. Your stupid armageddon turned out to be real. Happy? Can I have a glass of water now?

Water's all around you, says God. Go get it.

He laughs and curses and cries in rapid succession. This is bad. Hearing voices is bad. He needs some kind of plan, however basic.

First, regain strength. (How?) Find a house somewhere, raid it for supplies, then travel onward. (To where?) Encounter others, talk his way into their trust over weeks of mutual suspicion. (Sure.) Or they're cannibals, and he'd spend his last moments being mauled in a spectacular frenzy. (What?) Or just die without a word in the desert, alone. (Most likely.)

This dang tooth is killing me.

Normal people have an instinct to survive, don't they? They make plans.

So why doesn't he? Is he not a normal person?

Or: does he secretly know there's nothing left anywhere worth surviving for?

He doesn't have the stomach for any of this. He doesn't know what he wants. A spicy Italian sandwich would be nice. He remembers those: long, wrapped in checkered paper. Beyond a spicy Italian sandwich, his mind has no way of knowing where to go next or what to do once he gets there. How can he want anything when he doesn't even know what there is left to want?

He wants to pee.

He rises, unzips, and casts toward the bottom of the channel a stream warm enough to steam.

I refuse to drink my own goddamn pee, he thinks bitterly.

The pee won't stay long, now that the sun is rising in preparation for another inferno of a day. What kind of god forces a man dying of thirst to expel the little liquid remaining in his body?

He keeps an eye out. The embankment runs rail straight in either direction, smooth and white, interrupted only by the second bridge. No one around. No clues about territorial claims or ragtag alliances. It'd almost be a relief to see a flag of any color, flying from a tall pike of skulls rammed into the ground.

Maybe not the skulls.

He realizes he can't recall what year it is. How could he forget the year?

Maybe he'd time-traveled?

Speculative fiction.

He blinks. The day's becoming brighter and sharper. He reaches out from beneath the shade into the sunlight. Becoming warmer, too.

He looks closer now at the white slope beneath him. Small pipes jut out at certain points, marked by faint deltas of rust stains beneath their mouths. Soil drainage, he guesses. Maybe this whole basin was once a fertile crescent.

The only way he can find out anything is by traveling beyond the safe perimeter. The vandals could be waiting for him, crude scopes trained on the upper banks in a contest to see who could score the first puff of pink mist. He can just see them now. Bored, grimy boys leaning on their guns like oarsmen waiting for their heat. Boys hungry for sport.

He decides to stay low.

There's a small black thing the size of a crate for carrying that white stuff. Whatever you put in tea. Milk. He pictures a cup of warm tan liquid and the creamy nebula blooming from its center. A small flecked earthenware cup of tea sitting quietly on a kitchen table with rain pattering on glass somewhere. The memory throws him into a rage for an instant. You had to ruin cups of tea, even? What kind of bootleg god does that?

He digs his fingernails into a fist and the teacup flickers away.

The small black thing was a little cage. Inside it was a pipe, pointing up and out like a faucet.

A faucet?

He's on his feet and running. A stupid decision—within a few strides his legs crumple and he goes crashing down onto the uneven slope. Blood trickles from his nose. More precious moisture lost. He rises, panting hard, and steadies his step, like a determined drunk. He makes sure to keep his head ducked below the top of the channel and out of sight.

My name is Aorta, Anchor, Apple, I am somewhere between twenty and fifty years old, background ancestry from Asia, he thinks, although I do not speak Asian. I speak English. Pretty sure I do.

Water, he rattles in English, like a curse.

Stupid again! Advertising his presence like this. Although what's left for them to take? Clothes, a few pills, the meat on his bones?

The cage box is not a box, really, but a kind of little fence without a top designed to protect the faucet inside. He falls upon it at once, fumbling.

It's got no spin handle thing. No tap. Instead, it has a small square bolt inset into the pipe. He'll need a special tool to turn it. The head of the bolt has a small hole drilled into it, a circle within a square. It reminds him of something: dice, snake eyes.

He pinches the square, crazed now. Twisting, contorting. He jams a finger up into the faucet. First his index—too big—then his pinky. He feels wetness. He licks his fingertip and feels his tongue pucker the moment it makes contact with the metallic water.

A bonanza of water, just a few inches down the neck of this pipe, blocked by this nonstandard divine brainteaser faucet. *Here's that water you wanted*, says God. *Go get it.*

You want me to go get it? he mutters. Let's go get it.

He stutter-steps his way down the slope and strides to the middle of the channel to examine this grand puzzle better. Back toward the crawl space, he spies a dry cluster of flotsam nestled at the foot of the support monolith, on the other side.

He stumbles toward it for a few steps before realizing, jackass, you're walking in the sandy center groove, depleting your near-dead body of its energy reserves with each step. You do not want to be feeling the burn right now.

He moves onto the flanking concrete and shuffles easier there.

Little bitch-ass God, he thinks. I got this.

It's a nice big pile of debris. Large, crumbling foam floats, like a string of beads discarded by a desert giant. Plastic orange webbing. Something that looks like a bucket.

He's striding now. Good shoes. Red. I like these shoes. Shoes made of money you had to work to acquire, he never had enough money, he reaches the flotsam pile, he dances around it.

Where to begin?

First, a large metal bucket labeled PACIFIC RESTAURANT SUPPLY. The handle is still good, the interior unblemished.

He heaves the floats aside and hears clanking within: metal, plastic. Promising sounds. There's a length of corrugated hose, two glass bottles, small round lids. A useless lantern battery with corrosion frothing out one side. A nest of metal wire. A shattered bicycle lamp, a clear plastic to-go cup, its lid and straw miraculously intact, decorated with a repeating band of palm trees.

There is the seat portion of a chair wrapped in green naugahyde. The plywood underside reads MADE IN CHINA. He remembers that. Everything used to be made in China. And everyone used to joke about it, until they realized it was a national liability, until they realized none of that mattered anymore, and never would again.

His friend, the one who waved cigarettes around, he loved this topic of Made in China.

We don't make *real*-shit with our two bare hands no more, man, he would say. We make abstract *bull*-shit with our minds. Bullshit is nothing but fiat currency. We abandoned the real world of things a long time ago.

In the cool shade he set aside the green naugahyde chair and thought, Well, best friend of mine, welcome back to the world of things.

Then he spots something. Awestruck, he reaches for the object, brings it before his eyes. It is a wine opener. It has a corkscrew, still shining and unrusted. It has a little serrated jackknife for cutting foil.

Most importantly, it has that folding metal lever that would allow the wine drinker to coax corks out of bottles, if only there were still any wine in the world left to drink. Crucially, the metal lever is folded (by someone in China?) lengthwise into a U-shape for added strength. A square U-shape. One roughly the same size as the square bolt in the faucet head.

He feels like Prometheus holding fire in his hand.

SIX

WHEEZING NOW, HE HUDDLES OVER THE FAUCET TO GAUGE THE SIZE OF the bolt.

He swallows, and again his throat sticks. Thousands of years from now, his preserved skeleton will be on display in a museum suspended by invisible force fields. They'll totally have force fields by then. In his bony hand will rest a *primitive artifact of unclear purpose.*

He flips open the wine tool, inserts it into the faucet head.

It fits perfectly. Fuck me fuck me fuck me, he thinks.

What sort of grip is he supposed to use again? He absolutely cannot bung this up. The tool could break. Then the faucet would stay rusted shut forever. This is the ancient gateway, and he has but the one key.

He folds the tool into an L for better leverage, then remembers to pinch the point of contact hard to create a more stable fulcrum. That's the grip right there.

He pushes the tool counterclockwise. It doesn't move. He gives it a little more pressure. Still nothing.

He's sweating now. Why does he think this will work? Drips of moisture fall off his face onto the white concrete and evaporate almost in an instant. He shouldn't have gotten so worked up over what really was just a pile of trash. All that wasted exertion. Every drop of sweat matters now.

Before he can kick himself again, he hears a crack. Not the tool breaking—the faucet, snapping past whatever seal of rust had frozen it in time. He turns it counterclockwise a few degrees, then more. A bellow sounds from below. Orange water comes sputtering out.

He watches it run. The moment the stream becomes clear and steady he cups a hand and drinks. Cold. He drinks again. Every cell in his body seems to expand. The ache in his head subsides. He feels like one of those toys. Remember? Those little capsules that expanded in water to become dinosaur-shaped sponges. They were a lawsuit just waiting to happen, but the kids loved them.

Little toddlers at a party, splashing around in a shallow turquoise plastic pool on a green and brown lawn under the yellow sun.

Totally one-hundred-percent waterproof diapers, she said with a snort, and squirted the babies to prove it. They squealed with delight. Then the tiny humans returned to their very serious baby business. He used the break in attention to sneak in a kiss.

Stolen moments, she said.

He flings cold water on his face to bring himself back to the present.

He rolls onto his back, marveling at the infinite blue sky and his sudden luck. He feels grateful. There's no god to curse, no grand puzzle by design. That's all nonsense.

His shirt is beautifully soaked. He thinks he's in the clear, but then her voice comes right back unbidden.

Every parent knows the *waterproof* part is just marketing, she said.

Marketing is lying for hire, he said.

But who cares, she said. It's about the perfect dream of never having to think about pee in a pool. Or worse. Isn't it a beautiful dream?

He douses his head again to clear it. The water continues to pour silently over him and onto the slope, and he thinks, I'm sorry, I miss you, but I cannot hear your voice right now. I want so badly to hear it in person, and not in my head. Can I possibly walk to wherever you are?

He pulls off his shoes and socks and washes his feet. They feel better already.

He can do this. Gain strength, head out, find something. Who knows: maybe there's an army base still functioning nearby. He can find it, or something just as good, even if he has to carry that bucket filled with water for miles.

He gazes over at the second bridge in the near distance. There's a small pile of flotsam at its base there, too. Something to investigate later. He follows up the slope to the matching crawl space near the top, and stops.

A blanket hangs there.

He sits up now. He scrambles to put his socks and shoes back on his wet feet.

A gray blanket, hanging like a curtain in a doorway.

The water.

It flows down the slope like a black cape, a dark ink stain against the powdery surface. It's already begun to pool at the flat bottom of the channel.

He hurries to turn off the faucet, taking care to avoid overtightening with the wine opener and therefore dooming himself forever. Then he runs back to his shelter.

Whoever lives behind that blanket, maybe they're out foraging. Maybe the sun will evaporate the water in time and allow him to stay undetected. He peers out from behind his column, watching, willing the water to fade faster.

The tip of the black cape grows lighter, then begins to recede in the sun's heat. He watches, inch after inch, as the stain shrinks. He can barely make out the blanket beyond. It remains still.

An hour passes. The stain is now kidney-shaped, lightening at the edges until it becomes a set of small pools that finally contract into nothing. Only traces of orange rust remain. Hopefully they're faint enough.

He stays frozen like this until dusk, until he can no longer see the blanket in the dying light.

SEVEN

WHEN THE SKY DARKENS TO THE POINT WHERE HE FEELS SURE HE can't be seen, he creeps down the slope to the flotsam pile.

The moon is a brilliant disc in the black sky, bathing everything in its magnesium light. It casts razor-sharp shadows like the sun never could. The channel has become a world of polygons glowing from within, full of leftover heat from the day. He hopes that they will keep him warm all night.

He takes the bucket in one hand, two glass bottles in the other. Halfway back up the slope the bottles clink once. He freezes—*gaddangit*—as the sound hangs in the air. He glares at the blanket. If he's lucky, the shelter behind it is abandoned. But there isn't any such thing as luck anymore, good or bad.

Reading the words PACIFIC RESTAURANT SUPPLY on the bucket sends him into a catatonia for a moment as his consciousness breaks into freefall: Pacific, ocean, restaurant, utensils and plates and platters making their warm clinking music. Her hand holding his, her other hand doodling on the white butcher paper oversheet laid atop the tablecloth under a dim beautiful brass lamp. They called it dueling doodles. He remembered giving his baby a pencil to hold while he held her hand, a pencil inside a tiny hand inside a large hand, three people holding hands now at the table glowing. He showed her how to play the game: first Mama scribbles, then we add to it, then she adds to ours, see, then it's our turn again, and so on, look, now we have—what would you call this, honey—a sassy spectacled sunflower smoking a cigar in the pilot's seat of a starfighter—

He turns the bucket away and makes a mental note always to hold it with the words facing out.

He descends again to grab other usefuls from the debris pile: the to-go cup, the seat cushion, the wire. He'll find each of them a new purpose in this afterworld.

The to-go cup seems clean enough. He takes it and the wine opener and tiptoes his way to the faucet in the dark as quickly as he can.

The blanket remains invisible.

He opens the faucet with ease now. He holds the plastic cup at an angle to prevent any pouring noises and fills it without a sound. Doesn't spill a single drop, *yessss*. Back in his shelter, he rests the wine opener under the foot of the cup to keep it level and prevent it from rolling away in the night. He uses the seat cushion as a pillow.

Time to rest up. You got this. Remember when people used to say that?

You got this.

Turns out we didn't!

He claps a hand over his mouth. Now is no time to laugh, he thinks. But it's funny! he thinks back. And so on.

Sleep feels impossible. He expects a boot to come crashing down onto his face at any moment. The fresh influx of water into his system has made his mind supple and active again, racing with thoughts.

What are our known variables, he thinks. Let's assess.

We have a dependable source of water. That is huge for us. No food, though, which while fine for now will become an increasingly important factor in the next few days. No weapons yet. The few homes up there that had survived the firestorm might be a resource. Or, surprise, they could be an ambush from those depraved animals that left us for dead.

What else do we got, he thinks. Assess.

We finally failed on that catastrophic scale we'd always fantasized about, and now everything is this wasteland. Whatever theories you might have had about why and how don't matter now. Even the most cynical fanatic, down in his bunker for months surrounded by food and weapons and alcohol and porn while the neighbors above whispered their bemusement, even that guy can't possibly feel any sort of smug vindication as the new king of dust. No one can.

Byron!

Byron is his name. Was?

His close-talking, conspiracy theorist coworker friend. His best friend, he remembers now. He bets Byron made it. He's pretty sure Byron was (is?) a bunker type, the kind who would survive.

Not that survival has much point, unless civilization is being rebuilt on a miserable scale at a half-destroyed military base somewhere. The primary goal for now is to find answers. What happened, and why, and how many died.

And then, satisfied with this knowledge, to finally be able to move on to the next great wherever.

EIGHT

THE HUMVEE JACKHAMMERED THE WASH RUTS BUT HELD A STEADY line.

Where the hell are we? he said.

East of Coachella, said Byron. 'Bout ten klicks.

Byron flashed his round sea-glass-green lenses, old-timey things with the leather side shields. He looked like a Vietnam War movie extra in between calls. Half Filipino, half African American, he liked to confuse people by saying he was one thing, then another, then something else altogether, just to watch them squirm.

We could've taken 111, he said to Byron.

Byron cut him a smile. He'd recently quit smoking, so he took a vape hit instead. Which was still just smoking, but my God did arguing with Byron make him tired.

Where's the fun in a freeway? said Byron. Still can't believe you grew up in Cali and never been to the Salton Sea.

The Humvee hit the sudden silence of a concrete bridge, then resumed its rattling on the hard bare earth.

He fluffed his shirt in the heat. This thing's got everything but AC, he said.

Hey, said Byron. I was birthed in this *thing*—

—at Pendleton, he sighed.

—right there, continued Byron. He jabbed a finger at a rear seat. I know we like to joke and everything, but my mother lives on in this vehicle, which I have duly customized beyond its original mil spec!

He grimaced at the thought of baby Byron lying in that back bucket seat in a pool of viscera.

May the mother of Byron rest in peace, he offered.

I'm actually glad she didn't live to see the world turning to shit like it is, said Byron, exhaling a raspberry cloud. Oooh, I think we're near this decommissioned salt evap facility I've been meaning to check out.

Woohoo, he said.

You don't care, said Byron.

I do, he said. Fuck that pink Himalayan shit!

Byron thumped the wheel. It's so funny when you swear. No one swears like you do.

Like what?

Like the bad words are really *bad*. You're dad material. Makes perfect sense, you guys having a baby soon.

Imagine the world glitching, like the sky is actually a celestial computer screen with a loose cable. This is what happens now. He knows it isn't real—that all this is just a dream memory—but right now he can see Byron so clearly, down to every last hair on his patchy goatee.

And yet: He can't remember her face. Even the first letter of her name.

I guess it does make pretty perfect sense, he said.

Byron finally turned them onto a normal road, still far off the main highway but at least onto solid asphalt sprouting young half-foot-tall weeds, and in the distance beckoned beautiful little flashbulb glitters atop the beautiful little wavelets of a beautiful lake.

What are the girls up to? said Byron.

Spa day, wine tasting, he said. So, same as us.

Byron cackled before feigning composure. No, good for them. Sounds fun.

Deep tissue massages, too, he said.

Byron blanched. This road's bumpy like a massage?

Sss, he said with a grin.

They reached the sea, if it could be called that, and hopped out to stretch. It was a fake sea famously formed by accident—a giant stagnant mistake of a puddle the color of soy sauce surrounded by a narrow shore of fish corpses. It stank like it should.

My God, he said.

I'd offer you an N95 but I left 'em all at home like a dumbass, said Byron.

Is an N95 a teleporter that will take us back to the casino?

It's just 'cause I was so friggin' excited! said Byron, dancing to the back of the Humvee. He produced a bag with a special nozzle. He inserted the nozzle into the foul water, pumped a handle, and waited for the bag to fill.

This is a brand-new filtration model! shouted Byron, even though there was no noise to shout over. The holes are so small it can block microscopic-ass viruses!

And to his horror, Byron took a sip from the bag.

Tastes good! Byron cried. Way better than purification tablets. Mm?

Sounds really super tempting.

Byron straightened. Are you making fun of me?

Dude, stop.

I mean are you?

No! he said. I am not making fun of you.

You have a miracle on the way, said Byron. I was thirteen when my mom passed, okay? You wanna be around for your daughter no matter what, and I'm gonna make sure of it.

Okay, I'm sorry, come here, he said.

The two men crunched their shoes into the endless mess of bones and shells for a brisk embrace.

In this dream memory he can see himself in Byron's glasses, and yet: his own face appears as a blank oval. Another glitch.

You have no idea the batshit crazy stuff I've been reading, said Byron. He brightened as quickly as he had soured just a moment earlier. You *do not* wanna know what I know, and because I'm here, you therefore *do not have* to know. Come on, dude! To fatherhood!

Byron held out the bottle like it was a potion bubbling with magic, so he took it—*here goes*—and sniffed the opening. It smelled like nothing.

Byron rubbed his hands together. You could do your own pee and there would be no smell, he said. Purification tablets, on the other hand, by their nature are unable to remove odors.

Are you telling me, he said, that you drank your own pee before?

Byron didn't have to answer.

Byron watched him with that stupid smile of his. He really could've gone into Hollywood as a character actor, if he didn't believe American movies were an arm of the Chinese government.

He saluted with the bottle, touched it to his lips, and before drinking said: To fatherhood.

NINE

SOMETHING COVERS HIS FACE WHEN HE WAKES.

Plastic. He swats at it, and a translucent bag whirls away.

Arctic wind gusts all around him.

There is movement everywhere. Dust, paper, flocks of plastic bags bearing the words THANK YOU spin high until they scrape the bottom of the bridge above. The air smells dry and mineral.

He startles with relief at the sight of his cup—still there!—and takes a long pull of cold water. His head still throbs with pain when it moves, but much less now. Two pills left. He takes one with water, shivering, and the gesture makes him feel almost civilized.

Time again to pee. He's too loath to leave his little body-warmed patch of concrete, so this time he does it lying on his side to leave it trickling downward. He can't tell what color it is. Probably pale, and growing paler.

A ball of branches rolls down the channel. Tumbles. A tumbleweed, getting an early start on the day. Cartoon deserts had these things, he remembers. A tumbleweed and a cactus with one arm raised and a nearby cow skull, which sometimes would sing a song. As a very small child he used to get up early and sit in a compact meditation style and watch television. This was when televisions were boxy and paneled with wood-grain decals, way before they became flat and the local news began looking like Mission Control with spinning visual effects and video walls.

Then, in his mind, a newscaster, standing before a slowly swirling graphic. The newscaster opens his mouth to speak.

Stop, he pleads, and the newscaster dissipates.

The wind runs through his hair and up his shirt. The lone tumbleweed reaches the second bridge, where it joins another, and still another smaller one.

A family of three tumbleweeds, he thinks, just like the family I used to have. Tumbleweeds get to be together. They get to venture forth and roam around freely. No one ever bothers with tumbleweeds.

I wish I were a tumbleweed.

In other words, he thinks, I wish I could venture forth. But unlike me, tumbleweeds fear nothing, because they are *tumbleweeds*, which are *dead*. What kind of freak organism only becomes able to move once it expires? Undead plants, sure, okay!

He is stupid angry. The lack of decent sleep.

He dares a long look: the blanket ripples slightly in the air, revealing a sliver of darkness inside. It must be anchored down from inside somehow. He takes a long sip of his water, eyes locked. He watches. But he can discern nothing about its contents. Two hours pass. His eyes begin to close. He lies back, just for a moment—

—One time the baby had finally gone down, and running on nothing but two hours of sleep I squeezed toothpaste onto my razor and shaved with it, wasn't that hilarious, and yet I was crying at the sink because that was the last of the toothpaste and all I wanted was to feel normal for a moment—

—and a moment later it's already late afternoon. Hot, just like that. He must have slept for hours. He lifts his head, squinting at the dust flying around him, and gazes at the blanket in the distance. Still there, beckoning.

In ancient times, such a portal would have taken the form of a gate guarded by a minor sphinx dispensing cryptic aphorisms as clues. What has four legs in the morning, three in the afternoon, and so on.

But that was back when things made sense. This blanket, this gate, this whole puzzle operates on some new logic. Which is to say, no logic at all.

He thinks about taking his last remaining pill but decides to leave it in his pocket.

He knows he has to investigate the blanket. There's nothing else. It's either that or the houses, and he knows the clutter within those ruins will just trigger his mind like a multiball pinball frenzy. So he'll start small with the blanket shelter. With any luck, all it contains is a mummified body with eyes dried flat like a fish's. With any luck, it's long abandoned.

Which raises the question why. Maybe its supplies had been exhausted, and it was time to move on, which would mean he should move on, too. Maybe an empty shelter is the kick in the ass he needs to venture forth like the intrepid tumbleweed.

All this water he's been drinking only gives his stomach a clear glob of nothing to churn with hunger. The wind is not going to deliver a plastic bag filled with cheeseburgers wrapped in yellow wax paper. There is no choice.

The blanket continues to twitch. He formulates what can barely be called a plan.

1. Find a weapon.
2. Stand outside the blanket and make animal sounds.
3. Stab to death whoever comes out to investigate.

The first step is pretty funny. What's he going to do? Bucket them to death?

The rest of it is pretty funny, too. One of the few remaining *Homo sapiens* spends his final moments imitating an animal. What kind? A snake? Are there even any animals left?

He chuckles. This is stupid, he thinks.

You're not taking any of this seriously enough.

What is the point? I die now, I die later. A lot of effort and drama in the meantime.

You survive and find out what happened to Earth.

Civilizations come and go. Does anyone obsess over the final days of the Mayans? Nerds do. The Byrons of the world. Our sun will go red giant and burn those ruins and everything else up eventually. There's no such thing as immortality.

You live while you still can. You find that army base. You reach there and you write down the truths of your life.

And at this nonexistent army base there's a ragtag multiracial team of survivors, and they all cry *There you are!* when I arrive and there's plenty of weird little esoteric tasks to keep me present and engaged. And at night the sexy PhD life scientist sneaks out of her makeshift laboratory and into my tent because she has a thing for swarthy Korean muscle.

I'm Korean, he realizes. He examines this mental artifact for clues. It gives him nothing.

Be serious. If not an army base, then something else.

There is nothing else. Don't you remember?

The army base was a show on TV.

Yes.

And the hot scientist is played by my real-life wife.

Real. Life. Wife.

Yes.

No—

Listen—

Stop.

He claws at his hair. He wants to do something. Anything. But what? Even if there were a thing he really wanted to accomplish, what can he do about it?

He can remove this stupid rock from his stupid shoe.

He begins untying the laces, sneers at the pointlessness of such a fastidious procedure, and simply flings it off. He shakes it mouth-down into a cupped hand. Nothing comes out.

Frantic with confusion now, he digs his fingernails in to strip out the hot insole blackened with grime. He tips the shoe. An object plinks out. Not a rock, but a bright brass rectangle.

He stares at the thing with pure terror.

The brass rectangle is machined with rounded corners and a bevel to de-sharpen the edges. One end is covered in a neat grid of tiny, randomly sized dimples perhaps etched by a carbide drill bit, something. The other end is stamped with the word:

REVERE

His mind observes the word, makes connections: reverence, reverie.

Above the word is a little open hole.

He touches the metal with a fingertip, and his mind goes blank.

He can see an ingot-shaped remote control in his hand now. A tiny red light pip-pips on its face as he holds a button down, fast-forwarding through commercials on an immense screen across a room. He can sense her head resting snug in his lap.

She was half asleep with a pleasant boredom. What a luxury, to be bored. In the curve of her ear rested a single mole, tiny as a fleck on a robin's egg, in the shape of an ink-blotted D. Somewhere in the ocean there might be a deserted island in that exact same shape. On that island might be a single man, lost forever.

They had been watching that show. The one with the futuristic army base and the hot Black life scientist going over irradiated soil samples with the hot Asian platoon commander.

There's us, he said.

I'm way hotter, she said without looking, and smiled into his thigh. So are you.

He glanced at the portable monitor, where a tiny baby glowed. She really conked out tonight, he said.

But now his wife was asleep, too.

He hated this stupid show, and he was half asleep as well, but he enjoyed seeing themselves on a screen for once, no matter how dumb the story.

He opens his eyes again and finds himself back in his shelter. He stares at the brass rectangle. He knows what it is.

It is a key.

But it isn't the key to his house, the one he was familiar with. The key to his house was the normal kind, with a head and neck and teeth.

This brass thing isn't the normal kind of anything. This key, he knows, is filled with dangerous energy vibrating deep within its metallic crystalline structures.

The key is a mystery. One he feels he will never be ready to solve.

But he can't bring himself to fling the thing away. Maybe later, when he eventually finds a secure abandoned office or something in which to live out the rest of his blanked-out days, he'll seal it away within an airtight container where it belongs. For now, his sneakers will have to do.

He unfolds the little blade from the wine tool and gingerly slips it beneath the strange key, lest he touch it again, and flips it back into his shoe. Then he stuffs the stained insole into place. He puts it on, reties the laces, moving slower now.

Stand up, he thinks.

So he stands up. Takes a breath.

He shifts his weight left and right, to and fro. His right foot complains again about the discomfort of that foreign object beneath it, but it's fine. He can live with a little discomfort. He'd rather.

Maybe one day he'll remove his insole and find that the key has simply dissolved away.

Wouldn't that be nice? For everything just to dissolve away?

Beyond, the blanket holds still.

He could search the flotsam at the other bridge but might run the risk of being ambushed while rummaging. So no. He climbs the concrete bank, just until his eyes are level with the top, and peers out. He takes a moment. No sniper fire comes.

He climbs a few more steps. Still nothing.

He stands like this for fifteen minutes, waiting. The vandals must be long gone. They would find his precautions amusing.

At the top now, he sees a flat dirt shoulder running along both sides of the channel. One flank, the one with the wire fence, bears nothing but the blackened plain with its ruined neighborhood. Whatever blast happened there must have sent everything flying like toothpicks in a hurricane of flame. Is this flank the east? Or west? Who friggin' knows. He decides to just call it the right flank.

The left flank, with its cinder-block wall and scant houses peeking above, has tall reedy plants waving along its edge. Each about five feet tall, dried through, and tapered to a sharp point.

He steps down the bank and jogs across the channel floor to hit the opposite slope running. He stops once to breathe. No way can he run like this. He can't possibly manage a trek out into the wild. He needs more energy, energy only food can give.

At the top he flattens his body against the wall and hides among the whispering plants. They probably have a name that no one remembers anymore.

In the distance the blanket inflates and deflates like it is quietly breathing. No other movement.

He flicks open his wine opener and, using its small blade, cuts away at the base of a reed. It's like hacking at a chair leg with a nail file. He can see his energy level dropping fast like a bar in a video game. But it'll be worth it. He has to believe this.

After a hundred stabbing exertions he's finally cut the stalk enough to begin thrashing it loose until he falls backward to free it from the ground. He looks up: still undetected, still safe. It's already becoming dusk again. His arms are sore and sweat catches in his armpits. The sweat, he imagines, will become less and less salty with time as the nutrients and everything else of substance fades from his desiccating body.

No time to examine his prize—he trots down the slope again, only looking back once to check the blank attic windows of the dead houses.

Back in his shelter, gasping for breath, he whittles off the reed's feathery foliage to reduce it to a clean arc. When he's done he presses its tip into the palm of his hand. Nice. This could puncture flesh for sure. This was his weapon.

He lunges at the air before him with the dry reed. Jab jab jab. Man make weapon! I am man! Did I just figure this out, or is there some leftover Cro-Mag part of me that already knew how?

He sits back, exhausted. Sips water. No way he can approach the blanket tonight.

When evening falls, he tiptoes off to gather more water at the faucet, then unrolls his body onto the ground with a groan. It's been a good day, productive. He crashes into sleep tucked as tight as he can for warmth, clutching the spear in one hand.

TEN

EARLY MORNING.

The wind has died down, leaving in its absence a limitless silence under skies still dyed with traces of night. The world now frozen with cold. He realizes he is shivering hard.

He takes a long look at the last pill in his shuddering palm. It is round and elegant in shape like a miniature Go game stone. Who knows when he'll ever get more of these?

He swallows it with long gulps of frigid water, wincing at the thought of making his already cold body even colder from the inside. He grabs his spear and his wine tool, then rises—slowly, joints cracking—and hobbles off.

He keeps his eyes locked forward as the rest of his body now runs low to the sloped ground, spear tip leading the way. Right foot slightly less nimble than the left. Cold, cold as the proverbial brass monkey's balls, how can a place as hot as the desert be this cold?

More reason to run faster.

The blanket grows closer. He glances at the left bank. The abandoned houses, silhouetted by the oblivious streetlamp, remain abandoned.

He veers up the slope to avoid the faucet cage when something makes him pause. On the dirt shoulder at the top of the channel, a black shoe.

Not a shoe. A dead black bird. Blackbird singing in the dead of night. A crow.

He'd assumed all the animals were dead.

You don't know anything, says the crow.

He stares. The crow lies motionless.

You have no idea what is going on, it says.

Its beak doesn't move, but nevertheless he can hear it talking in the thin, raspy voice of a lifelong smoker. A woman's voice, murmuring just inches from his ear.

Hello?

I just lay down here one day, you see, says the crow. I just decided to close my eyes and that was that. Easy as you please.

A burst of crows appears in his mind, released by a dark tree beyond a window in the small early hours. There is the cup of tea before him again, swirling with milk. The child is asleep. The scene outside shimmering behind a moiré of flyscreen. Crows, he once read, are smarter than dogs. Dogs, he also read, have intelligence equivalent to a two-year-old.

He remembers marveling at the thought of his baby's brain dividing and growing in her sleep like a miniature thunderstorm, and how that thought would give him a peculiar surge of pride. She would easily become as smart as either of those creatures, and then rocket far beyond. She would become stupendous.

He looks down and frowns at something. From the crow's little chest protrudes a long thin something.

A nailhead.

Whatever blood had spilled has faded; whoever had committed this act was long gone along with the rest of the vandals.

This crow is not a good sign.

This crow must be erased.

He shakes his head to regain focus. He makes a silent vow to bury the crow later, if there is to be a later, and bury with it whatever portent it was supposed to have. Get straight to hell with that creepy omen, please.

He rears back, gathering strength, and launches into a sprint toward the blanket. Each step brings a tiny familiar ping of pain in his foot.

He charges silently as the sun peaks the top of the channel and draws a line of brilliant orange across its rim. The air feels good now, bracing, and his sinuses open with this burst of exertion to take it in and propel him forward.

He'll sweep the blanket aside and stab with the spear in a two-step motion. Sweep, stab. But now his energy begins to flag. It's farther than he thought.

By the time he reaches the stupid blanket, he's slowed to a ragged jog. It is suspended by hardware clips attached to bolts in the columns. Made of cheap acrylic fabric the color of horse manure. He inserts his spear tip into the gap and sweeps it aside with a strange ripping sound.

Before he can wonder what the sound is, he sees the stack of cans. Beside a towel, with utensils folded into it. Next to a lantern and a blanket, also folded. An object that looks like a water jug with a special lid. No—a stove, a little ding-dang camping stove. Everything rests on a flat portion of the slope providing a level floor his shelter does not have. There's even a maroon bath mat for a rug. He probes the cans with his spear.

Stop, he says aloud. He closes his eyes and reopens them. Everything is still there.

The air is different inside. Still and close and warm, warm enough to make his frozen fingertips tingle. What a difference a blanket only five millimeters thick can make. Someone has cemented strips of Velcro to the walls to pin the blanket to. Hence the ripping sound, which would also prevent surprise attacks. Clever.

He isn't sure how he's supposed to proceed. This is a trap. He'll be hauled to the ceiling by his feet the moment he enters. But he can see no line and pulley above him. He waves the spear around, as if purifying the space. No trip wires, nothing.

He realizes he's stopped breathing. He lets himself pant as quietly as he could muster.

Fuck me fuck me fuck me. It's so funny when I swear. Here is another challenge set forth by the grand puzzle. Think. Consider the possible moves.

Maybe the food has gone old and deadly.

Maybe a madman, craving fresh meat for weeks, hides patiently in an unseen rafter.

Maybe the bath mat covers a hole dropping to an underground hive of mutants gathered in wait.

Or maybe not. Maybe the previous tenant did what he could not, and simply possessed the uninhibited courage to move the hell out and the hell on with their lives. The army base is real, just beyond the channel's bend, and they arrived to high-five its attractive, multiracial crew waiting there. Why else would they leave behind a weapon as valuable as this steak knife?

Maybe a rug is just a rug.

He lifts the bath mat. No trap there.

But wait. Maybe they are many, not one, and are counting on him to enter before ambushing him through the shelter's only exit. They—hunters of infinite patience—will give him time to fatten up and relax with a nap before attacking, because relaxed muscles make for tenderer steak.

Oh, quit dithering already. There's no real choice here.

He lowers his spear and enters.

ELEVEN

HE LETS THE BLANKET FALL BEHIND HIM, WONDERING IF THIS MOMENT as his eyes adjust to the darkness will be the moment of his death.

But nothing comes. He sees sheets of cardboard leaning against the back wall, and a ballpoint pen. A single cinder block. Inside the hollow of the block stands a small action figure toy. A squat blue warrior with big anime eyes and horns for hair. His left arm some kind of cybernetic weapon.

Already a memory is coalescing around the little figurine. He can see the wheels of a shopping cart, a baby seated in it, rolling along the cool linoleum of an endless toy store. He can't make out the baby's face, but he knows it was his. It was *her*.

One side of the store was entirely pink for the girls, with sections like BATH & BEAUTY and CLEANING TOYS. The other half of the store was blue for the boys, and focused entirely on sports and war-play weaponry. The future paths for all children, laid out in binary. What bullshit, he'd thought. Take all that nonsense away and let them run free, for chrissake. Let the soldier style his hair pink! Let the homemaker tighten her shot grouping in her basement range!

He veered the cart to the blue side, standing atop the back axle for maximum danger and (therefore) maximum fun. She shrieked with delight, so he boosted off again. He stopped to let her feel the knobs of tiny monster truck tires, pretty gel green rubber around pretty chrome hubs, see? He showed her how to load a foam revolver, whip-slap the barrel in, and line up a shot.

Pff went the foam dart, sending a tambourine falling into a pile of rainbow ribbons.

Sir, said an employee.

Uh-oh, he said. She said Uh-oh, too. They said Uh-oh again and again as he skated off toward the wooden trains.

Let all the babies everywhere be whatever the hell they wanted. Life was too short for bullshit.

What would little-she have done? he wonders. Would she have loved nothing but pink, or blue, or some other hue? How would she have changed when she turned two, five, thirty years old?

Then he dares to think: what would she do *now*?

This is a tougher question. The previous world of choices—school, work, maybe a business, maybe a marriage—have been replaced by choices he can't even recognize as being choices: find water, find food, try not to get killed by crow-murdering trolls.

He hopes she isn't part of this new life. Or his wife. His heart wrings itself dry at the thought of his two beautiful girls picking through a shattered mall, flinching at every sound. They deserve gentleness and light and easy laughter. Not this world.

No one deserves this.

He once believed in this ideal tabula rasa notion of the mind, but in places like that toy store he became less sure. The mind is less like a stone tablet and more like a ProFlo HEPA automotive air filter, designed to collect everything in its path. Those things don't stay spotless for long.

The key—the one named Revere—is for his girls in some way. He can lose his weapons, his tools, even his clothes, but he knows he must not lose that goddamn key.

He punches his temples hard ten times in a row.

He has to be better about cutting short these memory triggers as they came. God knows how long he's been sitting here staring at a small blue toy. He snatches a square of cardboard and covers the cinder block. Baby goes poof, toy store goes poof.

A blank mind is a sharp mind, he thinks. Master your situation already, dickskin! Fear is a weed that can take over the entire garden if he lets it.

The stack of cans all boast familiar logos and colors, all triggers leading to triggers leading to still more triggers, like a speck of rain traveling down a windowpane consuming other droplets in its path to form a megadroplet.

He closes his eyes and rips the labels off one by one. Then he tears them into tiny shreds, which he sprinkles into the hollow of the cinder block before quickly covering it up again by slapping the cardboard down like it's some janky makeshift lid on Pandora's jar, whose original screw top has been missing for millennia.

He re-stacks the shiny metal cans. No labels means that every day for the next week or so will be a potluck. If the food doesn't kill him first.

Arranged behind him on the floor is a box of matches, beautifully dry. There's another blanket and a flashlight, dead but salvageable if and when he finds batteries. There's a spool of some kind of string made of clear plastic that reads NIIGATA MONOFIL PRO-CATCH LINE 30.8LBS 300YD, none of which adds up to anything that makes sense.

He also finds a curious strip of metal about an inch and a half long, scored along its length, with a notch cut into one side and an eyelet punched out of one corner. A flat hook, only a half inch long, swings from a tiny hinge off the larger strip. More perplexing words appear before him, stamped into the metal: U.S. SHELBY CO.

A company, in the United States, named Shelby? That brings nothing to mind, which is both a relief and a letdown.

Unfolding the tool locks the hook into place to form a rigid ninety-degree angle. Lifting the hook just a hair allows it to be folded back again. It seems like a trifle. But it's such a deliberately designed object, so particular in its details, that he can sense it is an entity unto itself and not the missing part of a larger machine.

Another puzzle. The challenge, he sees, is to find the role it plays in the world. Way easier, he muses, than figuring out his.

He slashes the corner of the tool on the concrete. No sparks or anything. Makes sense—with a full box of thousands of matches at the ready, they wouldn't need an extra spark-making tool.

They, they, they.

There was a picture book when he was very small: a scatterbrained cat wearing a tall red-and-white-striped hat who told a little boy and girl (whose parents never seemed to be at home) that the best way to find something was to check off everywhere it was *not*. With pink goo, no less.

He'll do something similar now, just not with pink goo.

He checks off the utensils: there is a spoon, steak knife, fork. The tool can therefore not be an eating device.

He tries cutting a cardboard sheet with the sharp end of the Shelby. With effort, he can only manage a ragged line. So not a box cutter, either. Check.

Maybe it's some sort of hanging hook, and the eyelet is meant for a nail in the wall? He gingerly passes his fingers along the concrete but detects nothing. The hook, while dull, is pointed enough to poke holes in fabric. Some kind of sewing tool? But then where are the needles and thread?

He eyes the stack of cans.

He presses the hook into the top of the can at its center. Harder and harder until his thumb tip becomes white. He slips and jabs his palm and lets the can fall. He sucks his hand and examines the can: nothing more than a pinpoint dent in the metal.

He turns the can over and over again. He is close. There's something here.

He matches the lip of the can with the notch in the side of the tool. The point of the hook rests right atop the can's rim, ready to pierce. He feels an inevitability of purpose here, and twists forward with his thumb.

The hook easily cuts into the metal to unseal the can. It sounds like a little kiss.

Immediately he can smell what is inside: some sort of beef soup.

He shifts the tool away from him a bit, then repeats the gesture to draw a lengthening arc around the can's rim. After a quarter turn he moves with increasing dexterity. His left hand rotates the can by small degrees while his right hand keeps a steady rhythm.

The loosening lid begins to jitter with each turn, and soon it collapses into the soup. He carefully lifts it out.

Chili with beans.

Goat shit, he cries. That's what U.S. soldiers would call their cans of beans in the war. The Korean war. His mom told him that when he was little. She is long gone but there's her face now, floating before him with wry eyebrows lifted. This memory will lead to others, he knows, but he'll let this one linger for a moment. She was a war child and had seen things no nine-year-old should see, and he habitually excused her strange immigrant behavior all his life because of this fact. The spare Tapatio packets she liked to keep in her purse didn't seem so eccentric once you learned she once walked for three days without food.

He sets her aside as gently as he can to focus back on the tool. U.S. SHELBY CO.

Very few people put full stops after each letter when abbreviating *United States*, and one of those people is the U.S. military.

He can see the base in his mind. There's no way to know how far it is, or which direction, or if it contains nothing but a pile of dry corpses. All neatly cross-stacked, ten or a hundred or thousand, a clear warning and grotesque flex, followed by a surprise hail of gunfire from a shattered tower manned by soldiers gone mad after years of nonstop fear and paranoia. He would have to approach carefully. One does not simply wander up to a base and buzz the front desk. Not before and certainly not now. But he'll have to accept these kinds of risks. He'll find this base, or a house, or a village, or goddamn any-thing. He will find Byron. He will find *them*.

But he can barely think about any of that right now, what with the can open.

All that is left is to see if the stove has enough fuel to light and warm the can to an appropriate temperature for eating.

Dude. You need a little dinner music, too?

He snatches up a spoon and takes his first bite cold. He lets the chili overtake his every sense with its savory tang. He can barely re-member how to chew. But he does, ruminantly, with import, and swal-lows.

Then he waits to see if he will die.

But he doesn't die. Which is super great!

He celebrates by taking another bite. That doesn't kill him, either, so he celebrates with another, and another, and another.

TWELVE

HE EATS TWO CANS.

The second one is a chicken soup that brilliantly balances daring levels of sodium and oil with hints of celery bitterness, carrot sweetness, and extremely extremely tender noodles, all infused with a bold minerality from the can metal itself. He gives it five stars.

He licks both cans mirror-clean, taking care around the sharp edges. A tongue infection would make for a truly stupid death. I cut my tongue and now I'm dead, aaaah, he would think as his throat swelled shut.

He finds himself smiling. His eyes become dreamy and he listens to his stomach go to work. He apologizes to it for his neglect. Go ahead and digest. You've earned it.

His eyes flutter and he sleeps with a loose grip on his spear pointed toward the curtain.

Hours later he wakes renewed. What time is it? He pins the curtain open and steps out to survey the channel. It's already almost noon, and hot outside. This time, the blanket keeps the shelter noticeably cooler. Hot, cold, hot, cold. He urinates. When he finishes he sends a rivulet of water down to wash it away.

That's the last of that. Time to suit up and head out.

Goodbye, Arroyo Plato Villa Estates.

He looks down the concrete channel, the pale gray geometries under a flawless sky, and apologizes to God.

Didn't mean to get so mad at you back there. Didn't mean to call you a bitch-ass. I just needed some food and water and for the swelling in my head to go away. My amnesia is still intact. And for that I thank you.

If this whole thing is some kind of book of revelation of yours, let's read it and see what happens.

————

HE STANDS ON THE DIRT SHOULDER OF THE RIVERBANK. FULL TO-GO cup of water dangling from a makeshift hip wire harness. Spear tucked into his belt. Cardboard in one hand, pen in the other. From the crook of his elbow dangles the bucket, which contains the Shelby, cans of food, the little camping stove, the wine opener. He wants to take the blanket, but it'd started coming apart at the slightest pull.

He'll find another blanket out there.

He begins walking and drawing, the dry crunch of his step the only sound anywhere.

He counts his steps and heads to the trio of storm drains embedded in the mountainside and draws small on the cardboard so he won't run out of space later. The gigantic end pipes, at least fifteen feet in diameter, gape open with no gate or grille to keep anyone from entering. Or emerging. The entire terminus has been sealed off with a spike fence whose tips bend inward, as if they had melted in hellfire. An ancient depth-level gauge has been painted into the wall and bears the stains of another era when water once flowed.

The entire drain assemblage creates a kind of huge wall that can't be scaled. So on the map he writes DEAD END.

He heads back past his original crawl space—which seems pathetic now—and farther past his current, luxurious curtained shelter. He draws the two bridges on his map.

Each bridge, he notices, carries roads that once led into the neighborhood but now are blocked by a line of Jersey barriers and high, makeshift plywood walls. The first wall is weathered past legibility. On the second, he can make out the words ARROYO PLATO VILLA ESTATES, followed by NEW HOMES AVAILABLE SOON—RESERVE YOURS TODAY. He marks these walls as ENTRANCE 1 (SEALED) and ENTRANCE 2 (SEALED).

He draws in the four house peaks visible above the cinder-block wall, followed by a question mark since he can't see how many other houses lie beyond. It's irrelevant how many, because even a single house represents potential ambush and death. He marks the houses with another DEAD END.

He edges up to the shoulder road at the top of the channel and spots the dead crow. For completeness, he places a dot on the map where it lies.

The crow is just a crow now. Ordinary as can be.

Amazing, the tricks a little hunger can play on the mind. He laughs.

The other ends of each bridge run into the fenced-off, blackened area, which he labels DEAD LANDS. The mountains beyond he names the DEAD RIDGE. He adds DEAD END there, too.

That leaves really only one direction to go.

He heads down the channel, away from his blanket shelter. He feels at ease despite being exposed high up on the shoulder. Maybe it's the full belly. He marks where the vinyl Arroyo Plato banner is, grateful to be looking at it for the last time.

I'll be gone by the time you get back, he thinks, addressing his attackers. Thanks for the supplies, no thanks for the headache.

Just beyond his shelter stand a few clusters of dry reeds in the channel below at regular intervals, which he marks: REED 1, REED 2, and so on. They form a meaningless constellation. None of what he writes down means much of anything, but he wants to keep a written record anyway. Maybe he'll show it to his girls if he can ever find them.

When you find them, you pessimist.

He continues on a hundred steps. A hundred more. Nothing changes. He can see an occasional half-constructed house poking above the cinder-block wall, little triangles of raw lumber framing nothing but blue sky. He marks those for a while and then simply writes: HOUSE RUINS CONTINUE.

He makes his way around the gentle curve of the river for the next hour, passing a graffiti mural on the opposite bank that's been nearly erased by years of relentless sun. He struggles to discern anything readable amid the spiky lettering. KROKOS? KAORCE? Why go through all the trouble of writing graffiti if you can't even read it? He marks it anyway.

Something in the remote distance catches his eye.

A flash?

He squints. Between the far end of the cinder-block wall and the curve of the channel, he can see a strip of desert horizon. He ducks and jukes slowly until yes—a glint. Something is out there. Could be a car, or a house, or an autonomous impulse-drive shuttle that can take him out of this multiverse timeline and into the proper one.

Could be a death trap.

Depends on whether that spot of light holds good intent, or bad.

Let's say Man is fundamentally evil, he thinks. All that greed and murderous sociopathic impulse, Man is born with it. He uses the word *Man* because he can't come up with any murderous, sociopathic Women on the same level as the Nazis, Pol Pot, that Virginia Tech guy. Names from a history book, a history book in a classroom, a classroom full of children, him standing at the front of it.

Stop, he tells himself. Memories are beginning to cascade. Stop. Let's go back to this topic of evil.

If Man is fundamentally evil, then evil is simply an inescapable part of nature. Man creates tools, discovers fire, leaps to the top of the food chain. Creates culture and science. Then sets about murdering himself in the pursuit of dominance.

If Man is fundamentally evil, is this apocalypse really anything to mourn? Any more than we mourn a leaf falling from a tree? It is only nature running its course, after all.

On the other hand: if Man is fundamentally good, then this all must be some terrible lesson from God, and the only sensible thing to do would be to start over and try again.

This place is not heaven, nor is it quite hellish. Is it purgatory? That would mean he died in a state of grace and needs to atone for his sins before being allowed to rapture. Which means suffering lies ahead. Or something. He can't quite remember the rules.

The faraway light glints again.

The reeds crowd together here to form dense little thicket islands huddled on the channel floor. Up ahead, they merge to form a maze of tall foliage, some of it even green. He marks his map. There are small flat rocks, too. A small stack of three or four of them in descending size.

He stops drawing. There is another little stack. And another, and another.

The whole trail is lined with them. Some stand seven stones high.

These totems. What are they called? Corns. Cores. *Cairns.*

The obscure word reveals no meaning. There they stand, like little spirits frozen in place. He can't remember if they are good omens or bad. All he knows is that they mean someone has been here. Only an intelligent creature with specific intent can make their presence known in such a manner.

But what the intent is, he has no idea.

You have no idea, says the dead crow, what you're getting yourself into.

The air around him falls silent.

There are so many of them. The cairns. He takes the tiniest sip of water, maintains a vigilant gaze.

Then one of the rocks falls. It tumbles down and disturbs the stack and sends a small group of stones sliding. Into one cairn and another the stones collide, sending a cryptic message in their mute language.

Time to go, time to go. He turns and hurries away.

THIRTEEN

IT'S _____, HE SAID.

_____? said Byron. I've seen her in the teachers' lounge. She's hot!

I know, he said.

Okay, well, dibs for you. So you're into Black girls.

Dude.

Or she likes Asian dudes?

Can you stop talking about race for one second? You're obsessed with race.

Why do you think we're here? said Byron. When it goes down, it will be precisely because of race. I don't want the Rahowa, you don't want the Rahowa, but Karen and Kevin sure as hell do, so we have to be ready.

He changed the subject fast. Byron could go on literally for an hour about the impending racial holy war. Two if he'd been drinking.

I'm gonna ask her out for coffee, he said. You looking for the tent spikes?

Byron took the spikes. If coffee is the custom, then fine. I would personally start with a series of questions, just make sure she's not some kinda cannibal. I need the mallet.

That's a low bar. Anyway that's what meeting for coffee is . . . for. Mallet.

People need any kind of excuse, I suppose, said Byron.

That's great, best friend! I'm so happy for you, best friend!

I'm sorry, I'm happy for you. She seems super nice.

One time I caught her all alone in the lounge making her coffee creamer scream for help while she was squeezing it empty, he said.

And she's funny? said Byron. Nice.

Have mercy, Queen Caffeine! The brown lake burns! Then she saw me and got all shy. It was the hottest thing ever.

Funny woman, hot woman, said Byron. He stood, slipped the mallet into a belt loop that wasn't there, and watched it fall to the soft grass with a thud. See how I angle the stakes inward?

She definitely keeps her funny side a secret, he said. That's why I asked her out for coffee. To hear more of that funny.

Ask her many many questions, though, said Byron.

I will.

Then give me the full debrief.

Full debrief was my nickname in prison, he said.

Byron laughed in his guttering way. That's a new one.

I've been working on some material for the kids. Aaah—

A bug had been crawling on his arm, and he flailed it away. What the hell was that? Did you see that?

That's an earwig, dude, chill, said Byron. Earwigs are very common.

Like crawl into my ear and eat my brain?

That's a myth, said Byron.

Can't we just read about plants at home, indoors?

We learn best using all our senses, said Byron. Like, what's that plant right there? Touch it, smell it.

He did as Byron said, plucked a strand from a giant nearby fluffy pincushion, snapped it, held the open end to his nose. A shrub? he said. Chaparral something?

It's actually a grass, said Byron. Deer grass. You're gonna learn all about the local flora and fauna, what's edible, what's poisonous, what's good for wounds et alia. What's this tree we're under?

He looked up and admired the little white flowers dotting the foliage. I know this one. Dogwood.

Very good! Extra jerky for the Boy Scout.

Are the leaves medicinal?

No, said Byron. Leaves are inedible, thing is useless to us. But—hear that? Home to birds, which you can eat. Also insects, which you can eat.

Isn't that just all trees in general?

That's a bushtit call. These trees are full of bushtits.

Kehehehe! He laughed into his knees. Kehehehe!

Byron's eyebrows fell flat. Jesus, look at this grown-ass man here. This grown-ass man just turned five years old, happy birthday.

Bushtits is what a virgin says to his first naked woman, he said.

It took a second, but soon Byron exploded through his nose so hard he had to wipe it. Two grown-ass men giggling in a park on a lovely late afternoon.

You are the worst student ever, said Byron, glancing at his armored multifunction orienteering wristwatch. Canteen time. Eat! Hydrate!

Byron opened his ruck and took out a flat plastic packet. He followed suit, opening his own ruck. He ripped one open and tore off a strip of jerky with his teeth.

Whoa whoa whoa, said Byron. First you absolutely must say out loud that you're gonna eat (a) what type of ration and (b) how many remain in your possession. If this were real we'd have to stay on the same page to avoid making harder decisions further on down the line.

Harder decisions, he said, chewing.

Let's just say people have killed each other over someone else's last piece of jerky.

He spoke through his food. I am eating beef jerky, he said, and I have twelve remaining rations in my possession. Sir captain major Byron sir.

Shut up.

You shut up.

Shut up more.

We got incoming, said Byron, suddenly alert.

He straightened his posture and watched as two women jogged by. 'Lo, ladies.

The ladies said nothing and continued their pace far along the dirt path.

Whoever put blondes in yoga pants, said Byron, give 'em a Nobel Peace Prize. Nobel Piece of Ass Prize, right?

I'm gonna choke. Stop.

They totally checked me out.

Because you said hi.

You could tell they're into Black guys.

So you're Black today, he said.

I'll be whatever it takes! You know Asian guys don't get any respect. They have excellent walking form. Jesus hang-gliding in heaven!

Look at 'em go.

Whatever, you're dying to be a kept man, said Byron.

He smiled. I'm a faller-in-lover, so what. He folded the whole sheet of jerky into his mouth. Byron frowned at this, but wound up eating all of his, too.

Then Byron's wristwatch beeped. Byron startled at it. How long did we put in for?

This part of Griffith closes at dusk, so I got six hours.

Can you please double-check? They ticket around here.

He nodded. Sure, he said, and began walking the hundred steps to the car.

Get the extra propane, too! called Byron. Our survival depends on it!

FOURTEEN

THE GLINT SEEMS TO GROW NO CLOSER.

He travels up and down gentle rolling hills of cracked dirt dotted evenly by neat brushes. Sagebrush? Some other brush? Something about the roots of desert plants spreading out, not down, naturally creating for each plant its own circle of personal space? He can't remember, and it's too hot to care.

About an hour ago he thought he could bear the heat of the day, but now he feels the penalty for having left while the sun was at its peak. He tries not to trudge his feet. He likes his sneakers too much for that. But they keep wanting to trudge. They get heavier with every step.

He daydreams about being back in the shelter and fashioning a smart hat out of cardboard. If only he'd thought of that, before getting scared off by a bunch of random rocks falling. Superstitious dipshit! He would've taken a piece of cardboard, torn it neatly to its middle, then slid it over to form a shallow cone like those hats you see (saw?) in Asia.

Is that racist? Conical hats were in every damn stereotype on TV. Can you be racist against yourself when you are one of the few people left on the planet? Does it matter? Does the concept of Asia even still exist?

You're obsessed with race, he'd said to Byron. Much later, long after he married _____, she would tell him: All of America is obsessed with race. We can't not be obsessed with race.

His foot drags a long flat line. A hat would be nice, sweetie.

That's what he called her.

Sweetie.

After what feels like another long hour his shirt sags with large ovals of sweat. He sips carefully from his bottle and gasps so hard a rattlesnake pauses with alarm. He looks down. He'd drunk half of his to-go cup in one swig.

Behind him, the infinite cinder-block wall of Arroyo Plato Villa Estates has become just a pink ripple in the heat.

Ahead, the glint grows no closer.

I'm a chump chasing a mirage, he thinks. I'm a walking cartoon cliché in a cartoon desert. Bring in the one-armed cactus and singing cow skull.

He shields his eyes and squints for a good long moment. Everything around him dead hot and dead silent.

He can see a black rectangle shape fluctuating next to the light. A scraggly tree, another tree, a heavy pill shape. A trapezoid.

A car?

A trapezoid atop another trapezoid atop two sunken circles.

A car!

He wants to run. But a million thoughts stop him. What if the same people who had smashed his head in now live in that structure? What if the glint he follows is a lure, and he's just a clueless little guppy headed toward the maw of a stonefish, too hypnotized to know any better?

He stands frozen, melting in the relentless sun for five minutes. Six. A drop of sweat runs down the center channel of his back and pools between his buttocks. He glances back. Maybe the bad guys live back in the houses he just left. He looks over to the Dead Lands.

Maybe they live somewhere in there. He has no idea. He's not a ding-dang tracker. He can't *read* the ding-dang land.

He would turn back, if not for that confounding car up ahead. He can drive that thing, yeah. Swerve around debris and outrun attackers. Gun it south—he doesn't know much, but he at least knows his house is south. Windows rolled up tight and AC blasting. To-go cup finally in a cup holder where it would fit just right. Maybe even music!

And his girls will still be there. Alive, as it turns out! She'll come running out, hysterical, with the tiny one in her arms, and he'll take them both and propel them far away from the ruined city.

He discovers he is jogging now. Probably sending up a little plume of dust for all the world to see.

But whatever, world—a car!

Legs burning. The bright dot grows closer. It's the side mirror! There's also a propane tank and bicycles rusted solid and the world's most heartbreaking plastic kids' playset bleached paper thin from the years. There is a disgusting barbecue and a big pile of chicken wire and garbage cans tipped this way and that.

Closer now. He's settled into a steady pace and can now allow himself to realize what a bizarre anomaly this building is. A square two-story condo with crumbling stucco and plastic Spanish tile on top, like something found among a million other low-end generic condos among the business parks and strip malls, except this one has been plucked by the hand of a mischievous god and dropped here in the middle of nowhere. Nestled in a nameless valley created by two low hills as if it were the ill-fated result of a bad real estate tip. There are trees—all dying, obviously imported from some verdant other-land, but at least they provide shade while they still stand. What kind are they? All he knows is that they are not dogwoods.

Now he can see the shattered plate windowpanes, and the poor illegible graffiti, and the hanging front door sprayed with a big red X.

The X means what—abandoned? Looted? Infected? A hex to keep bad spirits out?

How's that working out for you?

He slows. Because now he's close enough to tell the car's tires had gone flat—all of them.

Wunderbar.

He gathers himself, regroups. There might be a pump. At the very least there might be something useful here.

When he reaches the house, he rests his hands on his knees and breathes hard. The tire rubber has split with age. The car windows are gone except for a starred windshield and cratered back plate. Rearview mirror gone, stereo gone, steering wheel gone. All the seats have been taken out as well, probably for their valuable leather. Without thinking, he kicks the driver's-side door, and the hollow *pok* is swallowed up by the flat landscape.

He glances at the jagged windows of the condo. Nothing stirs, no shadows come running.

The car's side mirror is intact. For a moment he's tempted to see what his own face looks like. But no way. He feels a familiar dread, like he did when having to check out a dark cellar full of telltale rat pellets or a maybe an online video with the blurred warning: EXTREMELY GRAPHIC CONTENT AHEAD. He always left the cellar alone, left the video unclicked.

He leaves the car and its mirror.

He steers clear of the world's saddest children's playset, because the closer he gets to it the more he can picture her on it in another time and space where the set is brand-new, perhaps in a toy store with its shelves divided into blue for boys and pink for girls.

See what happened just there?

This is exactly the kind of bullshit he's afraid of.

Still.

He's come all this way, and already the sun is beginning its descent behind him, dyeing the south faces of everything orange. The front door hangs open on a single twisted hinge. Inside, he can discern something bright blue tipped with bright yellow. A hand tool of some kind. Be dumb not to check it out.

So he steps past the big red X—no magic force-field hex—and goes in.

FIFTEEN

HIS FEET SNAP BROKEN GLASS AS HE LETS HIS EYES ADJUST. HE STANDS in the open doorway where a dry breeze exhales a constant breath. A breeze is good. He sets down his bucket and billows his shirt. Maybe the shower faucets work.

Man, a shower.

The room—what would be the living room—is empty. There are bricks and crushed cans and thousand-year-old cigarette butts and—looking closer now—a bent syringe. Soot from a small fire blackens one wall; into the soot someone had written KEK SKWAD with a fat drunken finger.

Your squad lost, he says. Everyone lost. No more keks from you.

On the ruptured kitchen counter sits a microwave with its keypad peeled off. Next to it is a closed refrigerator—no way is he opening that fear vault—and next to that is a sink filled with more broken glass. Not even a trace of septic smell there. He checks below, and yep: it's hooked up to real pipes. But what are the pipes hooked up to?

He tries the sink faucet, half expecting dust to come puffing out. It gives nothing.

Every cabinet and drawer has been opened and upturned. Forks, spoons, a stupid slotted spatula. He has no use for those things.

Finally his eyes come to rest upon the blue-and-yellow object he spotted earlier. It's heavy and iron like a crowbar, but shorter. A prybar? Is that the term?

He hefts it. Hopefully it's not coated with a virus or anything. But whatever, he's handled cans and a wine opener by this point, and he is still alive and prancing around dung county here. The prybar has a good weight to it, and when he gives it a swing he can picture the condo as it once was—everything intact, ready to be destroyed all over again.

Crowbars were often the default weapon in video games. Is this a video game? He wants to smash a toaster to see if it'll give up a rotating heart or a green mushroom or ammo or some kind of goodie.

He continues exploring with ginger steps.

There is a horrible bathroom full of mirror shards—hell no—and a rotting closet. There is a family room with an exploded couch and a fireplace with a large shattered television hung above it. Carpet gone stiff with dried muck.

There is nothing else, so he heads up the dark staircase. He has to hold the handrail. The steps can give way at any moment.

But they don't, and now he finds himself in a small hallway blooming with mildew. In one room, a warped desk and luggage gone fuzzy with organic matter. Another holds a simple mountain of old clothing, half of it children's. He flinches at the sight. Hell no. Run away. To another bedroom—guest room?—which has a dresser and nightstand flanking a sagging queen-size bed stripped of its bedsheets holding a purple sleeping bag with a corpse.

He drops the prybar and picks it right back up.

A dead body.

The thing has gone so dry and black that he can't tell if it is a man or a woman. So crisp, no flies bother with it. It is bald. Does that mean anything? If he were to lift it, it would probably weigh only twenty-five pounds.

He bends over and spews a quick shot of watered-down chili with beans onto the impossibly filthy carpet. Everything in his stomach, not much.

Goddammit, he mutters, and spits and spits.

He has ventured out of a perfectly hidden, perfectly adequate shelter, put himself at the mercy of the elements and human-un-kind, to find but a single prybar and now a body.

Dead man high five!

He knows he should unzip the cursed sleeping bag—the person might very well still be clutching a go bag hidden within—but he cannot, never ever. This makes him a very bad survivalist, and he can see Byron frowning upon him. Wishes he can, anyway.

Is the whole world like this now? Are the cities even worse?

Of course they're worse. So much worse! Millions of bodies as tough and dry as beef jerky.

Without thinking, he fishes out his spear. Is this real? He probes the sleeping bag. It sounds like a sleeping bag sounds.

He nudges it. Whatever's inside has lost all elasticity, and simply shifts dryly like charcoal. With nausea he notices the skull shifting accordingly, because its neck bone is still connected to the back bone, the back bone is connected to the hip bone—

He reels in the spear and takes a deep breath to center himself. Thankful the only smell is that of dry mold. He manages a quick scan of the room. The closet doors have been bashed off to reveal empty hangers. The nightstand has been robbed of its drawers. There is more nothing here, and he's glad for that, because it means he can move the hell on.

He comes to another bedroom, much bigger. What they used to call the master. Another blank, ransacked place—all that remains of the bed is a splintered frame, not even a mattress—but at least the windows are intact. They give a milky view of the dead trees just outside.

Within a small fireplace sit a few remnants of candles. There is even a cup and a bowl with a spoon and a fork on the hearth. It doesn't smell of mold or urine or anything, there's no satanic graffiti or dead bodies. It's the best room in the house, and has been someone's shelter up until whatever solitary end they finally met.

The fireplace has ash, meaning it still works, and above it hangs the centerpiece of the room: a huge triangular assemblage crafted from thin branches knotted together with strands of fabric and twisted brown paper bags.

A giant white peacock tail?

A Christmas tree?

He sees ribbons tied with rocks and plastic pens dangling four feet long, and thinks yes, it has to be some kind of makeshift Christmas tree. Look: it even has ball ornaments made from wadded-up something—toilet paper?

He wheels around and sees the white cylinders in the corner. Toilet paper!

Holy crap! He stifles an actual laugh. How can he be laughing right now?

There's even a stack of chemistry textbooks, too, all in Spanish, all ready to be used as fuel for the fire.

Not much use for química orgánica these days, he says.

First the caged faucet at the concrete channel, then the shelter with its canned food, and now this place. He has to appreciate his good luck whenever he can.

Sure. The corpse in the next room is good luck, too.

Shut up. We're staying here tonight.

Also the apocalypse. Talk about a lucky streak!

This is a good place to stay.

Also everyone we lost.

I said shut up.

Hey. This is just us talking here.

I know.

It's just me.

SIXTEEN

DARK OUTSIDE. IT FEELS NICE TO BE ABLE TO SAY THAT, *DARK OUTSIDE*, like everything is normal again and he lives in a house that features a clear distinction between inside and out.

Getting cold, too.

Why, I think I'll light myself a nice little fire, he thinks.

He clears out the candle butts, checks the flue for breath, and stands three chemistry books up like a miniature Stonehenge. He stuffs wadded-up pages in the gap they create. They light beautifully.

While the covers curl and blacken and catch, he opens an unlabeled can of—*yiss*—chicken soup, eats, and enjoys just the smallest sip of water afterward. It's going to be a long day tomorrow, and who knows when he'll find water again. He's had good luck so far.

Aside from the end of the world.

Didn't I say shut up?

He shuts up. Exhausted.

He uses two more books as a pillow for his head. The fire is catching nicely.

From just beyond the window comes a rustle. He sits up, arms himself with the prybar. But he quickly realizes it's the sound of a small animal, and when he hears it he knows it's a bird.

Who-oo, who? Who? says the bird. The mournful call makes him smile.

That's a great horned owl, Byron had said one time.

Not a bushtit? he said.

I grew up with bushtits of my own, she said.

Pthhh, he said, spraying beer.

The three of them had been at a campground somewhere. Byron was there. Plus himself, and her. Before the child, before the wedding, just friends still. They sat staring into a campfire. He could barely make out their faces shadowed beneath the brilliant LED headlamps Byron had bought them, and that was fine by him as he lay there letting this memory play out.

You are so quiet at work, he told her. He can't remember what this *work* was, and he doesn't yet want to know. He lets it pass.

Does anyone know how hysterical you really are?

He knows her next line by heart.

I got 'em all fooled, she said.

He knows that even in the darkness of this memory she was smiling that crazymaking smile of hers: sly, perceptive, sexy but unaware of just how much. A world of possibilities in that smile.

Speaking of owls, she said, someone in _____ told me you sound like one.

He took a swig and blinked. Who said I was like an owl? Who? Who?

Byron kicked the iron fire drum and howled. She held on to her folding chair and gasped in between giggles. Someone stop him. I'm gonna die.

Oh my God, you guys, he said, realizing now.

Okay, so, she said. You know why crows in Boston keep getting hit by trucks? Because the only word they know is caw!

You must be stopped, he said.

Crows are predators, said Byron, suddenly serious. He hoisted his beer like a gavel. They'll eat baby birds, doves, oh yeah. Get enough of 'em together, they'll gang up on our great horned owl.

Byron had a habit of putting his feet up and turning those feet into a drunken lectern, but she didn't know any of that yet. She glanced at him—*is Byron okay?*—and he could only offer a bemused smile in return as an apology for his clearly weird friend.

He kicked Byron to break the silence. How many beers have you had?

How many beers have *you* had? countered Byron with mock suspicion.

Three.

More like six, said Byron, now tilting his head.

Alcohol doesn't count on vacation, she said, which got another laugh.

More like twelve, said Byron, now with his eyes crossed.

Whatever, two grapes, he said.

What the hell is two grapes? she said. Giggles now, and dangerously infectious ones too.

And you're really not red? said Byron. It's too dark to see.

I don't get red! he said.

All Asians are supposed to get red! said Byron. I'm only half and I know for sure I'm red.

It's a problem when drinking with racist best friends like you, he said, and he and Byron tossed back and forth a few chuckles with practiced ease.

He's red, she said, but not because of the alcohol. Her beam held steady. She was staring at him. It's because we got him good and now he's all shy.

I'm not shy.

He said shyly, she said through the light of her beam.

I gotta piss, said Byron. Add a perimeter check to the logbook for me?

Yes sir.

Don't *sir* me. I said no friggin' hierarchies, dude!

Byron stumbled away, waking the campground with the errant kick of an empty bucket, and vanished with a *Fuck!*

They giggled at his graceful exit.

Perimeter check? she said.

He could only sigh. Yep, yep, yep.

One minute we're camping, and the next it's like you guys are playacting some kind of army bivouac, she noted, accurately.

He started another swig, then stopped himself. He didn't need anything more to drink, because drinking more would only obscure this moment.

Byron's just Byron, he said.

You're indulging him! she cried.

I am.

It's sweet and kinda weird.

Thank you.

Well thank God, 'cause when I think of you I don't think prepper type, she said.

He smiles at this. Savoring those words. He remembers what comes next in this memory: he set his beer into the wild grass and forgot all about it because beer was nothing compared to her words. Nothing could be anything, compared.

What are your favorite horror movies? he said finally.

We're skipping straight to the horror category, she said.

I mean unless—

The Wailing, she said.

Get all the way outta here.

Mind-blowing, she said.

So mind-blowing, he agreed.

But funny, too, and sweet just as much as it was scary.

Right?

Also *Parasite*, she said. Also *The Host*.

You have a thing for Korean horror movies?

You got me! she said. I have a total fetish!

He paused. He'd never been an object of fetish before, even in jest.

Are you blushing again? she said. Please say I made you blush two times.

He touched his cheek in the dark, and yes, it did feel a little warm.

How about the classics, he said. Like *Dawn of the Dead*?

Hehehehe!

What!

I thought you said *Dong of the Dead*.

He laughed, too, just so absolutely thrilled at how fluidly this new history between them was writing itself across the parchment.

Totally different movie, he said. I'll send you a link.

Please don't! she said.

What's so funny? said Byron, and missed his chair by a mile to hit his ass in the dirt.

Time to sleep, he said, laughing, and she agreed, and he agreed.

So they slept.

They lay in their respective single tents, each pitched so closely to one another that he could hear her every zip, every rustle, every sigh. He zipped himself into his sleeping bag as well—the icy dew had fallen hours ago—and dared a whisper just for her, something he hadn't done since he was a little kid at a slumber party:

Dong of the Dead!

She immediately was beset by giggles stifled by something—her sleeping bag? Her slim smooth hand? Was her palm cool? Hot?

Stop, she whispered back.

Okay.

She fell silent for a moment, then fell into maniacal wheezing once more. You're making my stomach hurt, stop!

I didn't say anything! he hissed.

Her giggles subsided, and the night took over.

Good night, _____, she said.

He said her name right back: Good night, _____.

But he knew she was lying awake in her sleeping bag. Even as the dying fire crumbled apart, he could hear her awake.

He can't remember if her sleeping bag was red or green or blue or purple like the one with the corpse.

A sleeping bag with a corpse, nothing left to keep warm, no movement in the dead of night for all the nights to come.

And what nights are to come after this?

Her corpse in a sleeping bag and the child snuggled to her bony breast, too—you'd see her if you unzipped the thing—as their years-old campfire defiantly continues to burn with strange flames that never extinguish.

He flinches awake with all his limbs and is struck by a divine astonishment.

Before him, a blaze gushes tall enough to fan across the ceiling.

SEVENTEEN

THE CHRISTMAS TREE.

He should've known.

He kicks his way to his feet, runs out, runs back to get his stuff: the bucket, his to-go cup already softening in the naked heat. He must not lose his things. Runs back out, slams into the corridor wall as he turns to sprint down the staircase.

Don't give out on me now, he thinks, right as a step gives out on him.

The bucket flies forward. In a daze, he realizes he is stuck crotch-deep in the broken stair, leg dangling helplessly into the moldering darkness beneath, home to god-knows-what.

The Christmas tree!

What numbskull hangs a three-meter-tall fire hazard above a working fireplace?

From above, the sound of water, except the water was fire.

Push up, says Byron.

What?

Push up! he shouts, at himself.

He realizes he's still half-asleep.

He braces both hands at his sides and pushes hard, hard enough to let him snap a quick handgrip onto the stair rail above and pull.

Soon his leg comes out—uneaten—up to his knee so he can contort it out of the jagged hole.

Then he tumbles.

He reaches the bottom of the staircase, where he at least has the good sense not to move suddenly. Not a good idea when lying in a sea of broken glass. He gingerly rolls to all fours, stands, and shakes glitter from his limbs.

Death from a glass cut? Hell no, not today.

He doesn't have much time. Just enough to gather the things thrown from the bucket and run out. Heavier now with the prybar in there.

Finally he makes it out into the dry endless night. When he looks back, the bedroom window is flickering a bright orange-black. It is quiet. Out here, you can't really tell anything is wrong. You can't tell the house is vaporizing from the inside out.

Even the owl can't tell. It's just there, saying what it always says:

Who-oo, who? Who?

But now the glass spiders with a *ktk*, and the flames have grown large enough to shove the entire pane crashing out of its frame. The bird flaps away, unseen. Perhaps with a look of *nope* on its face.

But he himself doesn't move.

The flames—brilliant orange feathers, like a phoenix, huh—stretch and reach the thinnest tendrils of the dry, dead, obviously imported tree, igniting it with an easy caress. Kinda beautiful, he thinks. A singular conflagration growing so tall so quick—now four, now eight meters in height—sending embers so high they cool themselves blue into real stars just like they'd always dreamed of becoming.

Back on wretched Earth, a series of crashes come from within the house announcing three critical breaches through the roof.

As quickly as the tree had ignited, it dims, as if satisfied with seeding the heavens with new constellations. The fire moves on, room to room, thoughtfully. It takes care of the dead body. It and it alone knows who that person was and what they were made of.

What a quiet, lush sound, he thinks. No fire trucks come, no klaxons. The flames, as big as they are, are but a tiny matchlight in this vast black no-place. He could watch it burn all alone all night until the house is nothing but a shrunken sizzling heap.

He thinks about cities and their gas lines running everywhere. Whose bright idea was that? Running miles of flammable pipe all under and around people's homes?

He thinks about cities—how totally burned up they must now be. There's no way such a fragile system could hold for long.

There's no way *they* could've held out for long.

The phoenix feathers emerge from window after window, gripping the tops of the frames and pulling up hard.

Are his girls alive? Did they manage to hold out?

He realizes the flames have no interest in ripping up the house wall by wall. What they really seek is the much easier solution sitting beside the house.

The propane tank.

NO SMOKING

The flames grope at the base of the giant pill-shaped tank, then snuggle their way beneath it for a proper roasting.

NO SPARKS

He runs.

Ahead in the flickering dark is a rock barely big enough to curl behind. He hugs himself in the rock's mile-long shadow, tucks his bucket in closer, waits.

NO DIRECT FLAMES

NO SURVIVORS IN ANY CITY ANYWHERE

It is a beautiful still night—vistas so vast the light from the flames dies out before it can find any surfaces to touch—

NO YOUR FAMILY WAS NOT SOMEHOW SPECIAL

NO YOUR FAMILY IS DEAD EVERYONE IS DEAD

To make its point undeniably clear, the tank then explodes. A quick intake of breath, then a great sudden exhalation. Terrifying in size. And dry, too—not that wet growl found in idiotic movies. Shrapnel radiates in neat straight lines simply everywhere.

He dares a look over the rock; the house has been erased. Even most of the fire is gone by now.

In his bucket is the only surviving artifact from that place: the prybar.

Was it worth it? Your little excursion?

He takes a long pull from his to-go cup and then—hell with it—drinks off the whole thing.

He can always get more back at the shelter.

———————

DAWN IS BREAKING BY THE TIME HE REACHES THE CHANNEL ONCE again. He had kept a steady gaze on the tiny pinprick of the solar-powered streetlamp as he stumbled. Now he can allow himself a look back. The only evidence left is the tiniest wisp of black rising into the empty sky.

That could've been me, he thinks. A little bit of soot on its way to heaven.

Actually, would that be so bad?

He doesn't know what anything is right now. He needs water and food and sleep. He needs not to be freezing his ass off anymore. He finds himself *looking forward* to returning to the shelter.

He drags his precious sneakers in the endless dirt. Dirt everywhere, nothing but. Who gives a shit anymore. When he travels far enough finally to make out the distant familiar concrete channel and twin bridges in the dim rising light, he actually sings:

Home again, home again.

Jiggy-jig-jig.

You sent me a sign, didn't you, he says.

Did I? says the crow.

Big explosion visible from orbit, he says. Real subtle.

It was a little much, wasn't it?

Anyway, I got the message. Stay home, don't bother, nothing out there. Got it.

If you believe it to be a message, then let it be a message.

I'm not arguing about this, he thinks. Crows do not talk. You are in my head.

Me inside you, interesting. We could be each other.

Shut the hell up.

My work is done for now. Goodbye.

Work?

He waits, but there is nothing.

Hello?

He had stopped long enough to start shivering. Gotta keep moving. Almost there.

He arrives at the KROKOS graffiti, almost invisible in the predawn, and knows it is eighty-eight paces to the crow carcass, then thirty more to his shelter. Almost there. He'll give that dead little bird a good kick along the way.

Sweat glazes his frozen forearms, making the cold that much worse. He should've stayed home.

He says it again: home.

Eighty-five steps, eighty-six, -seven, -eight. It should be here. He looks at his feet. Where are you? He wheels about.

The crow has vanished.

PART II

THE OLD MAN

EIGHTEEN

WHEN HE WAS LITTLE, FOREVER AGO WHEN CHILDREN STILL WALKED themselves to school, he'd found himself lingering in a playground in the misty hours of early morning.

In the sand pit by the swings he found a pile of chicken bones arranged in a pentagram. He'd heard about this symbol from the news; his parents had warned him of Satanists. Devil worshippers. People who wore studs and listened to metal. They kidnapping you, said his mother in her particular English. They do so bad things. They forcing you take the drugs and kill the animal. Very be careful.

He'd gotten plenty of warnings like this from his mother and father. Unmarked white vans contained North Koreans on a kidnap-and-brainwash spree. Billiards were the game of gangsters and would land you in a choreographed street fight you had no chance of winning. Handling playing cards would turn you into a gambling addict. These warnings of course never panned out. As an adult, he rented vans and played pool and dealt poker and managed to stay alive, balanced, non-Communist. He would share these warnings with his White friends and together they would chuckle, ha ha. He didn't yet realize that his mother and father's paranoid warnings were roundabout attempts to say *We love you.*

Little him used to walk to school, without a fear in the world—until he came face-to-face with his first real pentagram. That was when fear became real.

Back in the shelter now, he warms a can on the camping stove and lets the image of the chicken bone pentagram stay in his mind for a moment like a freeze frame.

Now, of course, he knows the bones were a joke. Bunch of bored kids smoking weed in the park one night after polishing off a bucket of fried chicken, inspired by the Satanic symbols on the album covers of their favorite bands.

Therefore: when those cairns fell down yesterday? That was just simple inertia. Mountains crumble, sands shift, shit moves in the wind.

The crow carcass—valuable free food—was taken by a snake or kit fox or whatever.

As if to confirm his thoughts, a faraway bird drifts into view. The pentagram vanishes and his mind relaxes.

See? says the bird. My existence doesn't mean diddly-squat, craw! And the bird dips away.

He smiles to himself. The food is warm. He eats.

Think logically. Think about when the cairns were formed. If they're even just a few years old, their creators are long gone, leaving him safe. Sure, the safest policy is to assume they were recent. Think of all the new tribes that had formed after the apocalypse. Or the exodus of Arroyo Plato survivors, one of millions that happened all over the smoldering world. Maybe they left the cairns as parting mementos as they abandoned their homes in search of supplies.

Which would imply the houses near him have been depleted of anything useful, he guesses. Meaning, once his stack of cans are consumed, he'll quite literally be up a dry creek without a paddle. The only way to be sure of this theory would be to search the houses. No way he'll find any food. Maybe a bicycle or clean socks or a container with an airtight lid, though. You never know what you'll find.

A dead body?

He thinks about the human urge to account for each and every dead person. How that's a recent phenomenon. For much of history, after all, most deaths were not considered worth noting, because most lives were not considered worth noting. Kings and queens and archbishops, sure, but not common folk. It's only in the modern age that we deemed every life to be deserving of a spot on humanity's long scrolling record.

Whoever that was in the house—burned on a lonely pyre without a single witness—marked a return of sorts, to the way we used to do things. No one earns a marker now, least of all for living.

He finishes his meal, sweeps his shelter floor with a piece of cardboard, stands outside to stretch. In the distance hangs that vinyl banner, with all its promises and smiling dead. He'll have to take that eyesore down.

He takes a length of the clear string and tugs at it. It is surprisingly strong. He fashions a lanyard for his wine tool and wears it like a pendant.

He strolls over to the faucet and lets it run for a moment before stripping off his clothes and lying under the cold stream. The water cools his head. He prods it, finds no lingering sign of injury. Not on the outside, at least. Who knows what's going on inside.

No way anyone lives in these houses anymore. Why not search them?

We tried that already. It didn't work out.

So we're just going to die under a bridge?

He rinses his clothes, wrings them out, and sets them to dry on the hot slope. Naked but for the wine tool hanging from his neck, he walks to his old shelter. As sharp as the ground is, it's a relief to be free from his lopsided shoes.

This place is all his. Whoever attacked him hadn't exactly offered him a seat at afternoon tea, but they also hadn't cared enough to kill him dead. They'd probably reached a certain point. Where there was nothing left. At least they hadn't been far gone enough to carve his body up into travel snacks.

He tidies his bucket, seat cushion, and other things. He flips his drying clothes to give them a turn in the warming sun.

Then he crosses the channel to the vinyl banner near ENTRANCE 1 (SEALED). It's suspended by simple wire hooks hung on the edge of the cinder-block wall far above him. Easily removed. He lays the banner facedown and rolls it and its smiling faces up, bye-bye.

He stores the banner in the shelter. It's waterproof, and you never know. He takes a long drink from his to-go cup.

He lies on the slope and lets the sun fill his naked body with warmth.

He should figure out how to hunt. Craft better weapons. Just like in a video game, ha!

Next level's in those houses, you know.

Where's the pause button?

His hand-drawn map describes a narrow zone hemmed in on all sides by mountains, a wasteland, foreboding totems, and ghost houses. Houses that could burn and swallow him whole and draw not a single peep from anyone, because there is no one left.

We've only got a few days' worth of food.

I'm playing a level someone's already picked clean.

I'm just saying. You know we have to move on.

You first.

NINETEEN

THERE WAS THAT ONE BOOK (MOVIE?) EVERYONE WAS FAMILIAR WITH but no one had actually read (seen?).

The title, like lots of things in this new memory-free world, escapes him. He could probably suss it out through free word association, one cultural reference forming the edge of another until the shape of his past grew definite.

But he'd really rather not, thanks.

His shirt and pants are dry and warm and stiff and feel unfamiliar, like someone else's clothes.

So anyway: in this book, a man is stranded on a desert island after crashing his overnight delivery company cargo plane. He spends years there. He teaches himself how to spear fish and is eventually accompanied by a "Man Friday," represented by a volleyball with a bloody palm print that he worships. But also is like his best friend. Something like that.

He himself will never need a Man Friday, inanimate or not. It'd mean he's lost all hope. It'd mean he's decided to settle in and build a life on this deserted island. He can't do that. He'll venture out again. He has to.

He is pretty sure he'd been sleeping. What time is it?

Food time, that's what. He pierces a can and cranks it open, leaving the lid dangling. He sets it aside. He draws a match, closes the box, positions it sideways. He strikes the match on the side of the box and opens the camping stove valve a quarter turn. The flame lights without a sound.

He blows out the match, savoring its smoldering smell, and sets it aside six other spent matches by the spool of clear string.

He places the can on the flame and begins stirring in repose.

There seems to be no wind. And yet, just to his right he can see the reeds swaying just a bit. Maybe the swaying is an effect of the channel, which possibly amplifies air movement.

Byron would like this setup.

This river channel, he'd say, is obviously asymmetrical. See how the reeds on the left bank move more than the right? Probably an effect of the cinder-block wall. Eddies change depending on the prevailing wind direction and speed, but in general there's a pretty clear pattern to me. See that?

Now, he'd continue, most of the reeds grow on the side of the channel with that cinder-block wall. Maybe the eddies gather seeds there. Or maybe the seeds are shaped to bias that location. Or maybe both.

His chili with beans begins bubbling, and he dials the camping stove off.

He takes a bite, rests his spoon in the can until he finishes chewing. This way the can lasts longer.

Byron, he says. No offense, but I can't help thinking you're full of shit.

It is crucial that you learn about the local flora and fauna if you want to survive this, says Byron in the dark.

Eddies and biases and the shape of seeds, ha ha.

Byron pauses and smiles to himself. Okay, ha ha.

Okay?

Maybe I am full of shit, ha ha.

I'm just messing with you, he says.

I know.

You're good.

I am, thank you, says Byron.

It's just you're way smarter about shit like this than me.

I'm good at faking it.

That's not true, he says. You actually know things.

Not without data I do not, says Byron. I got no single solitary suck-ass clue except what my intuition tells me.

Byron's voice sounds funny, like it is now very far down a tunnel.

Byron? he says.

The wind in the channel probably means nothing, which is perfectly fine, just is what it is, says Byron.

I wish you were here, man, he says.

It's not like any of this is your fault or anything.

You'd know what to do if you were here.

Doesn't it feel good to watch the reeds move this way and that? says Byron. You'll figure something out, what I don't know, maybe you will, maybe you won't, but you could certainly watch these beautiful graceful plants forever. Could be some kinda puzzle, or you could turn it into one, why not.

Byron?

Byron is gone.

Byron?

He's stopped mid-can, something he's never done before. He is full. But it isn't like he has a fridge to keep things in, so he scrapes out every last bit, swallows, and fills the can with water and drinks the rest as was his usual habit.

HE STANDS AT THE BOTTOM OF THE CHANNEL AMONG THE SPARSE reeds. He notices it's early morning. It is twenty strides from here to the farthest reed. Each stride measures about five feet, and multiplied by six major patches of reeds that works out to be about six hundred feet.

A puzzle, Byron?

He has enough clear string. He ties one end to a reed and clambers back up to his shelter. He snips the string, ties it to the cinder block so it won't fly away. He does this for the other reeds, heading down, tying the string, and then climbing back up to anchor the other end for each, making sure they all have about the same amount of tension. Not too tight, but not so slack that they drag on the ground.

What kind of puzzle?

The strings, connected now, arc from the top of the cinder block to their respective reeds below. He cuts simple circles out of a sheet of cardboard—he has plenty of that—and notches them to mark each string. When the reeds move, the cardboard circles rise and fall smoothly. He numbers each one.

Everywhere in the world has its particular patterns, and those patterns make up the facts of that place.

That's what you meant, right, man?

On a fresh sheet of cardboard he marks the amplitude range of each disc. He does this by lying down to eyeball the distance traveled by each, counting steadily to ten, and drawing the estimated lowest point and highest point for each of the six points over sixty seconds, or one minute. From these numbers he can draw a graph to better visualize things. No data for direction, but amplitude is probably a good start.

Like: it's already obvious that reeds 3, 4, and 1 move way more than the others. Weird, because they are the ones farthest from the cinder-block wall.

What do you think about that?

Over the next few days here—his last before moving on—he'll keep on keeping track. Could be something, maybe not. Ancient people drew characters out of the stars for fun, and then it turned out

they could navigate whole seas with that quote useless knowledge un-
quote.

You never know.

———————

HE URINATES, SENDS WATER DOWN. ANOTHER DAY. HE LIES ON HIS
belly and counts the discs again, marking movements on the cardboard. The clear string is strong and performs with good response
and impressive strength. He remembers to mark the position of the
cinder block on the floor in case it shifts.

A ruler would be nice. So he tears a strip of cardboard and marks
the straightest edge. Now his measurements will be more precise.
Whole religions formed around observations of natural phenomena,
right, Byron? Talkin' 'bout Stonehenge, or those huge drawings in
Peru.

What am I even saying, he thinks. I'm just a dizzy little daisy. He
sees an open flower, hears a voice, and knows it's hers.

He squeezes his eyes hard for a moment, counts to sixty to blank
everything out. The flower spins shut. He opens his eyes again. The
discs undulate. He marks the cardboard. The ruler is good. He knows
it's bullshit, but it's pleasant bullshit that passes the time nicely. He
lets out a long, slow exhale.

It's finally hitting him hard that he could've died in that meaningless house fire.

He is not a hero in some adventure book about surviving against
all odds. He is the guy who hides away procrastinating with string
and cardboard. Last Surviving Member of Human Race Puts Things
Off. He giggles at that headline. But he doesn't giggle for long.

Because after the food is finished he'll have to move on. Not to the
desert—nothing for miles out there—but to the obvious choice he's
been avoiding all along: the houses.

He's already found a dead body; he'll have to get ready to find more. Or live bodies. He grips the prybar, swings it with an amateur wrist. Imagines landing a solid meaty hit, hooking into bone, ripping free.

Can you do this?

Can you sift through things like jackets, containers, tape? Can you take apart appliances and use the parts for other stuff, like—who knows—repurposing a stove rack to dry strips of meat or skin a rabbit or something?

Can you?

You can't.

He wants to shout it out: I can't!

Jewelry, flip-flops, digital meat thermometers, antibacterial pet ramps. All crap, useless now. Maybe it'd be better to incinerate it all with a giant homemade Christmas tree fire hazard. Watch it all go up. Monogrammed shot glasses. Wedding rings. Dreams catching under holiday flame. Now books, movies, photos, toys, papers full of dead people's handwriting. All this crap from all those years hidden away like a forgotten museum finally burning down.

It's not fair.

Someone is supposed to carry those memories. Death is fine—you are supposed to die—but then someone is supposed to carry you on.

If no one carries you on, it's like you were never there.

TWENTY

NEXT MORNING. HE WAKES, PUMPS OUT TWENTY EVEN PUSH-UPS, AND then lies there to take measurements. Again, reeds 3, 4, and 1 show greater movement than the rest of the group.

Let's say, just for ticklebums, that one of the houses up there has seeds. It's not so outlandish, is it? Not many people think to grab seeds when fleeing attackers. He could set up a small garden on the far side of the river channel using reed clusters 3, 4, and 1 as a windbreak. Tomatoes, cucumbers. And lettuce! It'd be a good setup. He could imagine finding a garden hose to connect to the faucet to provide irrigation. He could maybe even make a weather vane. Maybe the measurements aren't meaningless. With enough planning and patience, this dry channel could wind up being his lifelong shelter, he reckons.

Reckons?

He sets his pen down. He is losing his mind. He isn't staying here forever. He doesn't belong in this place.

He removes the insoles from both his shoes and—with eyes averted—transfers the brass Revere key from one into the other, to give his right foot a break. The feel of the warm metal grounds him by soaking up his staticky thoughts. He places the key in his left shoe.

The key can live nowhere else. Certainly not his pockets, which he is constantly reaching into with his bare hands.

He puts his shoes back on, heaves himself to his feet, and hears a far-off gong.

A dark bronze sound.

He freezes. Is it the blood rushing from his head? He lies back down, waits, stands up. Nothing.

After a moment the gong sounds again.

He peers out from behind the blanket. Gong, gong, gong. It is coming from the terminus. The sound grows steadier and louder: footsteps. No doubt about it. Someone inside the massive drain pipe, approaching.

He hastens down the slope. Halfway down he remembers his weapons. He crouches to a skidding halt and sprints back up to the shelter to retrieve his long spear, then his short prybar. He holds the spear tip steady before him as he dashes to the first bridge and conceals himself in the shade of a support column there. He slips the heavy prybar into the wire loop on his belt and hopes it'll hold.

The gonging grows louder and louder. He peers at the terminus: nothing. He ducks back behind the column.

His heart thrashes about in his chest, and he realizes he is suddenly damp with sweat. There is a moment approaching, he knows. A moment that may be his last conscious experience. On the column are words debossed into the concrete: MCPHERSON CONST. CO. 1995. A faint waterline marks the surface just below eye level. Water flowed here once. Down at his feet sits a looped hook of junk plastic. It is, he realizes, one of those tiny hangers used to display socks at department stores.

Brand-new baby socks with crisp tissue paper crinkling inside.

He had held socks like this once, in the palm of his hand, before she had been born. The sound of the crisp tissue paper was the first event that eventually led him here. But how?

This hopeless question could be the last ever produced by his panicking brain.

He adjusts his grip on the spear and watches the three pipes of the terminus in the near distance. Which one? The gonging comes to a stuttering crescendo, and stops.

A shuffling sound now. The sound of someone dragging themselves across a tin roof. A figure emerges from the pipe on the right, pipe number 3. A White man with crazed white hair wearing long black garments. Attached to each of the man's limbs are a dozen white shopping bags, each filled to bursting. The weight of the bags forces him to move with a swinging effort, like a deep-sea diver crashing his way out of the ocean. One of the bags bears the words THANK YOU THANK YOU THANK YOU THANK YOU.

The man scoots along in a seated position until he reaches the lip of the pipe. With the great care of a drunkard, he turns his body onto all fours in preparation to back himself out of the pipe. He seems to be considering how best to dangle onto the ground six feet below.

The man's foot slips. He falls onto his chest and slides, fingertips thudding against the corrugated steel, before dropping like a rag doll onto the concrete floor of the river channel. The man's head bounces once, and hard. He lies there with the breeze pushing at that mad hair of his. He lies motionless.

TWENTY-ONE

HE WATCHES THE OLD MAN FOR WHAT FEELS LIKE AN HOUR.

The guy doesn't move. Is he dead? He adjusts his grip on his spear again and again. There's no way the man could be dead from a fall so short. Unless he hit the ground at a freakish angle. Maybe his neck snapped. Maybe he is lying paralyzed and unable to call for help.

He watches for a few more long minutes. Still nothing. The adrenaline seems to be ebbing from his body, and in its place comes the gradual realization that he could be staring at a man helpless and suffering. He may have nothing to fear after all.

He can walk right up and finish him off with a single spear thrust to the eye.

He can pierce the white bags and sift through their contents at his leisure while the man stares in horror.

He can simply stand there and gawk. He'd never seen a dead body before the world ended. Now he's seen two in a single week that he's been allowed to remember. Two is probably on the low end of the scale for most these days.

The old man could also be a trap. Maybe the old man is not stupid. He had spotted him well in advance, this younger, clearly panicked, clearly inexperienced man in his obvious stakeout spot holding his pathetic weapon.

Maybe the old man has just taken a well-practiced pratfall. He has a full belly and a sharp mind and now lies awake and alive, listening for his mark's footsteps to come close enough for a solid surprise attack.

This pretend death, he remembers, is called *playing possum*.

Not today, old man. He settles deeper into his position and holds his spear tip forward. The spear is no toy, no sir. I can wait as long as it takes.

ANOTHER HOUR PASSES. THE LAST TRACES OF ADRENALINE HAVE VAN-ished from his body, and his clothes cling with sweat. The prybar is pulling his flimsy wire loop loose; he tightens it again and resumes his watch.

The old man has not moved.

He can't tell much from the shape of the plastic bags. They are round and fluffy and soft. Clothes, maybe? Food? Maybe the old man is far gone by this point, and carries a collection of found women's underwear? Marshmallows? Severed ears?

What about weapons? A small pistol, and a supply of ammunition that grows increasingly precious with each shot fired? Or maybe something more ordinary? Ordinary things now count as weapons in this new world. His clear string, for example, could cut into a throat. The foil cutter on his wine tool. And of course the prybar. He mentally practices drawing it out quickly for attack. It's good to have a backup weapon.

Then there is the question of where the old man has come from. The three storm-drain pipes stand unguarded and open, an enigma waiting for anyone willing to climb in and venture into darkness.

Three perfect cylinders set in a massive rhombus of concrete, punctuated by a body on the floor.

He can imagine whole groups of survivors heading underground, maybe to the safety of abandoned maintenance tunnels below. That kind of thing had been done before. There was an old photo of Brits huddled in subway tunnels, all still in their smart street clothes. Every time there was a bombing, or the threat of one, they scrambled below while sirens droned on, carrying whatever they happened to be carrying, no clue if they would ever live normal lives again. No clue if the world above ground would still be there when they came back up.

Maybe a new generation of underground refugee is within those pipes, huddled in the darkness. Their temporary shelter now permanent. Faces illuminated by leisure camping gear now rendered dire and crucial while fires razed the neighborhoods above into the blackened fields they now are.

Maybe, maybe, nothing but maybes.

Supplies dwindled. The underground survivors sent scouts out for supplies, and they never came back. So they turned on one another. Cannibalism. This old man has escaped one hell after another, only to fall six feet to an unceremonious death.

Maybe, maybe.

Hot now, even in the shade. He lowers his spear for a moment to wipe his brow and lies on the slope of the river channel to rest. He can still keep his eyes on the old man even lying down. See?

———

THEY USED TO HAVE THAT SHITTY FAN. A TALL, CREAKY FLOOR DEVICE with clear blue blades spinning within the torus of its wire cage, gently swinging its head back and forth in the heat. *Oscillating.* No one could have possibly known that word before these fans.

It was hot as hell, summer, lying in a bed in the afternoon. No AC in their cheap apartment. She lay next to him, and they were both naked, and they were both so young they had nothing else to do with the day except lie there and see where their minds wandered. This was way before any pregnancy or birth. The brown skin of her abdomen bore no scar. They'd just made love.

There was a place your body settled into while at absolute rest, in a pose of such stillness and contentment and inevitability that to move even the slightest bit would disturb its perfection. To rise, sip from the glass of ice water laden with beadlets of condensation by the window aglow with the sheer primrose drapes she obsessed over, and then attempt to regain that position of ideal repose, would be impossible. The cavity in the bed would have ballooned slightly. The bedsheets would have cooled just enough to mark your absence.

Thirsty as he was, he did not move. He lay there with her. A perfect black curlicue of her hair lay stuck to the sweat on his forehead and he wondered how long it would take to dry and blow free.

Their heads were touching. He remembered how they loved this: a small point of contact the size of a dollar coin, but potent nevertheless. They liked to imagine their brains' electrical signals rerouting and merging at this new nexus, little nodes of light slowing their pace to sync up these two systems now each mated with one another. They liked to imagine they were exchanging data.

On this warm, lazy day, she sent him a single bright rainbow-colored bit. He paused, smiled, sent a matching bit zipping back.

As the oscillating fan blew about the room, they knew they would have a baby.

TWENTY-TWO

HE OPENS HIS EYES.

No.

He'd fallen asleep. His hands sit in his lap, still cradling the spear. He hears a shuffle and glances up.

The face of the old man floats before him, a mask of crushed paper. Holding something in his hands, about as long as a human femur, hooked on one end.

The prybar.

He springs back, clutching the spear anew. The old man is on all fours and shrinks back in response.

Berries? asks the old man, and shakes the prybar in the air before him. Berries?

The old man's eyes grow wider as he holds his ground.

He renews his grip on the spear and aims the tip right at the old man's face. If the spear fails—fails to pierce the soft target of his eye and travel back into his hot brain, oh God—he always has the wine tool as a last resort. Although he'll need to get a few feet away to retrieve it and flick it open and ready. He tries moving back, but finds his legs are unable to.

Both his legs have fallen asleep.

He hears the old man murmur again, Berries, this time with

wonder, and watches as he shifts his withered gaze down the channel. The old man is staring at the blanket in the distance, covering his shelter. He seems to comprehend the importance of that place.

Oh no no no. He shifts to a low squat, almost tipping on his own unresponsive legs. You are not going to jack my shit.

He suddenly remembers a time when his arm had gone so numb in his sleep that he thought a stranger had tucked their hand under his face. Or a severed limb.

That's how numb his legs are now.

He watches helplessly as the old man looks back at him, then the shelter, then him, then back again. He jerks his spear in warning: don't you dare. The old man jerks the prybar—*his* prybar, dammit—right back at him.

The two of them hold this standoff for a long moment. It's almost polite, the way they wait for each other to make the first move.

The numbness in his legs begins to dissolve, flooding his nerves with thousands of white-hot pinpricks.

The old man turns—*ehh*—and begins hobbling toward the shelter.

Stop, he hisses at him, and each step in pursuit sends brilliant pulses of pain up his body, so impressive and sharp he wants to laugh. No one in the history of humanity has ever died from a case of pins and needles, but dang.

The two men shamble together for a few long seconds in silence. From a distance it probably looks like the old man is pulling him along with a stick. Some kind of tedious two-man Beckett play for no one in particular.

The old man is just one step out of reach of his spear. Just inches away.

Nuh, he blurts, not quite a battle cry, and lunges forward with a wild slash across the old man's legs.

He makes contact with the rod of the spear, not the tip. But it works: one leg crashes against the other, and the old man falls in a splash of noisy plastic.

Berries, he cries.

He's all over the old man now. Shut it, he breathes. He glances at the houses above. No movement. Shut your face hole or we both die. He snatches up his prybar, struggles to holster it back in his useless wire loop, tucks it under an arm. He stands over him with his spear ready.

Berries, whimpers the old man.

The old man's face sags with defeat. There is a son somewhere in that face, a father or husband maybe, its features scrubbed so thin by time and wind that he could be anyone. Like a corpse left in the sun. He could be any race, any age between forty and a thousand. His hair gathers in dirty ivory hanks around eyes like dented glass marbles, flat with tears now.

The old man slowly reaches for his shirt pocket. His breath stinks like something died in his throat.

He shakes the old man. Who are you? he says.

The old man pulls a piece of paper out of the pocket. Berries.

What is it he keeps saying: *Buries*, or *bears*? Or is it simply babble, meaning nothing?

Of course it's nothing. Everything is nothing here.

The old man unfolds the paper: a cracked department-store portrait of a man with a woman and daughter, around age nine. A snapshot from the world back when it was alive and clean and perfect. It looks cut out of a catalog. Maybe it is.

Or maybe it's real, and the man is this old man, and this had been his family. Until the plague spread, until the firebombs came to contain the infected.

Berries, the old man insists, touching the photo.

He risks a closer look, and sees the eyes are the same.

TWENTY-THREE

HE LOWERS HIS SPEAR A CENTIMETER AND TILTS HIS HEAD TO REEXAMine the old man.

The old man returns his gaze with the resignation of countless prayers to God gone unanswered. Come what may, say his eyes, as he returns the photo to its special place. It's all pointless anyway.

What were their names, he asks him.

Burrberries, murmurs the old man.

They your family?

The old man nods.

Are you looking for them?

No response.

Are they out there? He gestures about. Alive?

The old man nods faster. Then he winces and grips his shoulder as if in pain.

He feels his heart flash with concern for the old man, but zaps that bug dead. Do not even try that with me, he says. He takes a step back. The old man continues making a big show of looking wounded, and reaches for a bag tied around his thigh.

Do not even, he says.

Berries, whines the old man, tapping the bag, then tapping his shoulder.

I'm gonna punch that bag open, he says. Do not move. Understand?

The old man just closes his eyes and massages his shoulder.

What is this? This is crazy.

What are the chances of meeting someone here in the middle of nowhere?

He wants to slap the old codger and tell him he's onto him—onto the whole damn thing—forcing him to break character and yell *Cut!* so that bored camera crew workers can emerge from their hiding places stretching and bitching about shoot schedules and overtime.

This is no puzzle. It isn't even real. It's a show.

Get up! he yells. Cut! Cut!

But the old man doesn't get up. A tear descends his temple and disappears into the white of his hair.

He looks around with his spear, no idea what to do next. The channel is blank like always. No camera crew, no showrunner, no nobody. He shifts his weight. He feels the key hiding in his shoe.

Then he turns and presses the spear into the plastic bag. There are multiple layers to get through, and he works the spear in and around with small movements, as if probing a body. The old man watches with grim resentment.

Inside the torn bag he can see four unopened toothbrushes, a dried sponge, trial-sized packets of hand sanitizer. The brand names and packaging spark a flashbulb memory of a drugstore lit by a hundred fluorescent tubes hanging above. He swats them aside.

There are socks, underwear, a bag of throat lozenges. Finally he hears a rattle and spots an amber bottle of painkillers. He coaxes it out, sweeps it toward him, and holds it up.

Is this what you're looking for? He can't stand the sight of the label and its familiar EXTREME STRENGTH logo. He tears it off and lets the label swirl away in the wind.

Got windy all of a sudden, didn't it?

The old man points at a bag on his other leg.

So he pierces that one as well. Little bottles of water come tumbling out. They lie in the sun, clear as glass, and cast tiny supernovae of refracted light in their shadows.

Where'd you get these, he demands.

The old man labors to a sitting position. He points at the pipes of the terminus. Then he helps himself to some water and beckons for the bottle of painkillers.

He tucks the spear under an arm and opens the bottle of pills, pointing it away from his face as if it contains bees. But of course there are no bees, they are just pills, pink as chalk. He shakes out a couple and sets them on the ground.

Take 'em, he says.

The old man swallows the pills. He seems to relax. Berries, he says.

Then the old man places his sun-blackened hand on the tip of the spear, guides it to his ear, and waits.

What is this, he says.

Berries, says the old man.

I'm supposed to kill you now? That can't be what I'm supposed to do next.

The old man looks up with mild disappointment.

He moves his spear away. Get up, he says.

The old man gives the ground a single weak push, buckles, and sighs with defeat.

Goddammit, he thinks, and offers a hand. The old man grasps it—skin dry and cool as stone—and teeters to his feet.

If you were the one who gave me those pills earlier, he tells him, then thanks.

The old man frowns: *Not me.*

What the hell does this old man signify? He's no Man Friday. He is neither a vandal nor a walking corpse. He hopes the old man isn't a test. He always hated tests.

He chooses an answer and hopes it's the correct one.

I bet you're hungry, he says, and leads the old man to the shelter.

TWENTY-FOUR

A CAN OF CHILI SITS WARMING ON THE STOVE IN THE SHELTER.

The only way you get one of these, he tells the old man, is if you show me everything in those bags.

So the old man complies. What he's doing feels profoundly jerk-worthy, as if he were forcing the guy to strip naked, when in fact all the old man is doing is untying each bag, laying out the contents, and waiting at the far end of the shelter for him to examine everything.

Still. If it feels like a violation it's because it *is* a violation, and he knows it. The old man casts his eyes down at a vague spot on the floor.

But isn't this the world now? Better him and not me? I bet he even has stuff tucked under his clothes.

We are not going there, he says to himself.

Before him lies it all. Clothes, surprisingly clean. A can opener with a handle. Utensils, a small thermos, cigarettes in a tin, a long barbecue lighter. Small packets of instant mashed potatoes.

There are three pornographic magazines, easily ten years old, rolled up. He pushes those back into their bag with the toe of his shoe.

There is a small plush toy keychain from San Diego. Cute little thing. There's a whole history there, but hell no, thank you. He shoves it under the clean clothes.

There's a straight razor so sharp it becomes invisible head-on.

I'll keep this safe, he says, and puts the razor in his pocket.

The rest of the bags are filled with bubble wrap.

You carry this stuff around? he asks, and gives one a pop.

The old man whinnies with panic. He pleads with his hands.

So he hands him a wad of the stuff, and watches as the old man neatly rolls and tucks it under his head. Berries, he says.

A pillow, he says. That makes sense. Also makes sense that bubble wrap is now so hard to come by that idly popping it for fun is unthinkable. But that kind of thing used to be so totally thinkable! Just yesterday!

The can of chili is ready. Before offering it, he pauses. You eat, I get answers, he says. I don't get answers, you get, you know. He feels ridiculous adding this last threat. He has no idea how this sort of thing is done.

The old man nods. He digs into the can with relish.

Watching the old man eat like this stirs up a feeling. From when he was little, when there was that stray cat. It had claimed the gap under the deck at his parents' house. Probably flea-ridden or feral, but he hadn't cared, and fed it anyway. He'd lie on his belly and watch the thing lick the bowl clean. Then he would bike to the store and buy more cat food, which he kept hidden under his dresser. The cat was his secret and his alone.

Then the cat vanished. A part of him knew that was bound to happen. It was a stray cat. But the other part of him felt a little stupid. The way the cat circled the posts mewling with anticipation as he cracked open a new can, the way the thing ate with total gusto, it made him feel like the cat loved him. Even when he would tease the cat by pulling at the can's tab without opening it, again and again, driving the creature into a frenzy so bad that it bonked its head against those deck posts, the cat still stuck around to get its prize. He probably could've tortured the cat for as long as he liked, if he were that guy.

But he wasn't that guy. He only teased it once or twice before relenting out of guilt. But still, one day the cat was just gone. Was once or twice all it took?

He watches the old man eat. I want answers, he says.

TWENTY-FIVE

HE SHOWS THE OLD MAN HOW TO SWIRL WATER IN THE CAN TO DRINK
the rest, and the old man rests in the back of the shelter.

The sun is setting outside. The air is finally cooling. The old man's
eyes glint from within that ghost-white circle of hair in the dark. The
old man is real. He tackled him to the ground himself. Can't do that
to a ghost.

But still: look at how he floats.

The old man lets out a single fart that fills the room like a question.

What? No! he says, waving a hand. Jesus.

Berries, says the old man in apology.

Come in here and do that?

Berries, berries.

You're telling me something about getting old, aren't you?

The old man chuckles.

They are both sitting up now, just kind of staring at each other.
He can't believe it, but he wants to laugh, too. The old man's chuckling
gets louder and breaks apart into a thick gravelly fit of coughing. He
holds his withered head in his withered hands and regains himself,
and the shelter gets quiet again.

Listen, he says. I'm gonna ask you a question. Just nod for yes, and shake for no.

Silence. He did just talk out loud, didn't he? Not just in his head? The old man is really there? He wants to prod him with the spear to make sure, like he'd done with the cursed purple sleeping bag.

He tries again: Nod for yes, shake for—

The old man nods.

Here we go, he thinks. Okay. Answers to the puzzle.

Do you only know one word?

Shake.

Did you suffer a brain injury?

The old man is still. Then he gives an almost imperceptible nod.

Okay, he thinks. Keep a light touch. Spook this guy, and he could clam up forever.

The photo—it's you?

Berries, says the old man, nodding.

And that's your wife and son?

Nod. The old man takes out the photo now and extends it to him, but he refuses.

No, I can't. They're beautiful. I'm all messed up inside. Do you understand?

Berries, concedes the old man readily, touching his sternum as if he can very easily understand being messed up in the heart.

I know for sure I had a family once, too, he wants to say, but just the unspoken thought brings him to a brink that he doesn't want to cross.

Are they still alive? he says.

Nod.

Are they far away?

Silence.

You don't know.

Nod. Berries. He stares at the photo and swallows a sob.

You'll find them. Hey.

The old man's eyes meet his.

Okay. I need to know what happened. How everything ended out there. Can you tell me that?

The old man leans forward, eager to explain. Berries berries berries, he says. On and on, nothing but that goddamn word. Repeated over and over again so fast it all just slurs together into one long guttural susurrus.

Hold on. Please. So the world has fallen apart.

The old man nods.

When? Last week? A month?

No.

Longer?

Yes.

This is gonna take forever, he thinks, and settles in. Was it a virus?

Shake, a strong one.

This sounds crazy but I have to ask. Zombies?

The old man just gives him an incredulous look, crazy calling out crazy.

Just kidding. How about war?

The old man tilts his head to one side, as if to say: *No-o-o-t quite?*

A nuclear accident? Aliens?

The old man points at the sound of that word. *You're so close.*

He chooses his words carefully. So the world—from before—it's gone? Right?

Berries, cries the old man, nodding.

He is running out of scenarios. But . . . so . . . was it . . . ?

Again the old man offers his photo. But it's not the photo. It's a piece of paper.

Berries, says the old man.

He takes the paper. It is folded origami-style into a diamond-shaped tray. He opens each petal until the entire square is revealed.

The paper is dense with microscopic handwriting trailing round and round the page to leave no spot blank. No title, no beginning, no end, no letters even, just:

2418 1001 4038 8812 9909 4914 7156 7751 2999 2429
4319 4095 7350 5178 4530 4078 7467 7523 4296 7992
8733 2047 6994 9259 1994 5852 0523 2023 8129 4911

On and on. Beautiful penmanship.

So this is the answer, he says.

The old man claps his hands once and nods: *Bingo*.

This is a hell of a moment right here. It can go well, or it can go very badly.

This old man is one hundred percent insane in the membrane.

He had neglected to plan for the contingency of someone one hundred percent insane in the membrane. His decision tree shrinks away to nothing. The old man must've lost his mind a long, long time ago. Certainly long enough to write thousands of numbers in four-point text.

He realizes he has no idea what this old man has been through up until now, what he has *had* to do to survive in this new world. He doesn't know how to respond to his numbers, because he doesn't know how the old man will react.

If he hugs him, calls him a genius, he'll probably be stuck with him forever.

If he dismisses the paper with the numbers, things could turn bad in an instant. The man has no weapons that he knows of, but he does have teeth.

He feels nauseous.

There they are, two men in a small shelter, staring at one another.

Thank you, he finally says to the old man.

He holds up the paper like it is a torch lighting a cave and forces himself to say the words. It's a lot, very very dense, but I think you're onto something. You figured all this out yourself?

The man's face falls with gratitude. He nods. *Yes, all by myself.*

Thank you, he says again. I'll get these to other survivors, if there are any out there. This is very important work.

The old man startles him by grasping his hand. Berries, he whispers, and he can feel his pulse through his grip. The old man pats the photo peeking out of the pocket next to his heart: himself, his wife, his child, smiling from the beyond.

TWENTY-SIX

AS NIGHT FALLS, HE MANAGES TO COAX A FEW MORE SCRAPS OF INFOR-
mation out of the old man, most of it nonsense.

There are a scant few believable details. Something about heat, a great fire destroying buildings for miles around. The old man hadn't encountered many people in his travels, and those he did he avoided entirely. The guy didn't trust anyone until this encounter. He's tried showing his numbers to others before but only got shoved away and ridiculed.

What else?

The old man hasn't met any cannibals but is sure they're out there.

He figures the human population has been cut by as much as ninety percent.

There are no underground colonies. He laughed at that.

He loves his wife and child very much and hopes to see them soon. He's not sure if they are still alive but keeps a strong faith. When he reunites with his wife he will perform cunnilingus on her and have intercourse, which he now playacts in exact detail.

Why don't you teach me how to make these mashed potatoes, he says, if only to get the guy to stop.

This gives the old man sudden purpose. He takes an empty can and fills it with some water to bring to a boil. Then—carefully—he tears open one of the small packets and pours its contents into another dry can. He jogs the can a few times, explaining by way of gesticulation that this is his method of aerating the powder mixture. The old man's hand, he notices, is missing two entire fingernails.

As soon as the water is hot enough, he pours it into the powder mix, little by little, stirring with a fork—no spoons, he insists. When the mashed potatoes are thick enough to cling to the tines in a fluffy clump, it is time to eat. He takes a bite, licks the fork clean, and offers it to him.

We're going to become best friends, he thinks. This old man will be my loyal companion till my dying day, wunderbar.

Just take the fork, old man spit and all, and take a bite while there's a bite to take.

The potatoes are creamy, buttery, with just enough salt and grit to give it texture. His mind is hauled to a memory of pots simmering atop a kitchen stove, and he has to shake his head to clear it.

When he opens his eyes—when had he closed them?—he sees the old man waiting for his verdict. Eyes shining in the dim dusk light.

Rillyrilly good, he says.

The old man claps once and places the two remaining boxes of instant mashed potatoes next to the pyramid of cans. *For you. My best friend.*

TIME FOR BED. HE LETS THE SHELTER BLANKET FALL. THE OLD MAN gathers all his things and ties each plastic bag to his limbs, like he's used to being ready to flee at any moment during the night. Makes sense.

Could be useful having a roommate, however unhinged he may be. He could maybe learn things. If they get to trusting one another, they could share various burdens and tasks while on adventure far,

far away from this shelter. Lots of things are easier with two versus one: gathering firewood, standing guard, stuff like that.

If they become blood brothers, maybe he will even show the old man the key in his shoe. Ask what sort of box it opens, what sort of vehicle it starts. It'll be a long time before he can bear doing something like that.

The old man gives him a roll of bubble wrap to rest his head on. Lice can't nest in bubble wrap, he tells himself, and lies down. He'll wait until the old man drifts off. Then he'll clutch the cans of food and mashed potatoes to his chest before falling asleep himself. Just in case. He touches the wine tool in his left pocket, then the straight razor in his right, tucks both the prybar and the spear behind his back lying against the wall.

Good night, he says in the darkness.

The old man doesn't reply. His breathing deepens.

The bubble wrap crinkles softly under his head, and the pneumatic spring of it feels like an inner tube drifting in the warm perfect turquoise of a pool in the sun. Floating like just-born babies being held in warm water in the darkness of a heated delivery room. It's bigger here, you're outside now. Nothing to be afraid of. You're still connected, see? We don't cut cords here. We don't slap feet.

In the birthing class, they had watched video after video of women in labor, rocking back and forth in a delirious trance, howling out invocations that went beyond language. Beyond simple pain—something far more complex and impenetrable. The crowning baby's head stretched their vaginas until a point was reached, a ridge crested, and the entire newborn came splashing out: an ivory figure stained with viscera.

They watched so many of these videos, and each one left them exhausted. The exhaustion was the point, because they no longer saw birth as something terrifying but as the miracle it indeed was. And yet with billions of women having given birth throughout history, the miracle was simultaneously mundane. The weirdest paradox. He remembered touching her naked belly whenever he got the chance. How firm and full it got.

Baby's coming out no matter what, the birthing coach would tell the class. Baby doesn't care what's going on at work. Baby doesn't know what your plans are.

Just be ready for baby, she said.

TWENTY-SEVEN

THERE WAS THIS THING CALLED THE RUBRIC IN GRADE SCHOOL. IT WAS a writing prompt.

The rubric had an easy paint-by-numbers structure: an Introduction, three Supportive Paragraphs, and a final In Conclusion. They used to write about all kinds of topics in class. *What If You Could Fly? What If You Could Turn into a Cat?* But the rubric that always stuck in his mind was the one called *What If the City Were Orange?*

What Would You Do in an Orange City? went Supportive Paragraph One. Then came Supportive Paragraphs Two and Three (*Who Would You Take with You?* and *Why Would It Be Fun?*), then the In Conclusion.

He's much older now since *What If the City Were Orange.* He can't remember exactly by how much. Anyway: imagine everything orange, from the sky down to the whites (the oranges?) of your eyeballs.

The orange color was beside the point, he'd written In Conclusion. An orange world wouldn't be any different from a city of purple or a city of green. The important thing was that everything was in monochrome. In a monochromatic world, you'd have no other colors to compare against. There wouldn't even be a concept of color to begin with. It might as well be all black and white. And did people living in black and white worlds—like actors in old movies, or dogs—feel like they were missing out on something? If they didn't even know what color was, did it matter?

Once, we couldn't see ultraviolet or infrared or whatever else kind of light scientists hadn't discovered yet. Were we less happy, here in our world limited to the visible spectrum?

Were we?

Maybe he'd been feeling snarky, like that punk who just wants to troll his teacher with some outrageous come-at-me claim.

Because In Conclusion, he'd written *Yes*.

We *were* less happy.

If we somehow figured out how to see ultraviolet light with our own eyes, we'd pity those who couldn't. Then we'd make fun of them, call them plain eyes, close ranks, shut them out. Brag real loud about how we could see the true color of the sky. Oh man, if only you could see what we could see! It's so normal to us now!

That's just how people are, he wrote. People get superior and gloat and gloat—until another group of people figure out how to see something they heretofore couldn't, and then in turn make that first group feel like shit, all in a never-ending cycle of shit upon shit, forever and ever amen.

For this Conclusion, he earned an above-average grade of B+.

TWENTY-EIGHT

EVEN WITH HIS EYES CLOSED HE CAN TELL IT IS EARLY MORNING.
The air is moist from having cooled all night. The blanket curtain glows blue at the edges. Everything is still.

He opens his eyes. He looks.

The old man is gone.

He sits up, throws open the blanket. There sits the channel, silent as a tomb.

His pyramid of cans is gone, too. In their place is nothing but a single packet of mashed potatoes. And a sheet of cardboard, with a message written in a prisoner's scrawl:

> *God loves you + will carry you on your Jurney as I
> continue my own. You R 4 ever my Brother + I would
> nevr hurt you + a gift 4 U.*

As if to prove it, there lies the old man's razor, picked straight from his pocket in his sleep.

Everything goes white. His ears stop working. The cardboard is still there, and his wind measurement setup. The string, stove, and matches are still there. The paper with the numbers on it. He feels a growing rage at the sight of that paper.

He touches his pocket where the razor had been. His shoes remain unmolested. Same with his tools. This is the old man's idea of compassion.

Did he seriously sit there scraping out a note on a sheet of cardboard just inches away while he slept?

He emerges from the shelter ready to kill. Did my shit just get jacked?

He can't yell. He wants to run, but where? He ducks back into the shelter, snatches up his weapons—fucker hadn't taken those—and lopes to the top of the channel.

The path arcs out of sight. Behind him the terminus sits empty. No sound comes from its pipes.

Had he dreamed the old man? The empty houses look down on him with their pitiless blank windows.

No. There is the handwritten note.

The mother*fucker* could write.

That makes me king of the idiots, he thinks.

He could've had the old bastard write his answers instead of playing twenty questions twenty million times. At least some practical specifics. Like what city they're closest to. What year it is. What areas are safe, the names of the major factions.

He had the solution right there and he missed it completely.

Now it's either wail with lament, or chase.

He chooses chase, and launches toward the terminus. Mind racing. This is all probably pointless. Even hobbled by his bags, the slow-moving old man most likely had a few hours' head start already. And who can say where he went? Why would the old man go back to the pipes he first dropped out of?

No way that old man could pull himself back up into the terminus pipes. The bottom lip is easily six feet off the ground. He stops, turns, and begins running the other way.

Which other way? There are thousands of other ways!

He stops again. He turns. He stabs at the ground, blunting the tip of his spear. He wants to scream. He wants to kick something. But there's nothing to kick.

So he just runs where his feet would take him, back past the shelter, past the KROKOS graffiti, to the tall reeds where the cairns sit undisturbed. No footprints here. Maybe he'd left some in the dirt?

He reminds himself: he knows nothing about tracking.

He looks at the houses. Maybe he's in one of them, relaxing in a dead man's bathtub, his plastic bags floating in the water around him. But that doesn't make sense. He said he made a point of avoiding people. Too risky.

Maybe the Dead Lands? He imagines the old man trekking through the fields of charcoal whose color matched his clothes. In the distance he can see a low pass between mountains. Maybe there? God, it's far.

He squeezes through a break in the chain-link fence and jogs into the death zone. The ground underfoot looks as if it's been spray-painted with black. He notices a concrete bar, leaps over it, and realizes he is standing in a blasted cul-de-sac street, complete with five curb cuts and empty driveways radiating from its center, driveways to nowhere.

A road leads from the cul-de-sac, and he follows it to yet another cul-de-sac tied to yet another, like interconnected spoke hubs. There's no way he can tell which ones he's already been through and which ones he hasn't.

He could mark each one if he had some chalk or something.

Make a map.

Come on. More mapmaking?

At his feet is a manhole cover, stamped with the word WATER. And along the outer rim: MADE IN INDIA. He tries prying it open with his fingers. Impossible. He tries his spear, bending it until it splinters in two. He tries the prybar but only winds up bending the metal itself, because it's a cheap piece of crap and this manhole cover is rusted shut and the old man isn't beneath it because there are no underground colonies to begin with, unless he's lying—are you a liar as well as a thief, old man?

He flings the prybar away. It lands with a *chk* into a pile of dirt.

From far away, he can hear a great horned owl ask, *Who-oo, who? Who?*

TWENTY-NINE

HE STARES AT THE NOTE AGAIN.

You R 4 ever my Brother + I would nevr hurt you.

You took all the food, he thinks. You left one packet of mashed potatoes. You'd never hurt me, so maybe you'll just starve me to death instead?

The packet is labeled IDAHO SNOW, NOT FOR INDIVIDUAL RESALE in plain dot matrix letters. He knows Idaho Snow. He can see it in the chilly aisles of the supermarket, twin hexagonal snowflakes occupying each of the Os in the name. He tears it open, slides the powder into a clean can, and places the empty packet into the cinder block to prevent any more memories from precipitating.

He wants to crush the old man's note and stuff it in there as well. But part of him wants to keep it displayed as a warning: never trust anyone again.

He crushes the note.

That leaves the razor. White pearl handle, brandless, simple. Could be five, ten, fifty years old. The blade swings out with a push and shines like a mirror. He rotates it until the edge vanishes.

It'd be easy to drag it across his wrists and wait. Lie on the slope with his heart pointing downhill like a superhero downed in midflight, a red cape unfurling from his outstretched arms for the next wandering survivor to stumble upon. The curious crows would see it first.

Is this the old man's gift? A way out?

Or is it shaving?

This is a funny choice. He laughs, anyway.

He begins boiling another can of water, taking his time to properly perform the ceremony of lighting the stove with a match. He has routines to fall back on, at least. If not those, then not much else.

When the bottom of the can begins to teem with tiny bubbles, he turns the stove off and drops the razor into the water. Maybe it will sanitize, maybe not. Maybe seeds of plague live on that invisible edge. He doesn't give that much of a shit at the moment.

He takes out the hot blade, splashes some scalding water onto his face, and shaves. The quiet scraping sounds relax him a bit; his newly naked cheeks cool in the weak breeze. He dunks the razor, shakes it, and scrapes some more. He shaves under his chin with extra caution. How easily a single flick could end everything.

When he's done he feels a weird sense of normalness he hasn't felt in forever.

I guess thanks for the razor? he says. Asshole.

AS DUSK FALLS, HE PREPARES THE SINGLE PORTION OF MASHED POTA-toes just like the old man showed him, except he uses a spoon because who eats mashed potatoes with a goddamn fork? When the potatoes are gone—just a precious few spoonfuls—he sits scraping the can with a forlorn rhythm and realizes aha, that's why the old man used the fork, to make the potatoes last longer.

You lose again, he thinks, and flings the can at the wall.

Would he have done the same, if he were the old man?

He wants to say no, but knows he's not sure.

There is no trust left in the world. Has to be. Maybe the old man had trusted someone in the past and got betrayed by that outdated thinking, unaware that humans have lost their ability to depend on one another. Maybe trust itself was an evolutionary lark in the first place, and our true destiny is to be forever small and insular and alone like most mammals, and leave all that mass-society nonsense to bugs and fish.

Animals have no sense of loyalty, just survival. Except dogs, maybe, but then again their loyalty is probably just a human interpretation of canine hierarchy. Now we humans, after trying out the whole civilization thing and sucking at it, are finally joining the rest of the animal kingdom as peers.

He shapes the bubble wrap, his new pillow. Thanks for this, too, he thinks.

He examines his map: the channel, the houses, the terminus. He adds a dot for the manhole cover in the Dead Lands, then opens the razor to carefully scrape at the dot where the crow carcass had been until it's erased.

At a loss for what else to do, he decides to head outside with his containers to run his usual nightly errand at the faucet. He fills the to-go cup, then settles in to slowly fill the large metal bucket. Water running underground, in reservoirs and aquifers dotting the land, enough water for everyone now.

Creatures deep in the sea have no clue as to what happens up on the surface. Just like always. They know nothing of us land walkers, and we know next to nothing about them. Now we never will.

And what about life on Venus? Jupiter? Beyond? We'll never know about any of that, either. Like we're trapped at the bottom of a sand pit, forever oblivious to the crashing sea just beyond the crest of the dunes above. If only someone would lower a ladder for us to climb and take in the vistas.

He lets the metal bucket overflow onto the slope and the black cape stretches before him, where it merges with a puddle dripping into a swimming pool full of little happy screaming babies and their parents.

THIRTY

THE PLACE SCREAMED LOUD AND NONSTOP LIKE A SANITARIUM. WHITE
tiled walls echoed the peals and squalls of dozens of happysad children splashing in the half-size Olympic pool, with the parents doing
their best to control the chaos.

Controlled chaos, she said, and her voice could barely be heard
amid the din. *Controlled chaos* had been a catchphrase of theirs.

They'd had catchphrases! he remembers now, and stops himself
before he can remember any further. He lets her face be obscured by
all the splashing, for instance. Keeps focus on her beautiful brown
hands against the shifting turquoise blue and the beautiful brown baby
legs against the turquoise blue wearing her turquoise blue *absolutely
waterproof* diapers dotted with the orange starfish with the faces on
them.

Take a breath and hold it, she said.

Was she talking to him?

Take a breath and hold it, honey, she said.

He squinted against flying water. You can't just tell a baby to hold
their breath, he said. You have to use the trick.

She paused and he could feel her eyes on him.

Don't do that thing with your voice, she said.

What thing?

Arurr! said the baby.

In the water, the baby weighed nothing.

You know what thing, she said.

I didn't mean anything!

God, she said. Let's just get out of here.

He was losing her fast. He didn't want to leave. He wanted to stay in the pool. It was the first time they'd been someplace new outside the house in weeks.

Did the pool get all quiet just now? Why now?

I'm sorry, he said quickly. I'm sorry I'm sorry I'm sorry I'm a pedantic sack pube.

She made a funny face and said: I don't like you very much, mister.

I feel like I say the wrong thing all the time these days.

She heaved a sigh. You do not say the wrong thing all the time. It's just stress. Just remind yourself of that.

Are you stressed out, too?

She bobbled her head. Stress, what stress, durr.

She smiled. When she smiled like that, no matter how dead tired she looked, it was his whole world.

A far-off swim instructor screamed something, and a bell clanged, and a child stepped up to a podium to receive some kind of achievement ribbon. Everyone turned their attention to applaud. He took the sudden clamor as an opportunity to touch his lips to hers.

Stolen moments, he said.

Aha: *Stolen moments* was another catchphrase of theirs.

Stolen moments, she said back, and all was well again. This was happening more and more: moments of tension, reconciled quickly. It was a new thing between them. In the past, before the baby, they had the capability to fight for hours or even days, because they were a couple with all the time in the world. Now, every spare minute was as rare as mercury, and as slippery. Who could afford to waste precious coin on some dumb fight?

Whenever they got over a tiff, she would say: Onward and upward.

Downward and outward, he would reply, and pat his belly.

So many little catchphrases they'd had!

Bada dah, said the baby.

So this trick, she said.

Right, he said. You blow air into the baby's face, they seize up, just naturally, and rillyquick you dunk them in the water.

You saw this on the electronic intertubes?

There's a bunch of videos, he said, making a case. The babies get trained to associate holding their breath with being underwater and after enough time it's second nature.

They stared at their child, who was oblivious to their plan. She had never gone underwater before.

Maybe we should just get the classes, she said.

They're like ninety bucks a week, he whispered. Then he spun the baby around in the water: whee!

That's dystopian, she whispered back. Who charges that much?

He kissed the baby's perfect head, cast an eye up at the colorful banners lining the walls. *They* do. Because they can.

Because they can.

Capitalism. He kissed the baby again.

She blew out a lip, thinking. You're confident we can learn this from the intertubes? she said.

I mean people out there do, he said. Out in the sticks without a fancy community center in the big ole city. You just blow and dip. Give me your hand. Pretend it's the baby. Blow, and dip, just like that.

You so need a tan, she said. Look at you. You're like the Asian in Caucasian.

Come on, he said.

Also the Cauc.

Tonight, he said with a stupid grin. Now just blow.

You blow! I'm scared!

You!

You!

He suddenly wanted to slip her swimsuit to one side and take his wife right here in the pool. After putting the baby down, of course. And clearing out the other families. Also getting out of the pool and dry and into a proper bed. He never understood the fantasy of underwater copulation. Releasing a semen cloud like a minnow in heat.

Here goes, he said.

Hold her like—

Phoo!

For the world's longest *one one thousand* second the baby fell silent as he baptized her face first. When he brought her back up, she was bewildered, then smiled, then took one look at her parents' worried faces and began crying.

He handed her to her mother. Oh my little baby, she said, bobbing slowly. But to him, she was frozen in silent, maniacal laughter. How could you, Papa? she said.

You are so dead, he said.

How could you, Papa?

He splashed water at her.

No splashing! came the lifeguard's cry.

They stayed at the pool for the next hour. If younger-him told father-him that he would one day not only dip a baby into the water for sixty minutes straight but also love every second of it, he would have narrowed both eyes and asked for clarification.

Now, father-him said: If we had a house with a pool we could do this all day.

She smiled. We can dream.

THIRTY-ONE

HE CUTS HIMSELF A NEW SPEAR AND SITS GUARD, STAYING AWAKE AS long as he can in case the old man returns. But no one comes. He creeps to the lip of the channel and scans the distance for hours. He scans the bridge, too, in case the old man is hiding in plain sight. Holding the spear feels like fishing for nothing, no ocean anywhere but the one he can remember only with effort: wavelets lapping on a funny-shaped break. The community fishing pier, a pentagonal jut of concrete built by the city of Delgado Beach. There was always a handful of people gathered there to catch and release, catch and release the small barracudas lurking among the rocks. A family of three—just like his, with a baby daughter—grilled fillets on a barbecue the size of a coffee can.

The family waved to them—a cheery *¡bienvenido a la paternidad!*—and he wiggled the baby's hand back as he held her. How small she was!

Say bye-bye, he said. Bye-bye, Delgado Beach.

It's not bye-bye yet, said his wife. The mother of their new child. She squinted, her smooth brown face gone reddish in the sun. Curls doing whatever they wanted in the wind.

I know, but eventually. Soon.

You're really ready to leave, huh.

Wait, he said. What's wrong.

She watched as another family joined the one on the pier, and they began chatting softly in Spanish carried on the breeze.

It's gonna sound stupid, she said.

I love stupid.

We've lived here for so many years.

I know.

She shook her hair out of the wind. I just . . . wanna keep things real.

Real stupid?

Stop. She laughed, but without smiling. What if we move away, and everyone's White? What if we're the only ones? She kissed the baby's forehead. What if *she's* the only one?

There was a party boat now, blasting music. Nothing but rich college kids drunk and hollering at one in the afternoon.

We'd never let that happen, he said.

What? she said, wincing at the racket.

I said we'd never let that happen to her.

They waited for the boat to finally go away, and the serenity of the inlet resumed.

Why can't we find something around here? she sighed.

He waved a hand at everything. You know how it is.

She hardened her eyes with a single nod. Oh, I know how it is.

Hey, he said. Don't let yourself get all worked up.

But get all worked up she did: It's *either* some shitty overpriced apartment *or* a McMansion for two mil. It's *either* dollar tacos *or* a five-star prix fixe. There's nothing in between. It's not rags to riches, it's rags *or* riches.

Baby.

And then it's like oh, let's put all the White people here in the big *nice* houses, and all the *vibrant* Mexicans over here, and the *urban* Blacks here next to the Mexicans, and the *tight-knit* Asians way the hell out in East Jesus.

It's a beautiful day . . . !

Where's the place for *us*, right?

Let's let it just be a beautiful day.

This whole city's just *done*, right? This whole country, right?

He touched her chin and gave their baby a glance. She can hear you, you know. She doesn't understand the words but she can hear your tone.

Now they both looked down and saw her gazing up at them with her big tiny eyes.

He nudged his wife with an elbow. Come on. You're starting to sound like me.

She laughed. Mister grumpy falump.

Don't sound like me. *I* don't want to sound like me.

Bad mama.

Does that mean I'm a bad papa because I succumb to cynicism in the face of a heartless world?

No, she demurred.

Are you maybe allowed a moment of anguish now and then as the thumb of capitalism crushes your ribs with unrelenting cruelty, just to make the point that the cruelty is the point?

She smiled and elbowed him back.

Have some baby, he said, handing her over.

She did, and melted instantly at the specific perfume of her little forehead.

I mean I get you completely, he said. He began circling out a Venn diagram with her finger against the blue-green California sky. We want a place that we can afford, with people like us, that's not falling apart, preferably brand-new construction, cathedral ceilings, and yes, I am an asshole, but I think cathedral ceilings are pretty friggin' sweet.

And we get a pool, she laughed. She drew out another circle and pointed at the intersection. Right there. See it?

He kissed her. You are the optimist of the family. You are my sunshine.

In between kisses back, she said: Not your only sunshine, though.
The baby farted.

I'm on it, he cried. By this point, he remembered, he'd been able
to get the changing pad, new diaper, wipes, and soil baggie out and
ready in five seconds flat. He could have her changed in ten. It was a
funny sort of expertise to be proud of. Like a pit crew? he guessed.
Except not like a pit crew at all?

Much more necessary than a pit crew, and more beautiful?

You made a smelly one, didn't you, he said.

I miss the meconium days, she said, tweaking her nose. Oh my
God, Jesus.

Meconium Days is my new band name, he said. He hoisted her
little chubby legs with one hand like she was a piece of poultry, slid
the diaper underneath with the other, and then strapped her in clean
and fresh and oojee woojee nom nom.

Maybe it's just a fantasy, she said. The place we belong only exists
in, like, some kids' show where they celebrate a different heritage every day.

In song.

I don't mean like Baldwin Hills or Downey or Monterey Park, I
mean a place where everyone is all mixed up *together*, right?

So like Hawaii.

Okay, Oprah.

Orange County's supposed to be pretty diverse.

Oh hell—

—No, he said, finishing her sentence. Anyway, it can't be a fantasy. It's out there.

You really think so.

Just gotta look around and get lucky. This is America, dammit.

And I thought I was the optimist of the family, she said.

It's out there somewhere. Gotta be.

THIRTY-TWO

HE SNAPS AWAKE. THE CHANNEL LIES BEFORE HIM AS ALWAYS, DEVOID of water or fish or anything else. He'd been napping. He'll probably nap more and more as the hours pass and his energy depletes. He takes small sips from his cup. Again he begins to picture the nutrients in his body thinning out from all the water and lack of food. Just a few parts per million lost per minute, until his blood becomes a clear stream of inert liquid.

By the next day he gives up on any pretense of vigilance and dozes openly on the slope, almost willing someone to come finish him off. He touches his lips. Dry and peeling, just like when he first woke up in this place.

Back to square one.

Rotating his head produces momentary vertigo, like his brain is slow to catch up with the heavy syrup in his skull. He turns his head over and over, fascinated by his decline.

We never did find a place for us, he says.

He wakes with eyelids fluttering against the sun. When had he fallen asleep?

He looks up at the dead houses. He should go. It is time to go. But he finds he simply doesn't care to. He doesn't give two grapes, if he's being honest. He cares more about sitting in the shade and focusing very hard on pushing every speck of dirt out from under his finger-nails with the wine tool. That's something he can really do.

Will death be all that dramatic?

You did your best. You had a good run. You never did figure out much of anything. Never remembered how you got here or why, or what that key in your shoe was all about.

If he pretends it is all about nothing, then it'll be easier to let it all go.

An hour easily passes. The thought of getting up feels impossible. He's too tired. Or too depressed. The sun has moved in the sky, pulling shadows along with it, and he discovers his right arm is now exposed to a slash of light. He drags it back into the shade.

I wish I had someone to talk to, he thinks.

As if in answer, he hears a scratching sound. He raises his head one centimeter.

A crow peers at him from a slight distance.

Looking for your friend? he mumbles.

The crow cocks its head.

He's dead, he says to the crow. Or she. I can't tell.

The crow stares. It looks so real. Although: real or not real, who cares?

What does the key open? he says.

The crow says nothing. It is a crow.

Were you and your friend close? Like an item?

At this, the crow begins cawing and baring its wings.

He stiffens. Shoo. Get out of here. He places a hand on the wine tool.

The crow hops forward, cawing. Go away, he says.

The crow lunges and feints back as if inviting him to spar.

Hey: I don't know who took your friend's body. Back up, dude. Maybe it was the crazy old guy.

Caw, says the crow. Caw, caw. The crow won't shut up.

He sees his baby daughter again, this time cozied up in a blanket, among towering sycamores somewhere. Her eyes bright with fall morning sunlight gazing up at the small murder perched above muttering *caw, caw*. She pointed at them with her little hand: Look, Papa!

Her skin, he remembers, was the exact shade in between his and his wife's.

Caw, caw, says the crow, emboldened.

You trolling me? he cries. He whips the wine tool at the crow's feet just as it leaps into the air. The crow immediately falls back to earth. The wine tool must've taken a bad bounce, or something, because now it's sticking out of the bird's chest. He hadn't meant that.

The bird pinwheels on the ground—a tempest of feathers—then stops.

He stands to a crouch, creeps toward it. He can see it is still breathing.

The crow lies on its side trailing a thin line of blood.

What does this have to do with anything? he says to the crow. I thought I was done! Food's gone, I'm sick of water, I thought today was it!

The crow regards him with an unemotional eye. Do what you will, it finally says. And in doing so, reveal yourself.

Is this some kind of puzzle? he says. Hey!

He nudges it with his foot. The crow gives a weak kick, flops a wing. Do what you will. Is that not what your kind loves so much? Free will? It's all you ever talk about!

I don't understand.

Free will! Free will! As if there were nothing else! Ha ha ha ha!

What's that supposed to mean?

The bird falls silent. Just breathing and staring at him.

He stares back for something like eternity. Like he's waiting for the thing to die. He might have to wait for hours into the night. Listening to it fitfully rustle, or the scrape of predators closing in: first a sniff, then the prod of a snout, then the first live bite.

He doesn't need that kind of guilt in his life. What little is left of it.

He wants to carry the bird far down the channel and leave it somewhere. Maybe offer it to the cairns. But his weakened body complains at the very thought of such a trek. The cairns feel hundreds of miles away now.

He has no idea what to do. If this is some kind of puzzle—which it isn't—but what if it is—he's already bunged it up.

He decides on a mercy killing.

He labors down to the flotsam pile and finds a broken wedge of concrete. He drags it back up. It takes forever times two. But the crow is still there when he returns, and it blinks its black marble eye with a flash of white.

Caw, caw, look papa, says the crow.

I hope this is right, he thinks, and brings the wedge down.

THE CROW IS A MESS. IT IS BARELY EVEN A CROW NOW. HIS HEART pounds in his chest. Get up, he thinks, and does, but too quickly. He nearly blacks out. That would be funny, breaking his neck right after breaking the crow's. That would be prime-time comedy gold.

Shuffling, he drags his heavy bucket from inside the shelter, tips it slightly, and lets water merge with the red streak to thin it and carry it away. He pours again. The water spills down around the crow's still body.

How much blood would it take to attract scavengers? One crow can't have that much blood, can it?

He sets the bucket down and gives in to all his macabre voyeuristic impulses. Not often you get the chance to stare at a freshly killed creature without anyone around to think you're some kind of freak.

The thing's eye is already sunken. Fascinating, disgusting. The body, deflated of air and fluid, is almost flat. Gingerly he picks it up by its tail and hoists it dripping into the metal bucket. It feels like nothing more than a piece of junk now. A claw scrapes the side as it sinks to the bottom.

His mind begins to spin up a plan. The water, see, will draw out the blood after a while and dilute it. Then he can safely toss the remains some distance away without leaving a scent for animals to detect. Somewhere not too far. The last thing he wants is another pointless expedition.

The water, thick with black feathers, becomes as still as a mirror. Caw, caw, look papa.

This is no puzzle. It is torment. He is being toyed with.

The houses would be worse, much worse, full of baby shoes and toys and makeup and purple hair picks with perfect curlicues of black still caught between tines that reveal their traces of perfume when brought to the nose.

What Would You Do? And Why Would It Be Fun?

The surface of the water in the bucket ripples. He realizes he is weeping. It's not fair that he should be tormented when he's already so low. Nothing about this place is fair. But the world has never been very interested in the notion of fairness, has it? Why would it change now just because humans are gone?

To compound the cruelty, he's just bashed a creature to death. Don't fool yourself into thinking that was some kind of mercy killing, he thinks. You got dealt shit, so you in turn dealt shit to someone else to compensate. They say an eye for an eye, but what they forget to say is that if you can't reach the eye of the one who wronged you, then any nearby eye will do.

Remember the world before. How all its evil was just a ceaseless cascade of misplaced revenge!

I'm so sorry, he says to the crow.

I don't know what your death means. None of us do. Every day souls fart away into the air, imparting nothing.

He weeps and weeps. It feels good to cry, he guesses. We weep not because there's nothing else to do, but because there's no one around to care.

He wipes his cheeks, eyes the dead houses with something approaching conviction.

THIRTY-THREE

HE RESTS THE CROW ON THE SLOPE AND CARRIES THE BUCKET DOWN the upper path to toss out the water. He studies it again for a good long while, mulling an idea in his head. He thinks about that previous crow—the one that'd vanished after he returned from his disastrous walkabout. It hadn't sat long before some creature made a nice meal out of it. Unlike the vandals, who had left it to waste.

But nothing goes to waste in nature. It is perfectly noble and correct for one creature to become nutrients for another. There could be no better tribute than to—

Eat the bird, he says.

Eat the bird.

At the bottom of the channel lies the wine tool stained with a small brown triangle of blood. It's otherwise undamaged. He takes it and the bucket to the faucet to refill it with fresh water, breathing hard with the effort.

He sits by the crow and takes a moment. He opens the wine tool's serrated blade and sets it aside, gathering what little reserves of energy remain.

He holds the crow with one hand and tugs on a feather. It holds firm. He pulls harder, stretching the skin painfully far until the feather pops loose. He removes another feather, then another, going faster with each one.

The plucked crow looks pale and naked but for a conical ruff of black around the neck.

For the next part, he thinks about using the straight razor, but decides no. Better to keep that thing sharp.

Wine tool it is, he thinks.

He holds the stripped bird above the bucket and—exhale—jabs the foil cutter blade into its belly and thrusts downward. A tiny cupful of black and white and wet crimson entrails flop into the water. He reaches in, digs out some more, and dunks the carcass once to rinse.

He hangs the carcass on the lip of the bucket and takes a break. The sun dips below the lip of the channel just enough to paint everything in indigo rectangles of dusk.

Time to finish up. He saws off the wings and feet and twists the neck back and forth until the head separates. He gently sets all of it into the water.

What he's left with is a duck carcass in miniature.

At the flotsam pile, he breaks apart one of the long thin wooden crates into small fragments and forms a small heap. It's either taking forever, or no time at all; his heart is thumping so hard he can't tell. He cups a flickering match and holds it steady. The dry tinder quickly lights.

He impales the bird on a loop of wire and dangles it over the growing flame as night falls. The only campfire for hundreds of miles, he thinks. Thousands, millions, billions.

I wish they hadn't sent you. Or that other crow. Maybe you're just the same crow again and again. I wish they'd just sent voices on the wind instead. You can't kill voices.

She hit the pause button. Everyone on the television mute and still.

This whole movie makes no sense, she said.

Give me the remote, he said.

I'd know something was up if it was me, she said. I mean how clueless would you have to be?

I'm suspending your remote privileges indefinitely, he said.

It had been another night, another precious free hour on the couch with a drink in one hand and baby monitor in the other. He'd long since developed a habit of glancing at the miniature screen every sixty seconds like a stakeout cop.

When he took the remote from her, she cried, No, remote loves Mama more!

You realize you have a habit of anthropomorphizing everything, he said.

Only because they love it so much.

Hear my words, woman, he said. If the guy in the movie was born on a Hollywood set, and the reality show he's growing up in is the only reality he's ever known, how could he even be able to question it?

Kids naturally explore the limits of their boundaries. He would, too.

All the producers have to do is flip a switch and bam, there's a forest fire blocking his way or a big fake train or like a snake migration.

Snake. Migration.

Did I just say that?

How many of those have you had? she said.

This is my first second one.

Give me some.

He did. She took the tiniest sip and made a face. I don't know how you can drink that, she said. Hear my words, man. You don't think after the tenth or hundredth storm he'd maybe begin to suspect that everything around him is just for show? I grew up questioning reality every day. I know you did, too.

You think it's because he's White?

She only cocked an eyebrow in response.

He took his drink back, took a nice big sip. Byron was all, This is classic cinema. But I have to admit, it's, ah, you know—

—Stupid. You can love Byron and call his taste in movies stupid.

He laughed through a mighty yawn. Oh god, he moaned. Let me die so I can get some sleep.

She laughed back. I thought I was tired, but there's like this whole nother secret level underneath tired.

You wanna keep going with the movie?

She snuggled her head into his neck. I dunno.

You wanna just go to sleep?

I love you.

You wanna watch something else?

You are wunderbar.

You're making me decide, aren't you.

She didn't answer, because she was asleep. He scooched a kiss on her forehead without waking her. Every minute mattered so much now. He once made the mistake of charting their free time BB (before baby) versus AB, and the drop literally amounted to ninety-six percent. It put pressure on everything. Every meal had to be worth it. Every show a masterpiece. Every lovemaking session a tribute to the glory of romance.

He had a drink left in his hand, an unconscious wife on his shoulder, and no clue what else to watch, so he fast-forwarded ahead through the ludicrous movie on mute.

The man did indeed begin questioning his reality. A studio lamp fell out of the sky, mysterious little black domes dotted every surface. The man set sail in a boat toward the fake horizon to see how far he could go, and the producers did their best to dial in the deadliest storm available to them. But murder was bad for ratings—and illegal—and so they had no choice but to leave him be. The man escaped through a studio back door and saw the real sun for the first time.

Or *was it* the real sun? he intoned to the screen with radio suspense, and threw the remote aside. Stupid movie. Sure, he himself hadn't left the same six-block radius in a week, but he never doubted the houses in the distance weren't painted facades. They were real.

Everything in the world was real and swirling about with boundless energy. Only they were on pause, just for a little while—just for now.

He blows on the steaming crow before him.

He can't tell how well cooked it is in the low light of the fire. Which is probably best. He takes a tiny nibble.

It is lean, with a dense sinewy texture, sort of like duck, not as gamey or greasy as he'd imagined. He takes a full bite. Neither here nor there, really. Needs salt.

Not bad!

I'm eating crow, he says, and chuckles up at the bottom of the overpass. Who needs cans when we got crows! he yells, and his laughter multiplies back at him from among the concrete walls.

THIRTY-FOUR

HE LIES ON HIS THIN BLANKET BACK IN THE SHELTER. IT'S MORNING.

He places a hand on his stomach. Feels fine to him. No queasiness or anything.

He sits up and thinks, I'm a novice hunter now. I'm pretty sure I can kill again if I have to. Pretty sure it'll get easier each time.

He pictures roasting the old man's leg on a spit. Hairs growing out of milky skin bruised with tattoos gone all blurry with age.

Keep your nasty old leg, old man.

He checks his array of clear strings and is startled to see the cardboard discs dancing. He creeps forth. The curtain swishes silently.

Outside, the world is filled with the motion of the wind. The clear lines shimmer in the morning light but hold strong. There is the tumbleweed again, moving with greater haste this time down the channel. Definitely got an aerodynamic bias to one side, he observes. See how it pulls to the left?

He knows it's not the same tumbleweed. But isn't it nice to imagine it is, come to visit him every day from its little home perhaps deep within the pipes of the terminus? Let's say it was the one that chased the old man away from here that day. Good tumbleweed.

He urinates, taking care not to spray himself in the gusty air. Hard to tell what color it is. Probably a nice yellow today, dense with nutrients from the crow. He pours water down to cleanse. The slope bears no evidence of last night's dinner. Even the black pockmark left in the sand by his small campfire has been erased by today's wind.

He'd left the bird bones and other parts in the bucket of water, to hide the scent from scavengers and keep ants away. He hates ants. They get into everything. Once an ant discovers a bit of food, the whole damn colony will build a freeway right to his shelter. Tiny little ants that bite, leaving itchy microscopic white pockmarks on the skin. Especially when you fill an ant hole with water out of curiosity. Ants pouring out from the vast network beneath his feet one summer decades ago when he was little: his feet wearing flip-flops like the ones his own daughter wore, on a similar summer day, as they sang to her:

The ants go marching one by one, hurrah, hurrah!

Play the drum, too, he said, but she pushed it away.

She doesn't want the drum, honey, said his wife.

It was a little finger drum with a triple yin-yang symbol: three swirls of blue and yellow and red in a circle. It was Korean. His mother's? Father's? They were both dead. He couldn't remember how or when, only that they worked hard and left him with a bank account whose number he once wrote down in triplicate in exchange for the brass rectangle now living in his shoe. He can see his parents in the wings of his memory, shadowy hunched figures waiting for their cue.

We can tell you all about that drum, they say.

I don't mean to be rude, he tells them. But not yet. I just can't right now.

The toy drum was the size of a small jar of cold cream. Small but important. Meant to be passed on? An heirloom? It wasn't old or fancy or anything. It was new, it was cheap. A trinket from a souvenir shop somewhere with one of those gold oval MADE IN CHINA stickers on its back. Where it was made didn't matter.

What mattered was its precarious journey at the crest of a wave of history. This was a wave that had traveled some distance for some time, crossing generation after generation before, finally and inexplicably, delivering this toy drum into his hand. The rim of the drum skin crowded with a ring of fat rivets, the shell decorated with colorful lotus blossoms.

The rivets represent something, he wanted to explain to his daughter. I think the lotus means something, too. But the three colors, it's red for earth, blue for sky, and yellow is—yellow is—honey, look it up.

Right now? she said. She had the baby strapped in to her chest. Can we please just enjoy our walk?

This little drum, he wanted to say, came riding to me atop this great big wave across millions and billions of miles, and if you keep it long enough it'll take you for a ride, too. All the way to the strange city of your ancestry, full of customs that are beautiful and nonsensical and embarrassing. But also true. It'll drive you crazy how true they will sometimes be.

But all he could say at the moment was: Play the drum, sweetie.

She pushed it away with her small hand.

She's too little, said his wife.

They turned a corner, the same corner of the same six-block radius they'd turned about within over and over.

Come on, sweetie, he said. Play with the drum?

Nnn, cried the baby.

She doesn't want it.

Fine, whatever, he said.

What is wrong with you today? she said.

Nothing. Let's walk, walk, walk, walk.

I'm gonna just let you keep doing whatever it is you're doing right now, she said, and later you can explain what is going on.

His ears burned and he had the urge to fling the drum down a storm drain. Why hadn't his parents explained more about symbolic shit like this? Why didn't he know anything about anything? Why did he keep feeling like he even should?

My parents gave me this drum, he finally said.

She froze her step. Oh honey, she said.

They never told me what it was for, he said, before his throat seized up.

Oh honey, she said.

The baby picked up on his tears—which babies did—and began to worry. It was adorable.

Don't cry, he said. Papa's fine.

Cars zoomed all around them in the brilliant magnesium morning light. To him, they were all strangely silent.

Try showing her again later, okay? she said.

Okay, he said.

But he never did—life was busy like that—and the great big wave wound up crashing at his feet like any other ordinary wave dissolving into the hissing sand.

THIRTY-FIVE

HE MARKS WIND MEASUREMENTS FOR AN HOUR, IMPRESSED BY THE animated movement of the discs, and checks his growing chart of data that is beautifully devoid of meaning. The hour spent collecting it is also beautifully empty.

He hoists the metal can and, armed with his wine tool and freshly sharpened reed, sets out to dispose of the crow remains. He climbs the bank and begins walking.

The wind continues to stream around him. It scrubs the channel clean and rattles the chain-link fence along the Dead Lands where his prybar lies hidden somewhere. No planes fly overhead, no cars grumble, no horned owls sing their sad song. He walks eight hundred strides, reaches the cairns. Double-checks his map: eight hundred strides, that is correct.

The little stone towers stand fast in the swirling air. The thick surrounding reeds sway in hypnotizing unison.

He gets as close to them as he dares and presents the bucket with an outstretched arm. He feels he should say something. Like what? He stands until his arm begins to hurt.

Forgive me, he says. His voice vanishes into the wind. I was, uh, in the throes of betrayal.

The throes of betrayal?

Your bird did not die in vain, he continues. I made the best of him? Anyway, he was very delicious?

What else?

I think the crow was your message, he says finally. Which I definitely got, so okay, it's time to go and check out those houses. I may or may not make it. Either way, goodbye. And thank you, for . . .

He trails off. He is talking to *rocks* right now, *out loud* using his voice.

Jesus.

He dumps the water and its contents into the thick undulating reeds, which swallow everything right up. He thumps the bottom of the bucket—*poomp*—and heads back.

Eight hundred strides to the shelter plus three hundred strides to the terminus means the channel is a little over a mile in length by thirty or forty strides in width. If he plumbs the depth he can calculate the overall volume. The channel is a trapezoidal prism, like a dent made by a massive ingot pressed upside down into the earth and lifted clean away.

A ping-pong ball is about one and a half inches in diameter, so the channel could contain at least four and half million of them. The orange kind. He could let himself fall back into the bright river of spheres. He bet they'd cushion his fall. He'd just sink smiling into their whispering mass.

He rinses his bucket, fills it with fresh water, and brings it back to the shelter. Takes another round of measurements. It's good to have a model of the universe.

Pff. This ain't no ding-dang model of the universe. It's all made-up bullshit. Like every model ever was or is or ever will be, forever.

He fills an empty can with water, draws a match from the matchbox, lights the stove, sets the spent match alongside sixteen others, their wooden shafts each equally blackened and contorted up to their shrunken heads.

After a while he dials the stove off and takes small sips. Imaginary soup. His stomach isn't buying it. He moves outside to survey his surroundings.

Blue of sky, vast whiteness of the channel, tan strip of earth above him. Beautiful. He knows he's going to miss it, oddly enough. His reeds wave and his lines sparkle in the sun. Let's call the whole mess of string an art piece and leave it at that.

The sun sets and the sky deepens into a vibrant pink, casting the surrounding mountains into silhouettes sharp as torn sheets of carbon. The wind continues to shimmer his brilliant man-made web until finally everything succumbs to the void of night.

THIRTY-SIX

HE DOESN'T KNOW SQUAWK-ALL ABOUT BIRDS. HE KNOWS TO BE LEERY of crows, quirking shitting pigeons, those nervous little bark-colored sparrows, but that's kind of it. He can hear the *Who-oo, who? Who?* of the great horned owl but has never seen one.

There was a hummingbird once, though. It built a tiny nest outside their bedroom window. Amazing, how bird saliva and random twigs could form a perfect little egg cup balanced on an ever-bobbing tree branch close to the sheltering eaves.

After the nest was finished, two little white eggs appeared, each the size of pine nuts. Fleshy blind baby hummingbirds soon after. Day after day the mother fed them in her revolting bird way, and the babies' down became ruined with a spiky plague of young feathers that eventually filled out, flattened, and made the young birds beautiful again. Every morning they could hear them crying softly for food.

Their lovemaking had changed during this time. It was scheduled, part of a plan now. Far from ruining things, it gave them a thrill. A sense of mission.

Spring came. One day he noticed the little gray nest was empty. A week later, a thunderstorm dissolved it with thick bullets of rain spattering the windowpanes. And that was that.

WITH NO FOOD REMAINING, THE SHELTER TAKES ON A SORT OF DEAD feeling.

The evening sun bathes facets of concrete in gold and bronze while the sides still sit in shadows of charcoal blues and purples. The wind has calmed. His reeds stand lethargic, as if exhausted from the activity of the previous day. No movement to measure there.

He stretches long and tall, thinking. He'll plan on an early-morning departure. Before that, prepare for any unknown contingencies.

Unknown contingencies? How can you plan for what you can't even imagine?

He takes stock. Wine tool, straight razor, matches, and stove. A few empty cans to cook in if needed. Drinking containers and utensils, the pen and some of the cardboard. All of it he wraps in the blanket for easy carrying. Leave larger stuff like the seat cushion, the metal bucket, the ball of wire. And the old man's note: let the next guy ponder that.

Leave the reed measurement apparatus—as a kind of monument—but take the string.

There isn't all that much to prepare, really. He lies on the slope and considers masturbating. The idea floods his loins with dread. How miserable during, how desolate afterward.

He instead strides with his containers to the faucet for probably the last time. Good old faucet. He opens the spigot with the wine tool as usual. No longer usual after tonight. He'll come up with new usuals, although god knows what.

The containers fill with the white sound of streaming water. He admires the simplicity of the faucet's construction. He closes the tap to silence. He feels like he should bid it farewell, or something. He clears his throat and ponders what to say when a small *tic tic* interrupts him.

Tic tic, scratches upon the concrete right behind him. He whirls about.

Another crow.

It is suddenly night.

He stares at it for a moment, with a quiet disbelief he is unfortunately getting used to.

Listen, he says. I'm sorry about your friends. I don't know how the first one died, but the second came looking for a fight and I just reacted. I was in a bad place at the time. For the record, I have apologized and tried to make amends with the powers that be.

The crow takes a single step to one side.

Call me crazy, he says, but I think you really are the same crow being sent to me over and over again. Like there's some message to all this that I'm too stupid to get. Probably because someone knocked the memories out of my head? Or did they knock the part of my head I'm too terrified to examine? Am—am—

The crow waits for him to find the word.

Amnesia, he says. Aah, aah.

The crow cocks its head. He shivers. The desert cold is creeping in from the hills.

Anyway, I'm sorry I'm too messed up to pick up what you're trying to tell me, but don't get too mad, because after tonight I'm gone. So thank you, good night, you can go now.

The crow cocks its head the other way and does not move.

What is this you're doing? A curse? You want revenge? Or you gonna troll me again and force me to remember everything? I don't *want* to remember everything. Get it? I don't want to remember *anything*. That's why I even stayed here so long in the first place.

The crow does something strange. It lowers its body and sits, as if on a power line, but right on the concrete slope. It seems to be making itself comfortable.

You're getting close, the crow says.

He falls back on his ass and stares.

You know I'm not here for revenge, says the crow. None of us are. And I know you don't really want to kill us again and again. There are thousands of us. Although that could make for a sustainable food supply for years to come.

I'd really rather not.

You say that quite a lot. What would you rather do?

I don't know. Fall asleep in a big bed of ping-pong balls and never wake up. That would be nice.

To rejoin them, I see. Her, and her.

Don't you dare mention them.

Also to apologize.

Apologize for what?

Would you like me to provide all the details? says the crow.

He holds out his hand. Stop right there. I know they're gone. I know it was something to do with a car crash. I would rather die before having to remember any of the rest of it.

Oh, you know that's not the real puzzle here, says the crow. You know the car crash is not all that happened.

He freezes up, clenches his fists. The crow is right. But he doesn't want this.

You know it's not, says the crow. But we do.

I'll kill you again if I have to, he says. He stands and raises the wine tool blade.

You know the crash was just the start. There are millions of doors in this world. You will one day find the one marked with your very special number. Unlock it and you'll see.

I'll kill all of you and hang your bodies one by one on the fence as a warning. A mile long if I have to. Provoke me.

All of us mourn them, too, says the crow. It doesn't flinch even as he towers above. We mourn you and your family and the demise of your whole society.

He slowly lowers the blade.

We mourn your carelessness, your hubris, violence, selfish neglect, your hard cold hearts. What an abomination your project became. We mourned you while you were all still alive, and could do nothing but watch as you busily destroyed one another with that idiotic sense of purpose you were so famous for. Don't you remember how we would observe you so closely from high above? From right up there? When that old man robbed you in the small dark hours, we were absolutely mystified. Why would someone do that to the only other person around? And a good person, too?

You think I'm a good person? he says.

Just mystified! says the crow, distracted. But we can't do anything about that, because of course we're not allowed.

I don't think I'm a good person, he says. But if I am, then does that mean you could just leave me alone?

I can't, says the crow, finally rising to its little feet. And I wouldn't want to besides. I have a job to do. All of us do. Between you and me, by the way, the powers that be are rooting for you.

What?

They seem confident you'll be able to find the portal leading out of this place. I myself have a secret wish that one day we can be friends. Maybe when this is all over? What do you say?

He is utterly lost.

Goodbye, says the crow, and vaults into the night sky.

THIRTY-SEVEN

HE CARRIES THE WATER BACK TO THE SHELTER AND SITS FOR A MO-
ment. He gives his head a shake to see if anything might rattle loose
within. He's just spent the last hour talking to a crow. A crow whose
mouth did not move. He touches his own lips.

Hello there, aah, aah. Yep, his lips move.

But he can talk without moving his lips, too. Hello, there. They
sound in his head.

Hoo boy. Not good. Crazy doesn't happen all at once. Crazy happens gradually. If his then-self could see his now-self, he'd run. Crazy
is shouting at God and hobbling around naked and getting cozy with
increasingly vivid hallucinations.

Maybe the crow was a hallucination?

Maybe the vandals thought he'd been a hallucination? And tried
striking him out of existence just like he did with the other dead
crow?

Or the old man? He touches the straight razor. No. He touches
the handwritten note. No way. He pictures scrawling the note himself
in his sleep, channeling some lost spirit.

The old man was real, keep saying it, the old man was real.

He can see himself from afar right now, and is embarrassed to
death by the sight. Crying over a goddamn crow. Eating it—come on,

man—and having a heart-to-heart with a bunch of rocks. He's just as unhinged as those half-naked contestants on that island survival show they used to laugh at.

That type of show that had been categorized under *Reality.*

Bunch of first-world assholes cosplaying third-world struggles, he said. So absolutely stupid.

Although I want you to put your judgment aside for a sec, she said. She paused the show and he resisted the urge to play-wrestle her to the ground for the remote.

But look at them! he cried.

Of course they're stupid, she said. But *why* do we even have the impulse to create a show like this? And why can't we stop *our* impulse to watch it? Mm?

Huh, he said, too stumped to say anything else.

You know people do stuff for a reason, even if they don't know it, she said. I think what's going on here is a bunch of privileged people sick of the day-to-day, sick of all the expectations, and they all just wanna feel something beyond their job title. Having a guy with a camera direct your every move makes it all real easy and safe.

Frees you from responsibility, too, he said.

You just saw it, didn't you, she said. The appeal.

Stop being so smart, he said. Give me the remote.

No!

She was being too much already up until this point, and her look now sent him over the edge. He grabbed her with both hands, kicked out her legs, and flipped her onto him. She flung a cushion away to better straddle his hips. It'd been weeks, and they were both so very ready. While the TV flickered on pause, she said, We have to be quiet.

He can't bear to let himself remember the rest.

The river channel is an inverted trapezoid, he thinks, as hard as he can with his eyes shut. It is windier on one side. It can hold four and a half million orange ping-pong balls.

He opens his eyes again. At the channel's bottom, yesterday's wind had scooped a series of ripples in the fine sand in a sinuous pattern untouched by footprints or tumbleweed tracks.

One last meal, then time to get a move on. He enters the shelter, fills another can with water, and sets it aside. He reaches for the matchbox.

He likes this matchbox: CROWN BRAND MATCHES, a red sash across plain blue. He doesn't know any Crown Brand, so the box's design elicits nothing in his mind. Three bullet points read *for Camp, Picnic, Emergency.*

Well, this is all three. Below them, look, Byron, the words MADE IN CHINA.

Each match has a hard dab of ignition material, whatever it was called. He's not a match expert. Or an anything expert. Anyway, staring closer at it in the dead quiet of the shelter, really taking his time now, he notices the blue match head is topped with a small white dot, like a balding pate. The wooden shaft is square, which makes sense. Easier to grip when striking than, say, a round one. Probably less waste and effort during manufacturing, too.

The striking strips on the sides of the matchbox aren't solid abrasive rectangles but instead an array of two-millimeter dots, hexagonally arranged with about one millimeter of space between each. He imagines the machine that printed these strips has to be pretty sweet, like a giant inkjet printer with nozzles the size of eyedroppers, all marked up in futuristic Chinese characters and moving with relentless precision.

He looks closer and closer and closer until he can see nothing but perfect dots.

He could make it to China. Head west to the coast, then north to Alaska, then pilot a boat across the strait. Head south, find the factory and its big-ass printers, and study them and the rest of the perfectly intact machines forever and ever.

He's never going to China. He's never going anywhere again. He can't even make it past this stupid stain on a map.

He strikes the match.

Once the can is heated, he sits very still and sips hot water as slowly as he can to hold in the silence of the moment. Then he reaches the end, and it is finally time.

He spreads out his blanket and begins packing things up when he hears a scratch outside. He flings the blanket open. It's not a crow, though.

It is a boy.

PART III

THE BOY

THIRTY-EIGHT

THE KID IS ABOUT SEVEN-EIGHT-NINE. HE WEARS MINIATURE JEANS, miniature sneakers, and a miniature T-shirt with little distress marks designed into it. Impeccable and clean and hip, like a tiny rock star. He wears a small backpack that is small for even him.

Dark walnut hair drapes flat across his narrow face the color of pale tan somewhere between White and what—Asian? He stands staring at him with big eyes outlined by the darkest, most dramatic eyelashes he's ever seen on anyone, let alone a kid.

Those eyes of his look like he could lift him into the air with just a blink.

The boy stands there with such ease. Like all this is normal. But then again, he knows how fast things can become normal, and how it's twice as fast for kids.

If he even is an actual boy, which he probably is not. He's most likely another provocation in a growing line of provocations: first the old man, then the crow, now this.

Berries, he says.

The boy stares at him.

Wasn't expecting a kid, he says.

The boy says nothing. He shifts his feet, just as the crow did earlier. Even his hair is flat and shiny like crow feathers.

Nice try, he says, and throws an empty can at the boy. He misses badly, or maybe the can sails clear through him, but either way the boy runs off.

———————

THE CAN ROLLS TO THE BOTTOM OF THE SLOPE. HE CALMS HIMSELF down. He evens out his stance.

For a panicked moment, he thinks he can't feel the brass key in his shoe anymore. Maybe the hours of constant pressure have numbed his nerves there. Maybe Crow Boy stole it in the night. Maybe the sweat and moisture thinned the brass into foil thin enough to melt on the tongue.

He digs a fingertip into his shoe, reaches the humid strata beneath, and with relief feels the front of the key. He knows it's the front because he can feel letters stamped there like he's felt many times before. Beheld it, admired it, noticed how his fingertips smelled like brass afterward. Tiny brass molecules deposited into the colossal winding canyons of his fingerprints.

Everything here is a provocation, he thinks. Key, crow, boy, old man, abandoned house going up in spectacular flame. You're just trying out one form after another.

Who is this *you*? Please don't tell me it's me. Because then I'd really be stuck here forever. I'll see my wife come rising up out of the ground, my baby, too.

They'd come up again and again and ask, Why didn't you stop it? There's no answer to that.

He rubs the key in his shoe again and again, oh God, oh thank God, it's still in there. That very important object so warm to the touch that he can't let it go and just stands frozen, crouched in place like one of those poor Vesuvian souls.

He sees a pop of invisible light all around him.

In the next instant he remembers tossing empty cans, this time into a tall steel trash bin, using their kitchen wall as a backstop. Two points. She hated when he did this.

But she hadn't been home that day, had she.

He fetched another from the fridge, cracked it open, took a sip of something. A margarita, from a can.

A long while later—who knew how long, it didn't matter—the police called to confirm his address. Using the first number in the favorites list is a common tactic we use, they said. We just need to confirm your relationship with your wife. There's been a crash.

What crash, he said. He'd been watching a movie about warring tribes of acrobatic vampires versus muscle-bound lycanthropes, and there was a big face with bloody fangs stuck on the screen.

What about the baby? he said. What's going on?

Sit tight, sir, said the police. We got someone coming over right now.

A trio of officers arrived. Two men led by a woman, who did all the talking.

Your wife, she said, heard the sirens of our squad cars in pursuit of the suspect and she followed absolutely the right instinct when she pulled over to the right shoulder of the flyover.

Good, okay. So she did the right thing. He offered them water. They refused.

The suspect was traveling over ninety miles an hour when he struck her vehicle from behind. So unfortunately, sir, while pulling over is absolutely the right instinct to do, the stated procedure on a single-lane flyover is actually to stay put, which not many people know. I mean not many police officers remember that.

So wait. She did the wrong thing.

Not at all. What I'm trying to explain is she followed what would otherwise be correct procedure when encountering an official emergency vehicle, which is to pull over as far to the right as possible, except in this case she was in a rare crisis-type situational.

Can we go see her now? Is the baby okay?

Sir, her particular vehicle was struck from behind by the suspect individual traveling in excess of ninety miles an hour.

The officer grasped at the air with her hands, out of words.

He remembers buckling at that moment, like someone cut power to his legs, then how the two male cops reflexively dropped their hands to their holsters. How the world took a tumble before it clicked off to nothing.

THIRTY-NINE

THE BONFIRE SENT EMBERS INTO THE NIGHT AND UNDERLIT A RING OF faces in its shifting orange glow. Happy faces. Grins, the glint of earrings. Someone was strumming a guitar. A staccato song in what— Spanish. The Spanish teacher, right.

Now he remembers: it was a gathering of teachers. They laughed and gossiped and drank wine and gin and whiskey from big red cups. They picked at cheese and chips and store-bought cake from a folding table hidden in the shadows.

A cellular telephone played its little melody. A ringtone! My God, he's forgotten about all that crap: tiny thumb boards for texting and horrible phone photos and that idiotic but irresistible brick-breaker game played using a pea-sized trackball that constantly got gummed up, remember those? Beyond the fire floated a young man's blue face illuminated by the tiny rectangle of light cupped in his hands. He wanted to slap the device into the embers, then slap the face: You have fire right in front of you! Look at that instead!

He'd been a couple two three drinks in by that point.

A sudden roar: the belly of an airplane ripped through the sky right above them and rumbled off into the lustrous clouds, ascending to become one of the traveling stars silently blinking beside the moon.

They were at that one beach, he recalls. The one at the end of the airport runway almost no one knew about.

Tarheel Sands, she used to call it. Because of the jet exhaust residue.

He'd been talking to Byron. Byron leaned in close, because Byron was a close talker.

Just try to take a picture of one of these planes, man. Byron exhaled gin. See what happens.

Okay, he said, and reached for his pocket.

Do not even think about it, Byron said. You press that button, it'll trigger a triangulation data event. They can pinpoint your location with that thing, and they store copies of everyone's photos.

Who's they?

They are everywhere. *They* are the exact reason why all of this, everything you see, is, I forget. Dude, I'm wasted.

They snorted with laughter. But Byron stopped and drew him close again.

We laugh now, murmured Byron. But just by being here we're automatically added to some kind of airport security watchlist. Location and demographic data tracked, then sold to the highest bidder. Welcome to 2006, baby.

Come on, man, he said.

It's true, said Byron.

It's not true!

Whatever, I'm okay with just the one time. It's not like she was even aware she chose a high-security perimeter for this party.

He looked past Byron, across the fire, and saw her face floating there surrounded by friends. Her eyes flashed, looked away, then held him again with resolve, as if playing a game of chicken. Who would look away first?

Can't believe my party idea got only one vote, said Byron.

You know I always got your back, he said. He held on to her eyes.

The river channel, man! No reception, concrete walls ten feet thick. I'm talking Eisenhower-era shit!

I'm gonna go, uh, tell her about this area and the tracking and stuff.

Her mind is not ready to accept that level of truth, holmes!

He patted Byron and headed forward.

Her surrounding friends made way for him. I need more drinks, one of them blurted, skittering, and suddenly he was standing alone with her.

Happy summer break, he said.

Happy summer break.

This place is perfect. Great idea.

Thank you. She sipped her cup with eyes aglow. In this light, her brown skin touched with the sun from earlier in the day looked like the most meticulously burnished bronze.

Another airplane lunged across the night sky, propelled by mighty jets. They could see Byron duck his head at the sound and almost take a tumble.

Is Byron still with us? she said.

He's fine, he said. He just wants all of us to smoke out and get naked and form a movement. Live in a big naked commune and no one's super sure whose baby is whose.

Naked Byron, she laughed. Dang, I just said *naked* and *Byron*.

He laughed, maybe a little too long. He paused. This fire good, he said, stumbling.

She squeaked out a laugh at his goof. Fire good! Fire good!

Shut up, he said, and used the moment as an excuse to gently elbow her.

Fire create, fire destroy, she said. Some primal bullshit, right there.

She retied her garlands of black hair against the breeze.

From this, she said, pointing to the fire. All the way to that. She pointed at the airplane in the distance. There's nothing like us in all of biology.

You should teach your students that.

Biology and planes?

'Sway more interesting than, like, the angle of takeoff is adjacent to the ground, which we'll assume is a flat zero degrees, so if the plane is going this fast then we can calculate the ground speed, and bam, I just put my whole class to sleep.

Come on, let's get refills. She led him to the table in the dark. They poured whatever they could find into their cups, didn't matter. He filled hers the way the pros did it, by pinching the bottom of the wine bottle.

She cocked an eyebrow at his gesture and exclaimed, Hor hor hor!

Oui oui hein hein, he said in retort.

She's funny, he realized, and it made him want to be funny, too.

Let's go check out the waves, she said.

Yes, he thought. He remembered this moment with exact certitude. Let's go.

The sounds of the party receded behind them, and when they reached the ocean the bonfire was but a distant match flame. As the waves tumbled onto the flat shore he could see a faint white glow at the fringing foam, too bright to be from moonlight alone. Had to be something else in the water.

I think my students are bored with me, he said.

Maybe that's just geometry, because it can't be you, she said, and touched his arm. I bet you have some closet math nerds who are too scared to show it. I bet some even love showing up to your class more than any other class.

You're sweet.

And you never know, maybe drawing angles leads to writing proofs leads to analytical thinking which could lead to a career in policy making.

Toward what, though? he said. We start out all pure potential, and then we study hard, we build on the wisdom of our ancestors, all to get a job and so we can buy crap.

Not all jobs! Come on!

Another plane climbed above them.

You don't think so? You work yourself silly for money but not time? And so you spend all your money to buy a ticket to board that plane to go on vacation somewhere to buy more crap? Then fly right back to the job you want to escape but never can?

I dare you to teach your kids *that*, she said. They laughed like a couple on their third date.

Bad teacher, he said.

She slapped his knuckles. No apple.

He glanced at her hand. The hammered silver bracelet sparkled against her fine wrist.

It's just you have work and rent and career and it's always just busy busy busy, he said. In my ideal perfect future I have tons of time, tons of space, a house probably, all that. I feel like I should be there by now, but I'm not.

I feel that, too. I think plenty of people do. She paused, chose words. But that's shoulda-woulda-coulda thinking.

I guess.

There's no shoulda-woulda-coulda in the world. There's only *is*. Like, there's two hundred species of squirrel. It doesn't matter if you think there *should* be more or less, there just is what there is.

Two hundred is way too many.

We evolve so quickly, she said, still driving her unstoppable train of thought. Just yesterday we invented fire, and today we can hang out in a virtual 3D world. I personally think it's too much for our minds to keep up with. Like, *slow it down*. But like I said, we're biology, too, and biology doesn't care what I think things *should* be. The *is* just keeps on going.

A wave came hissing up right to their feet, then slunk back into the black.

So basically you're saying there's no meaning, he said.

Not anything beyond what we try to ascribe, she said. But isn't that the fun part?

Ascribing, he said.

Yeah.

He held her hand.

Your bracelet is pretty, he said.

Thank you, she said.

I don't know why I believe it to be pretty but I do, he said.

Then it is, she said.

That was the moment. He kissed her.

FORTY

FOR A SECOND, HE SO BELIEVES HE IS STILL ON THAT BEACH THAT HE says aloud:

What makes the waves glow?

He blinks his eyes up at the shelter ceiling. Why are they doing this to him? Dipping him into some cozy memory and then jolting him back out? Why are they obsessed with torturing him?

He lifts his cheek from where it's stuck to the roll of bubble wrap and tells himself to just stop spewing nonsense already. Torture? Pff. Vainglorious delusions of grandeur. No one is torturing him. There is no conspiratorial intent here. He is a nobody in the middle of great big nowhere.

This situation doesn't mean anything, he thinks. It just *is*.

His memory is simply reconstituting, dormant seeds pushing up bright and green after a forest fire, and there's nothing he can do about it.

What caused the fire, though?

He takes his time rising. Always amazing what a day without food can do. Vis-à-vis starving, he'd read that the first couple days on an empty stomach were the hardest. It'll be weeks before the body begins to eat its own fat. After that it eats its own muscle. He read this online in a cavernous darkness lit only by the screen before him.

He quiets his complaining stomach with a long drink of water. He draws open the shelter curtain.

Three metal cans sit before him like little visitors.

He looks up. A few paces away stands the boy. Different outfit today: bright blue jeans and a red shirt with a yellow grenade on it, all fresh and clean. The kid regards him without emotion, his eyes darkly ringed with mascara-like eyelashes.

He needs to urinate, but not with Crow Boy standing there. He kneels down and, keeping one eye on him, pats the cans with a finger. They are real. The labels have been removed.

How long do you plan on keeping me alive, he says.

The boy only shifts his pack.

I know you're just doing your job. I have no ill will toward you.

The boy says nothing.

He takes the cans into his shelter, eager to open one and see if it really has food inside that he can actually eat. But he can't, because through the crack in the curtain he can still see the boy standing there, refusing to go away. He pins it open and speaks.

I'm sorry I threw stuff at you earlier. That was wrong. I will stop doing the wrong thing from now on. I have to pee. Look away or something.

The boy does not look away.

Okay. He turns himself away, urinates, sends water down. He tries a stretch. Does he feel thinner already? The boy's gaze doesn't waver one millimeter.

Creepy.

He takes a step toward the boy, who immediately takes a matching step backward. Another step. A tango, he thinks.

We're going to talk, you and I, he says. How about a grand tour? Nothing has meaning but for what you give it. That's how the world works. Not that the world works or anything, it just is. Chew on that for a sec.

He waits. I'm going this way, he says finally. Come or don't come. Feel free to do your vanishing thing or whatever.

He begins walking toward the terminus. He glances back. The boy follows, but keeps his distance.

This is the Arroyo Plato river channel, he says. The habitable portion is about a mile long end to end with a slight curve. It's about twenty paces wide and maybe twenty feet deep. By my rough calculations it could hold about four and a half million ping-pong balls, or about forty-five million gallons of water. That's a lotta berries, crow.

He keeps walking. He can hear the boy's small footsteps behind him.

He calls over his shoulder. So sometimes you talk, and sometimes you don't? I get like that, too. Today I'm a talkie. And a walkie. A walkie talkie.

The boy walks strangely, without moving his arms, because he is not real. A glitch.

They reach the terminus. Obviously water once used to flow out these big pipes, he says, but that's all over. I don't like it here. Let's head back.

He passes the boy, who's crossed to the other side of the channel to let him go by. He points at his reeds and their lines.

This is my wind measurement system, he says. I have a bunch of notes and data based on the geometries, but I gotta say I think it's all complete bullshit. When I'm gone you can dick around with it. Maybe you can get something out of it. Like, the wind's carved beautiful patterns in the sand down there. Isn't that nice?

The boy looks at the sand, then him. He seems to be studying the way he shifts his weight to relieve pressure on his shoe containing the key.

I hurt my foot, he says quickly.

The boy loses interest in his shoe.

I'm figuring out what happened here, by the way. Some kind of blast destroyed everything over there, but not those houses over there. Something to do with the aerodynamics of the channel like I mentioned. I'm going to those houses today. Still curious about how I got here, though. I'll find out soon enough whether I want to or not, I'm sure you'll make sure of that.

They walk for some time without talking. Every time he glances back, he expects the boy to be gone. But he's still there.

These stacks of stones are called cairns, he says. Do not disturb them. Hey—stop!

The kid had reached a hand out, but freezes at his sharp tone.

Sorry, crow, he says. I'm sorry. Touch them all you want. It's your world, right? Or maybe it isn't. Does it matter?

The boy, unsure, draws his hand back.

I'm gonna head back now, crow, he says.

When they reach the shelter once again, he sits and begins his customary preparations before heating one of the cans. If this is all a dream, then it's a damn impressive one.

Thank you for the cans, I guess. I don't know. Part of me thinks I should just let myself die.

The boy moves to stand in the shade, hot from the long walk.

But I'm too scared, to be honest. So for now I'm gonna eat this. You do whatever you want. No hard feelings.

He lights the stove, places the match aside the others, sets the open can upon the flame, stirs, et cetera.

"I'm not a crow," says the boy.

They are the first words he's heard in ages, besides his own. *Berries* doesn't count. Disembodied crow whispers don't count.

This is a real sound vibrating at him through the air and echoing high and sweet across the walls. It comes from within the boy's narrow chest. It has mass.

"I'm Clay."

FORTY-ONE

THE BOY INSTANTLY CHANGES.

Or does he?

Is he himself the one who's changed, suddenly grasping what's right before him, like the moment your eyes unfocus past the noisy black-and-white optical illusion to finally see the three-dimensional object hidden within?

He turns off the stove and holds the can and clears his throat. "You're Clay."

"You were low on rations," says the boy. "I took off the labels the way you like it."

Oh Jesus. Has he been watching him this whole time?

He thinks about the times when he walked around naked, waiting for his clothes to dry. Urinating down the slope.

Okay.

He looks at the boy, at the can.

Okay.

His mind is spinning. He needs to eat. He takes a spoonful, takes another, faster and faster, shoveling all of it down in seconds. It's some kind of astounding lentil soup. Soon, his intense hunger seems trivial. First he had no food, now he has a shit ton. How can that be? Is this luck? Something else?

The boy raises his eyebrows at him. "You eat fast."

"Not usually," he says, feeling self-conscious now. He wipes his lips. "Where do you live, Clay?"

This is, he realizes, the question all parents warn their kids about.

The boy pauses, thinking.

"Actually, don't tell me. You're not supposed to tell stuff like that to strangers."

Clay nods.

He silently begins freaking the absolute fuck out. A clean, well-groomed boy wearing new clothes has just brought him fresh supplies. From where? Were they right there in the houses this whole goddamn time, with not a threat in sight? And meanwhile here he is, burning down derelict houses, chasing crazy old men, and eating crows?

Stupid!

"I live right there," says Clay. He points at the houses.

Officially stupid. Perfect.

Or maybe he's not so stupid? He has no idea who the boy lives with or what mental state they're in. This kid could be escaping a madhouse with no future. There's a great slogan for the country right now. *America: A Madhouse with No Future!*

He feels sorry for him. He didn't ask to grow up in this world.

"How old are you? Actually, don't answer that, either."

"I'm eight. How old are you?"

"I don't remember."

The boy began to say something, but stops.

"What?"

"Nothing."

He fidgets. The boy. Clay. Children make such terrible liars it's adorable.

"Do you like the bivouac?" Clay says.

Bivouac? "It's great."

They pause. A little school of question marks swim between them. Clay looks as perplexed as he does.

Finally he speaks. "Is your, uh, family surviving okay?" He winces. More personal questions. But he has to at least try to get some useful information.

"I'm not allowed to—"

"—talk to strangers. I'm sorry. Can I ask one more question, though? Not about you. About all this."

The boy cups his arm dangling at his side and waits. Skinny kid. If he were his uncle he'd nickname him Bean Sprout or something similar.

"How'd everything get like this?" He gestures around.

"You mean all empty?"

He nods. *Empty* is a modest way of putting things.

"Everyone took off because it's not good here anymore."

So, an exodus. Okay. He pictures harried suburban moms and dads packing up their SUVs with the usual haste, this time not for swim practice but for forever.

"But why?"

He knows it's not fair to ask a kid a question like this. He can't possibly understand why. Most adults couldn't. There's a whole web of politics and greed and fear leading up to a neighborhood reduced to ash across the empty river. A world of ash, who knows.

Clay frowns for a long moment.

"I don't know, it's just not good anymore," he finally says. "Mr. Shaw used to say we need to succeed."

"Succeed?"

"Make our own country."

Secede? As in civil war? "Who is Mr. Shaw?"

"They moved away. He's a conspiracist."

"It's conspiracy theorist."

"That," Clay says.

"Did your dad teach you that word?" It's worth a try. But Clay falls silent, just like he's probably been trained. Good kid.

He decides he should stick to simpler questions about the here and now. Byron knew basic interrogation techniques. He'd even tried to teach him during one of their drunken overnight *training* camps.

Sorry, Byron. Should've paid more attention to your dumb ass.

He feels himself missing Byron and everything else and shuts that shit down hard.

"What did you mean by berries?" he tries.

"Huh?"

The kid knows nothing about all that berries nonsense. He is real. He has to be.

"What did you have for lunch?" he says.

"What are you measuring?" Clay says abruptly, pointing at his clear string setup.

He sighs. Patience.

"Wind. But it's all bullsh—bull caca. I was hoping to see patterns, maybe glean some insights, but eh."

"Were they dirty?"

"What?"

"You wanted to clean the insights."

He can't help but chuckle. He likes this kid. He wants to tell him that, but knows he couldn't-wouldn't-shouldn't.

"Are you an optimist?" says Clay.

"Good question! I'd say no, probably. It's complicated. Why, are you?"

Clay glances at the dipping sun, at the shelter, and at him, drawing an invisible triangle in the air with his eyes.

"You live here all alone, so either you really like the bivouac, or you really don't like it because something bad happened and this is the only place you can live."

Before he even begins to address this convoluted non-question, Clay hits him with another. "You're Korean, huh."

"I'm supposed to be. What about you?"

"I'm happa, half Japanese, half Anglo."

"Which side is your mom and dad?"

Once again Clay checks the vanishing sun. "Gotta go, bye."

This very real boy, Clay, hurries across the channel. "You need to shave," he calls as he runs. "You can't come to my house, okay?"

Clay reaches the cinder-block wall, expertly locates small grab points on its textured surface, and climbs up and over.

FORTY-TWO

A TINY HAND REACHING FOR A GLASS DOORKNOB.

A coffee table, a TV, a baby fence.

Her bursting in through the front door, kicking her shoes flying from her feet with a laugh. Those flyweight sequined Chinatown flats she liked.

I found us a neighborhood to check out! she cried. They're not even done *building it* it's so new.

She liked to aim for his head. Usually he thought that was hilarious, but not that day.

That day, he'd barked: *Watch the baby!*

There went that moment.

He should have been gentler then, about letting go of some things, and never letting go of others.

"I'm sorry," he cries, and looks around the concrete shelter. It's morning.

His sorry goes unacknowledged. His whole self goes unacknowledged. Too much crap bubbling in his head. Maybe he should meditate or something? Doesn't that involve knotting his legs under him? Or maybe pray to God? Which one? A bearded White knockoff Zeus painted on some chapel ceiling?

Byron wouldn't meditate or pray. He'd get up, fuel up, and get on with it.

"I'm having breakfast," he says to no one. He rises, performs his morning constitutionals, and sits down for a blank-can potluck.

Chili with beans this time. His favorite.

He cracks up at this idea of having favorites during this unprecedented time. His favorite is anything he can eat without dying.

He heats the can and eats and lets that warm luxurious feeling melt throughout his body. Eating from a steaming can in the free open air of the morning like a man in charge of his destiny. Food won't be the problem to solve from now on, he suspects. It'll be something else, and probably more difficult.

Wish you were here, man, he says to Byron. Two heads would be better than this one right about now.

He doesn't wish his girls were here. He'd never wish this kind of place on them. For them, he wishes he could un-explode the world and make it whole again.

Look in the margins, Byron liked to say.

Byron liked army surplus clothing, which he ribbed him for since the guy thought the military was a huge waste of taxpayer dollars. He also liked any and all military gear and gadgetry.

I contain multitudes, Byron would say, quoting some poem he read on the internet.

He pauses midbite at that word: *internet.*

He hates that word.

Why?

Forget about that for now. For now, just eat. Eat and eat and eat till the can's dry as the day it was made. If only he could eat the can, too, and shit it all out and just walk away.

In the afternoon Clay returns.

"I brought you a mirror and shaving cream for your razor," he says. From his pack he draws forth a white plastic bag. Within it, an oval of light shines. He makes a note to discreetly smash the mirror later. But for now, he is astounded. How many supplies does this boy have, that he can give them away with such ease?

"Thank you very much," he says to the boy.

"Aren't you going to shave?"

He has to avoid that mirror. So he says, "I just ate. You're not supposed to."

To his relief, Clay seems to accept this. "You pee over here."

He grimaces at the thought of being seen. "Yes I do."

"And you rinse it after."

"Listen," he says. "You seem to know a lot of stuff about me. Could I learn a few things about you? Only if your mom and dad won't mind."

Clay cocks his head as if receiving instructions transmitted from afar.

"It's just me and Mom," he says.

So no dad, then. He had expected bald bearded men, or face-painted boys bearing weapons fashioned out of sporting equipment, but never women, much less a single woman.

"Me and Mom have to be extra careful," says the boy.

"Does your mom mind you talking to me? Does she know you're here?"

Clay hugs himself and frowns. He is losing him. Keep the questions simple, he reminds himself.

So he brightens. "You guys seem like you're in good shape," he says. "Tons of supplies and stuff, right?"

"Tons," gushes Clay all of a sudden. "We have limited comms and weps but I can improvise ammo on highly short notice."

Weps? Weapons? And comms? Does that mean a working radio?

"Everyone's gone," Clay continues, "so we're pretty much on our own."

"What happened to your dad?"

He knows it was a dangerous question the moment he lets it slip, and Clay's face falls again. But he answers, in a strange voice that sounds scripted.

"He's searching for something better. He'll be back before you know it," he says. "His job is exploring natural resource opportunities. Mom's job is knowledge research."

"So your dad is alive out there?"

Clay nods.

He wants to leap at the poor boy with questions. Where is he? Are there others? How many? Are they there, too?

Are his girls there?

Then he remembers the wet road clogged with cars and the police and the pop of metal.

"Are you sick?" says Clay.

"No," he says.

Clay looks puzzled.

"Did you see the old man," he asks. "With the bags?"

Clay freezes and nods. "He was creepy."

"Well, he's long gone now," he says.

And lying dead in the sun, if there's any such thing as karma.

Clay is cowering a bit. He's been staring at the boy harder than he realizes. He presses on, gently.

"Did you have neighbors?"

"Mom says there's nothing left to stay for here. She's making our escape plan. She says it's gonna take some time and hard work but she's not taking any shortcuts this time."

Shortcuts?

"I'm not gonna live my life in fear," says Clay.

"Does your mom say that a lot?"

"We're gonna take back control," says Clay. "They can't have everything."

The world expands in that moment. Of course. If there are survivors, then there must be factions fighting over the scraps of civilization. That's just what humans do. If humans lack a common enemy, the nearest village will do just fine. Maybe secession is actually the norm now. If he walks the thirty miles to the mountains and sees what he can see, he'd see a battlefield raging for many more miles on the other side.

He feels like he's about to be recruited for a fight. He needs to figure out which side he's on.

FORTY-THREE

CLAY SITS SOME DISTANCE AWAY AND CRANES HIS NECK AT THE FAUCET.

"That's cool that you figured out how to get water."

"Where do you think you'll be going once your escape plan is ready?"

Clay frowns at this. He's getting sick of questions. "How did you open it?"

He shows him the wine tool. Clay scoots forward, leans in. Examines it like it's a magic wand.

He knows he should stop with the interrogating, but he just can't. What if he wakes up tomorrow and Clay and his mom have vanished?

"Are you gonna meet up with your dad someplace safe? With all the, ah, others?"

Clay only stares at the tool. Yep, the kid is done. He tells himself to be patient. But still: so many answers, all locked up in the mind of a single weird boy? Why couldn't they have sent him an average grown adult who could speak in complete sentences?

Stop. Nobody sent this kid. Nobody sent the crazy old man. Nobody sent the crows.

Be patient.

"Lemme show you how I opened it," he says.

He turns his attention to the faucet. He glances back at Clay, who has scooted forward an inch but still stays distanced as if he were infected. Maybe he is. Wouldn't that just be wunderbar?

He places the wine tool onto the square spigot bolt. "The first time it was so frozen stiff I didn't know which would break first, it or my friggin' arm," he says.

When he looks back at Clay, he sees he's moved in so close to look he nudges him with a knee. Pure curiosity on his face. He can smell the sweet citrus of his hair: shampoo. Things can't be that bad if people are still bathing, can they?

Clay squints up at him, eager. He's seen a similar hunger for attention before in neglected children among the teens he used to teach. Clay isn't a messenger, or a metaphor, or a spy. He's just a kid.

A kid with a paranoid survivalist of a mom who is probably neglectful at best. The thought of Clay's home life breaks his heart.

He opens up a space so Clay can see better.

"You pinch the fulcrum, that's what this point is called, so now it's stable and transfers energy smoother. And just push away from your body." Water gushes forth.

He closes it again and hands Clay the tool.

"You try."

"Pinch the fulcrum," says Clay.

"HOW DID YOU MEASURE THE RIVER?" SAYS CLAY.

"Ain't no water, ain't no river," he says, going for at least a little laugh, but with this kid ain't a damn thing funny.

"I estimated the length of my stride and walked around," he says.

"How did you measure your stride?" says Clay.

"Well, you know how long a foot is? Turns out my foot is about a foot. My stride is about five feet."

He does a little soft-shoe shuffle to demonstrate, and finally Clay smiles.

"Did water use to flow through here?" he says.

"No."

"Never?"

Clay shakes his head. "Ping-pong balls could. Like you said you wanted."

"Bring me a bunch in your truck." He watches the boy and telepaths his real query: *Do you have a vehicle?*

"Mom's always saying 'road trip.'" Clay pauses. "You can come."

His risk has produced a small payout: Clay must have a working vehicle. They are going somewhere, which means some cities still exist.

Makes sense. The chances of every single human being dying all at once are cosmically slim, the stuff of science fiction. Cities and towns almost never got completely wiped out. The closest mental model he has is of massive warfare, followed by stricken citizens piecing what they can from the rubble. Mighty superpowers aren't exempt from becoming hardscrabble third-world countries late in life. Shit happens. Happened. Is happening now.

"I guess I should probably meet your mom at some point."

"Okay."

"What's her escape plan?"

"How do you measure the wind?"

Clay walks ahead of him to inspect the delta of clear strings, out of avoidance or curiosity or both.

Just as he's about to track footprints in the fine sand ripples below, Clay leaps at the last second onto a clean patch of concrete. He looks back at him.

He jogs to catch up to Clay. "The reeds do all the measuring for me. See?" He wiggles one and the string bobs up and down.

"What do you do with it?"

He leads Clay back up to the shelter and shows him the discs.

"I take the cardboard and get down way low to mark the data."

"I wanna do it."

Clay wedges himself between him and the discs, taking the cardboard and making marks in the chart. The boy takes great care to closely imitate the style already drawn.

"Nice work," he says when Clay hands him the cardboard.

"So now what?"

"You just keep collecting data. I don't really have a hypothesis yet."

"What's a hypothesis?"

So he explains scientific theory.

AFTER CLAY LEAVES THAT EVENING HE EATS YET ANOTHER SPLENDID can of chili and watches yet another radiant sunset. What would baby have been like at Clay's age? he wonders. A miniature curmudgeon like me? Smart but wary but also tired of having to be wary, like her mother?

Tall? Stocky? Thin?

Shrewd? Stoic? Naive?

Kind?

Violent?

Kids are strange beings. He's seen enough to know that they become totally different people every couple years.

His mind races with so many theories he can't sleep.

Clay's mom has sent Clay to lure him into their house to his doom.

Clay lives with the dead body of his mother, waiting for her to wake up.

Clay and his mom's plan is to find and kill his dad for ditching them.

Eh. All crazy. How about:

Clay, fatherless, wants him to marry his mom and give him the little sister he never had. The resulting little girl will look exactly like the very baby he lost. Clay's mother will look just like the very wife he lost.

Eh.

None of these are it.

Maybe he'll never know what's really going on with Clay.

Or maybe, he thinks, all Clay wants is a friend.

FORTY-FOUR

HIS BABY: JANE, JUTE, JAW. HE CAN'T REMEMBER THE NAME. HIS OWN child!

In a panic, he takes the brass key out of his shoe and polishes it over and over with his thumb, willing memories to return. This whole time, he's been avoiding any triggers—but now he is growing terrified that if he keeps the past at bay for long enough, it will give up and go away forever.

He can't bear to do that to his wife and child.

Jean, Jam, Join?

Maybe if he finds the thing the key unlocks, he'll remember. What else will happen then? Will his head explode?

When he's finally able to close his eyes to sleep, he finds himself back at the apartment lying in his bed next to his wife.

It was so late at night. Hard to tell how late. The baby had woken up crying for the million billionth time. She's at the stage, said his wife, where she's waking up and not quite sure where she is. She's becoming more aware.

He swung his legs out of bed for the million billionth time.

She needs to know we're still here, she explained. Did you hear me?

I knew that already, he thought. I knew it, we studied all this baby shit to death, please do us all a favor and shut up, bitch.

He clapped a hand over his mouth in the dark, as if to stop more such venomous mean thoughts from spewing. He was so far gone he hadn't realized how far gone he was. Or her. Nothing but one-hour bouts of sleep for four days straight did that. Very well, in fact. Yesterday the power went out for fifteen minutes, and he wanted to run out into the street and rage at everyone and everything.

They used sleep deprivation for torture, didn't they?

Naked, he pawed his way through the darkness. He opened the nursery door by feel.

The world beyond it was a different one entirely. Full of dim blue starlight strewn across the walls by a little plug-in turtle, full of the scent of lilies and powder and the sour tinge of dirty diapers stuffed away in plastic bags. He bent down into the crib and slowly swept his arms about. His hand found his crying baby girl.

He lifted her into the crook of his neck and the viciousness brought on by his fatigue instantly dissolved into something else. Not that sentimental parent high on baby love he'd see on diaper packaging. What he felt was more serious and real. What he felt was duty.

Because dammit, without him, without her, the baby would cry for hours, soiled and abandoned, her tiny buttocks growing red and inflamed from the acidity of the urine and stool. The baby would cry and cry in the dark. She would sense the magnitude of this strange world she had suddenly entered—the absolute hugeness of it—and wail harder until her tiny throat became raw.

Eventually—God—she would stop crying. The nursery would fall forever silent with only its little turtle lighting the way for nobody.

Why in the world would anyone ever let that happen to a child?

No way. Hell no.

He stood there holding her with tears burning through the corners of his eyes.

Then he changed her diaper. He did so quickly and efficiently; he could've done it with his eyes closed.

I love this goddamn baby, he thought. I love my goddamn wife.

I'm a grown-ass man standing butt-ass naked in the dark and it's three in the morning and the whole world can go straight to the tenth add-on circle of hell because this is the best day of my goddamn life.

He rolled the soiled diaper into a tight triangle and twisted it into the special trash can, then rocked her back and forth, patting and shushing, patting and shushing, until she calmed down enough to be carefully set back down like a little blind baby bird.

Then he collapsed onto his side of the bed for one more desperate hour of sleep. He felt her fingers crawl into his palm and grasp tight.

You're the world's best papa, she whispered.

You're the world's best everything, he whispered back, and caressed her exquisite knuckles with his thumb.

FORTY-FIVE

"YOU SAID 'FIRST WORD,'" SAYS A VOICE.

It's Clay, from outside the shelter blanket.

"Are you okay?" says Clay.

He sits up. He'd been having a nightmare that she was saying her first word, but he was across town, across the world, and rushing home to hear it. He kept thinking if he ran fast enough he could still make it in time to hear the word before it vanished into the air.

The key is still in his hand. All night he'd slept, squeezing the thing.

He scrambles to stuff it back into his shoe before emerging into the light. He and Clay stare at each other for a moment.

What was her first word?

Did she ever have one?

He shakes his head to clear it, takes a long drink of water.

"You should keep track of the sand patterns, too," says Clay, and shows him a pad of paper.

He looks at it. It has a dense drawing, full of intricate wavy lines like a topographical map.

"You copied the lines in the sand?"

Clay nods.

"How long did that take you?"

"You slept forever." He pauses. "I can show you how I did it." He walks off.

He hurries to follow the boy. Along the way, Clay spots a small rock, snap-judges it, and deems it worthy for collection into his pack. He casts a sheepish look back at his grown-up friend, as if he's been caught stealing. Then he whips the pack back on and keeps walking.

At the base of the channel, Clay has marked off a square area with orange chalk in regular one-foot intervals, effectively creating a grid with X- and Y-axes to help him mentally slice the sand into smaller squares to make for easier drawing.

"I'm gonna tie strings across so you can actually see the grid lines," Clay says.

It is marvelous. "This," he says, "is the exact same technique used by muralists."

Clay stares at him flatly, uncomprehending.

"Clay," he says, "if you don't know what a word means, you can always ask. Don't just stare. It's creeping out the rest of the class."

The rest of the class? He says the words without thinking. Muscle memory.

"You're a teacher," Clay states.

He can see his classroom. The festive squares of patterned fabric draped beneath the fluorescent ceiling lights; the walls crammed with diagrams; the big circle of desks he'd pushed together himself. He'd wanted to foster personal space for discussion, as if geometry could be like therapy.

"Yeah," he says.

"You taught math or science or something."

The kids blip in and out of their desk chairs. He glances out the tall, thin door window reinforced with wire—*we called it prison glass*—and sees her go by: his future wife.

He can't do this right now. Not in front of the kid. He changes the subject. "How you gonna hang the strings for the grid?"

Before Clay can answer, something black tumbles into view on the slope above. A crow.

Clay gives the bird a single look, then quickly draws from his pockets a rubber band outfitted with a notched square of metal and something else. A nail. He seats the nail, draws it back, and looks at a blank spot on the slope away from the bird before firing.

The nail vanishes into the bird's chest without a sound.

He's too stunned by what he's just seen to say anything. Clay runs up and bends his head down to inspect.

"I got it," says Clay, beckoning now. "Come see."

So he does.

The bird is still breathing. There is the fine red line trickling from its chest that quickly turns brown on the hot concrete slope. This is history repeating itself. This will lead to nothing good.

"You have to look away when you shoot," Clay says. "That way you catch 'em by surprise."

The bird's chest pumps up and down with silent panic. You shouldn't have come back, he thinks. Please stop coming back.

"Their eyes are so black," says Clay. The boy is almost mumbling to himself. "Their feathers are all shiny like spring steel and their eyes are so black like big black fish eggs. I don't think they're supposed to have feelings."

He nudges the bird with a toe, and when it weakly claws the ground he presses down on its neck with the edge of his shoe until the bird pops softly once and stops moving.

"There's tons of these around here. They eat mice."

He stands staring at the crow long enough to jump when Clay nudges him for his attention.

"There really are tons," says Clay, as if to imply that there are plenty to go around, and one won't be missed. "They do nothing all day. Just sit around, all day long, doing nothing. I don't even think they know how to play with each other."

"What should we do with it?"

"Just leave it," he sings.

"Shouldn't we use it? For food?"

"Ew."

So Clay hadn't seen him eat the crow, obscured as he had been by the overpass and the night.

"There's tons," he says, "but you don't eat them?"

Clay becomes unusually animated with incredulous bemusement. "We have snacks and chips and cookies! It's a flippin' stockpile for all time!" He giggles. "If you ate crow you would start going *caw caw!*"

"Clay."

"Caw, caw, caw!" he says, giggling louder.

Caw, caw, look Papa. Her tiny outstretched finger reaching for the sycamores.

He squeezes his eyes shut so hard he sees stars streaking out from the center at warp speed. A vacuum is threatening to pull his mind apart and expose its entire stringy web for the universe to gawk at. He knows he can't stop it. He knows it will soon be time.

"That's enough," he snaps. "I get the fucking message already."

When he reopens his eyes, regret floods his every pore. If Clay were a normal kid, he'd be tearing up at such an outburst from a grown-up. At least look hurt.

But Clay's face has gone as blank as stone.

He instantly worries if very, very bad things are happening to and around Clay on a regular basis.

Has to be, he thinks. Growing up in this world. God. He read about this somewhere in the before time. Abused kids don't cry. Not once they learn no one will come running.

"Hey," he tries, even though he knows it's already a losing battle. "Sorry."

Clay turns away and begins walking up the slope.

"It's not you," he says.

Clay heads back to the shelter. "I'm hungry," he says.

THEY SIT IN THE TRIANGLE OF THE SHELTER'S OPEN CURTAIN AND share a can of chili with beans Clay brought for lunch. They pass the can back and forth.

"My favorite," he says.

"Nn," says Clay.

He sets the can down. "I'm sorry I freaked out on you back there. It's not you, it is not you. I'm just, ah, dealing with stuff."

"Nn," says Clay.

Clay had already fully shut down a while ago. He gets why. He is protecting himself.

Just like you did after the crash?

When he looks down he realizes he's been pressing the spoon hard enough to bend it. He promises to be vigilant and careful from now on with Clay.

He inhales, exhales, bends the spoon back. He hands it to the boy.

"I'm full," says Clay. "I had a late breakfast."

Breakfast? In a kitchen, stocked with food? He has to at least try for more answers. There's no such thing as a *good time* for interrogation, Byron said. Which means anytime is the time to begin questioning. Just don't make it seem like questioning. Make it seem like conversation.

"It must've been weird when everyone left," he says finally.

Clay nods. "There was the Shaws, and the Saitos, and the Reeses."

"Small neighborhood." He takes a bite, feigns being distracted by the food.

"They never got to finish it and only a few select approved zero-down applicants got in early, but then everything stopped and no more families came. We were first in, gonna be last out."

He licks the spoon with as much nonchalance as he can muster.

"Mom says it like," says Clay, "everything's gone to shit and we have to survive, no one's got your back but our own." He catches himself. "I'm not supposed to say S-H-I-T."

"It's fine."

"I'm not supposed to swear."

"You're good."

He looks at him with dispassionate eyes that can be read either way: Please don't tell my mom I said shit. Or: Go ahead, tell my mom I said shit, what difference does it make. The fact that it's hard to tell makes his heart pang with pity.

"I sure as shit ain't saying shit to nobody, shit," he tries, but Clay doesn't seem to register the joke.

"Mom's so mad all the time." Clay is talking through his teeth now. "Not mad, okay, frustrated." He says it *fusstrated*. "Not with me but the situation."

"Because everything's gone to S-H-I-T."

"She wants to make it clear she's not frustrated with me," says Clay, and then stands suddenly. "Gotta go, bye."

He watches Clay walk his strange armless walk. When he reaches the opposite slope, he picks up the crow by its leg and flings it somewhere over the wall. Then he hustles to his climbing spot and vanishes up and over.

In the shelter the discs shift up and down. He studies Clay's sand drawing, which while intricate and beautiful reveals nothing of any significance.

FORTY-SIX

MORNING. HE STARES AT THE SPOTS ON THE CINDER-BLOCK WALL THAT Clay had used to climb. They are so clearly lighter and smoother than the rest of the surface. Why hasn't he noticed them before? They're a totally obvious sign of life—benign, too, given the fact that he's been left alone and alive for so long. Meanwhile, he's been cowering in the shelter for god knows how long like a chump.

He could've been having breakfast in a kitchen by now.

He tries piecing together the details mentioned by Clay, like reconstructing the whole dinosaur from just a few key bones. The house probably isn't the outpost for some crazy new cult or anything like that. Apart from a bit of homebrew fortification, it's probably nice and boring.

He bets he can even walk up to the front doorbell and introduce himself.

Hello, my name is ____! I don't remember! Long story! I moved in recently under the bridge right by the Dead Lands. Your son's really good at killing crows!

Clay's mom would lean on her shotgun, dressed in—fatigues? A bathrobe? Plastic armor? Eyes glinting clear with the tough grace of frontier wisdom. Or who knows what. Maybe she is crazy-eyed with shell shock. Maybe she'd welcome him, or shoot him in the face, or simply not answer the door.

He feels the similar—and yes, comfortable—paralysis settle into his bones. Instead of deciding what to do next, he thinks, it might help to review what's happened up until this point.

You got hit on the head.

You were left for dead and woke up remembering nothing except that the world had gone to shit.

People have fled, betting that anyplace was better than the place they were in. Some of them wander the earth with all their possessions tied up in plastic bags, saying *berries*.

You had a wife and baby, but they died in a car crash before the apocalypse. You're not ready to know their names just yet, and don't know if you ever will be.

You are one of just a roomful of survivors.

You care about Clay, and not just because he's your only real source of information. You know you'll be more than a little forlorn when he and his mom pack up and vanish one day. You know it's impossible to ask them to take you along, and even more impossible to actually go with them. You're too scared to do much of any damn thing.

The sky has filled with clouds. The air has become fragrant with moisture.

Out of all the things you're scared of, you're most terrified of going back to your apartment and seeing its few small rooms now shattered and burned and leaking rain, because that would be like killing them all over again in your heart.

You could just stay here forever.

Use fewer and fewer words each day, until the only one left is *berries*.

Fuck's sake, he mutters.

He throws all the water from his metal bucket down the slope in one large arc and strides off. He walks across the bottom of the channel and drags his feet through the sand pattern there, ruining it.

I'm sick of sand.

He climbs to the other side and, avoiding Clay's house, searches for a good place to climb. There has to be another somewhere. He chooses a spot behind one of the unfinished houses. The wall there, he's frustrated to learn, is smoothly textured, with no bumps big enough to get a decent hold on.

A running leap might work. He sets the bucket upside down at the base of the wall. Takes a few steps back, jogs forward, and leaps off the bucket to catch a finger on the top ledge before slipping to the ground. The bucket tips from under his feet as he falls onto his side.

He shakes it off, resets the bucket, takes another run. His fingers grip the edge. He scrambles his feet up the wall, good old sneakers, and hooks an arm over. He hoists up his torso and rests a moment there.

He finds himself dangling at the edge of a fragmented labyrinth of walled backyards stretching for a mile in either direction, each filled with sand. Before him stands the wooden skeleton of a house. A half-open window has been installed in one of the gaping unfinished walls. There's a once-new pile of lumber still strapped together. Dozens of nested plastic buckets. Little orange flags half-buried in the ground.

The sand has piled up in one corner in a perfect dune, and he uses that to slip down—whee!—into the backyard. Beyond the naked beams and studs he can see more skeleton houses across the street. Beyond that? Nothing but desert plain ending in a low rolling ridge. The destroyed condo is out there somewhere, hiding charred human remains no one will ever claim. He marks it on the map in his mind: SAND HILLS EXPLOSION.

He steps through the house and onto the street. Drifts of sand have gathered in sugary curves on the flawless black asphalt. Of all the lots, only four have actual finished houses on them. Clay hadn't been lying about that. Dead brown grass sits in front of them. The other unbuilt houses are barely more than parcels of raw dirt and sand fluttering with more little orange flags. No cars, no movement, no sound. Everything filtered in monochrome by a sky getting thick with clouds.

No corpses, either, thank God. Just imagine if the neighborhood had been full of people and life. People and life plus death equals mass tragedy. He feels fortunate there's so much nothing here.

Thank God for all this nothing.

He thinks about strolling down the middle of the street, but stops. What if he runs into Clay's mom? *Hey, how's the knowledge research going?*

That'd be enough for her to shoot a nail into his chest and crush his skull with her foot, like mother, like son. There's tons of these crows, Clay would say, hanging around with nothing to do all day.

One of the houses has something out front: a flag. He looks closer.

It's a snowman wearing a red Santa hat. The flag says MERRY CHRISTMAS.

He feels a drop on his face. He looks around to see rain falling around him.

"It's Christmas?" he says.

FORTY-SEVEN

HE HUSTLES BACK TO THE SHELTER, SHIVERING. THE RAIN STRENGTH-ens, thickening the air with a huge soft applause. He thinks of the snowman flag dripping with wet.

Is it December? Or is it not? Has that flag just been hanging there forgotten for months? Looked pretty new, though.

In the best version of this world, people are good and keeping traditions alive as best they can. In another version, the flag is a lure designed to lull wanderers like him into a false sense of normalcy.

Who knows. When Clay appears over the wall and approaches the shelter, he calls out: "Merry Christmas."

Clay says "Merry Christmas" right back without any hint of weirdness. So it really is December. Time is still being marked down. That's a good sign, right?

Clay wears a parka. Man, a parka would be nice. And a coat, a blanket, those zinc tablets you take when you think you're getting a cold, and before I forget, a gun, the keys to a military chopper, and flying lessons too please and thank you.

Clay gazes at the bottom of the channel and frowns at the ruined sand pattern.

"What happened?" he says.

He plays it off as best he can. "Probably a kit fox."

Clay approaches and removes his wet parka. "What?"

"Probably a kit fox ran through the sand in the middle of the night."

"Then we should record the pattern."

Clay opens his pack—revealing pens but also a sizable collection of rocks—and gets out a notepad.

"You collect rocks?" he says.

"They're concrete chips, not rocks," says Clay.

"Cool," he says.

"Don't ask," says Clay, with a sudden sheepish smile that he can't help but mirror back to him. Had he been this awkward at Clay's age? Probably. Worse. Anyway, it's nice to see the kid smile for once.

Clay spends the next ten minutes drawing what he sees. He uses a fresh sheet and marks it NO. 2, follows the lines of the sand, and leaves wild ovals where it's been disturbed. He adds a note: RAIN TODAY.

"It looks like eggplants crossing a river," he tells Clay.

They eat another can. The line of spent matches numbers over twenty now.

He wants to ask Clay more questions to get more intel. Do they still give gifts for Christmas? What month did it all go down? But Clay is more reticent than usual today, like he's literally dampened by the weather.

"We should track rainfall with a bucket," Clay says with a yawn, and abruptly lays his head down in his lap: okay. In seconds he starts sleep-twitching; seconds after that, he is good and asleep.

He sits there with Clay slumbering on as the river channel grows musty and dark with the increasing shower. He studies the boy's perfect miniature ear: a tiny soft channel leading right to the vulnerable brain. He wants to think he is watching over him—that he has the right to brush a stray hair away from his closed eye—but Clay isn't his kid. No one is his kid, and he is no one's dad.

He can't say any of the things he wants to say right now—*You're gonna be okay, you're a good kid*—because he has no right to.

It'd be so nice to have a right to something, though, wouldn't it?

Anyway. He figures it's best to keep his arms propped to either side and just watch the boy's chest rising and falling until his own breathing falls in sync. So he does that.

THE RAIN DRUMMED AGAINST THE WINDOW OF THEIR APARTMENT. OUT-side was an empty lot where people abandoned large awkward things, like broken washers or refrigerators with the doors diligently re-moved. He found that hilarious and ironic. People smoked their lungs away or drove drunk or shot up a school, but they always remembered to remove the doors from a broken fridge.

People always remembered to pull over for emergency vehi-cles, too.

Inside, he and his wife sat stirring tea in the gray light. The baby was asleep in the other room. The house was filled with the kind of quiet they were no longer accustomed to, and they wordlessly savored the moment like a small sweet piece of hard candy.

This is nice, he said finally.

She smiled back.

He studied the way the milk swirled into the water, every second of it. The mugs were flecked earthenware, he remembered. The tea was still too hot to drink.

The tea was totally beside the point.

A droning sound approached from the distance.

They set down their spoons and gazed at the ceiling with irrita-tion and dread.

The droning grew in volume and began to rattle the whole house. A helicopter.

God, another one, she said.

I wish I could shoot them dead out of the sky, he said.

Stop, she said, and put her hand on his. Let's just enjoy the quiet while we have it.

They're gonna wake the baby.

Just as the helicopter began receding away from them, another helicopter came flying overhead. And another, filling the sky with its awful music.

It bleeds, it leads, he sang with disgust. I hope it's worth it.

Calm down, they'll pass over, she said. Another helicopter joined in the rumbling chorus. What the hell is going on out there? she said finally.

They heard a small whimper coming from the nursery then, one that bled into a wail that paused before erupting into a true cry.

He slammed down his tea. How can this be allowed? People have babies and entire lives down here. People are trying to sleep. It's like they want to torture us for ratings.

Honey, it sucks but there's no conspiracy here. They're just careless. We're moving soon, right? It'll be so much quieter. She reached for a nearby key on a string—a rectangle of brass marked REVERE—and touched it as if it were a warding talisman humming with power.

Careless like they could not care less, he said. I'm going to drive her to sleep in the car.

He snatched his jacket and keys and marched to the nursery. But she stopped him.

You're too crazy right now, she said. I'll do it.

They step all over us, he spat, and the only thing we can do is take it, like, if you can't afford it then you deserve to get stepped on.

You need sleep. I'll go.

I want it to be you, me, the baby, and that's it. They can all go ahead and stomp each other to death, but leave us out of it.

The baby continued to wail. She gathered her things.

Jesus Christ, get your ass in bed, put in some earplugs, and take a damn nap. Once we move, all this noise will be just a distant memory. She squared her gaze. Right?

I'm trying. They're so slow over there.

Hey. I'm not blaming you.

What the hell else can I do? Stalk the real estate agent? I call every day.

I know you do.

They can't get the most basic shit together but they can sure take our money.

Honey, I can't absorb your anxiety on top of my own anxiety. I'm full. I'm just as tired as you.

He stood, choking his jacket in his fist for want of direction.

You don't owe me, there's no blame, everything's gonna be fine, she cried. You just need sleep! Sleep!

She vanished into the nursery and reemerged shushing frantically. The baby was bright with tears now. He stroked her perfect miniature ear with a thumb, barely holding it together.

I'm gonna drive the loop a few times till she sleeps, she said. She muffled the jingling car keys. You can tell me sorry when I get back.

What about what I need, he wanted to shout. I'm last on the list now, and probably always gonna be. He wanted to sing through his gritted teeth: baby comes first, then mommy, and last is daddy if there's even anything left.

Instead he said, Just everyone leave me the fuck alone.

She stopped, incredulous. She left with a slam. The apartment froze with a stillness that was absolute.

He screwed earplugs in tight against the next wave of helicopters and poured himself a margarita from a can, thinking to hell with everything, he was probably in the wrong again as usual. He was always in the wrong. The arrival of the baby only seemed to make him more wrong more often. He'd never been very good at being a person walking around on a planet full of other persons. He preferred geometry, with its ideal angles and proofs.

He finished his drink, went to the kitchen to get another. For a moment he stood staring out the window at the empty lot. The rain had pooled in the dented top of a washing machine, creating a shimmering triangle of water. It was a pitiful sight.

He scowled down at that stupid brass key on the kitchen table. What a scam. He wanted to grind it into glitter in the garbage disposal.

Up-and-coming neighborhood my ass, he said, and flicked it beneath a napkin to get it out of his sight.

He traveled back to the couch, each footfall booming in his insulated ears. He lay down. He grew drowsy. He closed his eyes for a second.

He woke hours later in the dark. How long had he slept? He felt groggy but refreshed and sane again, his raging anger from before now nothing more than absurd and embarrassing, and he sat up with a clarity he hadn't enjoyed in weeks since the baby. He blinked, eyes fresh with tears from a mighty yawn. Maybe she took the baby to her friend's house, he thought, juggling guilt and gratitude.

He owed her.

He would apologize.

He was not last on some list. We all came first, we would all take care of one another.

He just needed sleep!

He got up, crushed the can in the kitchen. He twirled the futuristic new house key between his fingers. He'd never seen a key like this before. It was an entirely new, entirely cool kind of key. He marveled once again at the marketing brochure, thick with frictionless satin varnish and filled with images of perfect Spanish villas.

They were going to move on to their next stage of life. It was going to be perfect.

He studied the sweep of the wall clock for a moment. He would apologize up and down to her. God he would.

Time passed, and to kill it faster he began watching a movie about vampires, the young attractive fast-moving type, not the old slow kind. He sat there tasting his tongue. Man, how long did he sleep?

A few minutes later his phone began ringing and it was her: an unrecognizably pixelated photo on the tiny shitty outer screen of the flip case. But yes, there she was like always, bravely smiling in her hospital smock—exhausted!—after surviving hours and hours of labor.

FORTY-EIGHT

YOU KNOW THAT THAT IS NOT ALL, THE CROW HAD SAID IN HER SMOK-er's voice.

She's right. There is more. But please, not today, he begs.

That's fine, says the crow.

"Thank you," he whispers.

"Huh?" mumbles Clay. His eyes are still shut.

He nudges the boy awake. "Probably time to head home, buddy."

The boy blinks and rolls his eyes about, as if initializing their functionality. "What time is it?"

Time, he wants to scoff.

"Your mom doesn't know you wander around outside the house, does she."

Clay sits up and stretches.

"She doesn't know you come talk to me about secession and stuff."

"There's nothing around here to hurt me. So." Shrug.

Nothing? Not roving gangs of vandals armed with bludgeons? Maybe those same vandals had been his ex-neighbors. Mr. Saito wielding a bloody golf club against Mr. Shaw.

"Besides," says Clay, "Mom needs alone time to work on the es-cape plan."

"I should go wish your mom a Merry Christmas," he says. "Ho ho ho!" Clay doesn't smile, though. Hardly anything makes this friggin' kid smile.

In fact, Clay now frowns. "Why do you care so much about my mom?"

"I just wanna hear about what happened to everyone. Also how she plans on escaping."

"Is this because my dad's away?"

"What?"

Clay tucks his knees under his chin.

"Whoa, buddy," he says. "It's not that. Hell no, I promise."

The rain falls at a steady pace. The sand at the bottom of the channel has begun to pool here and there.

"She thinks I'm in my room or in the backyard. But I finished playing with everything! I finished all my video games like ten times!"

"You have video games? You have electricity?"

Clay shrugs.

Holy shit. A house full of light, humming microwave ovens, and music. Cold drinks for when it was hot, hot drinks for when it was cold.

His mouth goes dry. "Is it . . . solar?"

Clay shrugs again. God, this kid.

No choice but to keep plugging away. "So where does she plan on escaping to?" he says.

"She doesn't tell me. Doers don't waste time talking, that's why they're doers."

Who is this woman, self-helping her way out of apocalypse?

"She has her job," says Clay, "My job is to stay out of her hair." His face darkens. "I'm eight."

He wants to tell Clay something useful or comforting. That his mom loves him, even if it comes out all wrong sometimes. She is scrambling every day just to keep them alive.

But he can't, because like he said: he has no right.

Clay shoots up. "Bye." He slips out of the shelter and walks away. He abruptly turns back and calls out from under his dripping parka.

"I had fun today," Clay says.

––––––––––

HE SITS IN THE RAIN LATER THAT EVENING WAITING FOR HIS BUCKET TO fill at the faucet. He's getting all cold and wet but barely notices. He is busy constructing a theory about Clay.

Clay, to start, is a multitemporal actor.

Let me explain, Byron, he says, for this is definitely a Byron-type conversation.

When he himself was Clay's age he never saw his father, who was always working at the auto shop on the edge of the Latino Quarter. Dad would already be gone for the day when he woke up, and he only came back home after he'd already gone to bed. His cash cow was installing mismatched replacement body panels that he found at the junkyard for almost nothing. He spent half his life in his truck scouring all of Southern California.

His mother, meanwhile, holed up at home running one random scheme after another. Arbitraging imported Korean cordial glasses for twice the price, growing live cultures for a lab, selling cosmetics to climb, then slide down, the side of the great pyramid scheme. She spent half her life on the avocado-colored kitchen phone gossiping with friends on where the next vein of gold might be found.

He himself spent half his young life in his room, building and rebuilding moon bases out of blocks.

Later it turned out his father had been having an affair with a customer for months, and once that came out he hardly ever saw him again. All around him invisible walls of silence rose up and deadened the air in every room in the house. His mother turned to stone, his dad a stranger. As he got older, he vowed never to be like them. He would get a steady job—leave the hustling to others. He would find an awesome wife and proceed to be the best husband ever in the history of the world. Never argue or stonewall. Never ever cheat, hell no. And then he would become that most best father all abandoned children everywhere dreamed of. All day every damn day. Amen.

So yes: Missing-Dad Missing-Mom syndrome is something he and Clay share. Clay is, therefore, a modern-day version of his own boyhood self.

Take it a step further, he thinks. Getting wetter in the rain as the bucket overflows next to him. Clay is a vision of a future self, too. But not mine, Byron. By the way, how is it that I remember your name but not those of my own family? Or my parents'? What's that all about?

Oh, Byron. It'd be so much easier talking with you if you were actually here. If you won the same cosmic lottery as me, that is. Maybe you're in your own river channel shelter. Way nicer than mine, I bet. There's no way of finding out now. I could spend half my life scouring the land for you, totally unaware you now have your own little cult way out in Florida. I really should accept the fact that we are forever separated—that the planet has opened up millions of little holes to swallow people in—because that is easier than thinking you are dead.

Anyway.

Clay isn't just a vision of my past self. He's also a vision of my baby's future best friend. That's why Clay is so sad all the time. He knows he should be playing with my daughter. Adventuring and collecting. He's sad because he's the last of the kids.

Clay's mom is the future school parent friend my wife will have never have. Or wait: Clay's mom is a future grown-up version of my daughter struggling to survive with her son. That would make Clay my grandson. Or something. I'm getting mixed up with all these might-have-beens, Byron. But I've realized something about this temporal clutter. Quantum nodes branch off to infinite other nodes, see, but they're never supposed to touch. If they did, then the actors within each node would be able to see a whole nother world of might-have-beens. It doesn't matter if that world is better or worse than the world seeing them. No matter what, just seeing the other world will make all the actors sad.

That's what happened to me, man. My node touched not just one other node, but another, and another, and another. A full-on chain reaction collision disaster. Better or worse, it makes me sad because I know I can never cross into any of those other nodes. I'm only allowed to live in this one.

That's why we have *regret*.

FORTY-NINE

HE SHIVERS AND SNIFFLES. HE SHOULD'VE LIT A FIRE TO DRY HIS WET clothes, but he's been out to lunch, mentally speaking, for god knows how long. Just staring at that crate in the flotsam pile as it soaked all the way through to become worthless for anything, much less kindling. Slept in damp clothes all night, so now here he lies like the amateur survivalist flunky he is. Blowing his nose into his hands: yep, sick. Being loath to soil his only towel, he wipes his fingers right on the concrete floor.

The rain eases enough to become mist. It's pretty. The river channel is now a couple inches deep in some places, fed by the terminus pipes upstream. He tries picturing the old man's drowned and bled-white corpse flopping out with the rainwater, but his yearning for vengeance is no longer there. Vengeance means nothing in a randomly spinning world.

"Are you sick?" says Clay.

"I think so."

"Well, stay the hell away from me, then," Clay says flatly, as if reciting a joke assigned as homework. He could see that line coming from his mom, whatever she looks like.

Maybe I'm dead, he thinks. And this isn't purgatory. This is my afterlife.

Pretty shitty afterlife.

He retreats into the relative warmth of the shelter. Clay lies on the ground before him, studying the movement of the discs while humming a tuneless tune with simple contentment. He adds the words: MORE RAIN TODAY.

Clay puts the data sheet away, sits up, and seems almost sad that his measurement task is now complete.

He turns away from Clay, sneezes, sneezes again, and feels a tickle at the back of his throat.

"Great," he says.

"I can get you some medicine," says Clay.

"You have medicine?"

Clay shrugs. "We have everything." The kid shrugs like he does. He shrugs at dead crows. He shrugs at the end of the world.

They sit for a long spell, simply listening to the rain.

Then Clay slaps the ground with his hand. Weird, how he does it: first pointing his hand straight up at the ceiling, then slowly tipping it to fall. He watches closely the whole way down until it lands flat on the floor with a splat. Then he does it again, and again.

"What is that?"

"I have to show you something," Clay says. He darts from the shelter into the rain.

He watches Clay from the entrance with the blanket wrapped around his face to keep the cold air from coming in. Clay is already at the bottom of the channel looking up at him. He points to a spot in the center and calls through the lines of raindrops.

"This is where I found you."

His mind stops.

Clay is pointing at the spot in the sand where he woke up, an eternity ago.

"You fell here," says Clay. "Actually you let yourself fall. Not like a jump. Like this." He raises a hand, lowers it, and lets it land flat into the other.

Clay grows smaller and farther away and it's getting harder to hear his high little voice. He can't tell if it's because the rain is growing loud enough to shatter the triangle pooled atop the abandoned washing machine.

"You were drunk so I took that away from you and gave you headache pills. Mom takes a ton of those."

It had been night. Of course. The streetlamp, keeping its pointless vigil. The happy faces on the vinyl banner smiling at all the no one and nothing in Arroyo Plato Villas.

"Are you mad at me?"

No. He tries again, this time out loud. "No." En, oh.

Clay clambers back up to the shelter, panting and dripping wet.

"I took it because I thought you were dead," he says. "But then I could see you the next day. I thought you were a ghosty."

"Were you watching from the attic?"

"She doesn't know you can go up there." He is silent. Clay tries again: "I was scared to tell you because I thought you would get mad."

Whiskey, straight from the bottle in the night. He stepped onto the ledge and looked at the darkness below. *I bet this is high enough.*

"Are you sure you're not mad I took it?"

Falling backward into the empty volume. Just letting it happen.

"Took what?"

Clay climbs up the slope and ducks past him, heading to the back of the shelter. He moves the cardboard sheets aside to reveal a small rectangular hollow. From within he produces a little yogurt container. He hands it to him. It's heavy. It rattles.

He opens the plastic tub. There are keys. His car fob. The metal key flips out at the press of a button like a miniature switchblade. He opens it, closes it. Right: he liked to do that when he was thinking.

Beneath that is his wallet.

He remembers the blue toy figurine trapped in the cinder block. He'd have to fish that out and give it back.

To Clay.

"This is your shelter, isn't it," he says.

Clay nods. "In case things don't work out."

"In case things don't work out," he says.

"Mhm."

He holds the wallet in an upturned palm like it's about to flap its wings and fly away. Clay snatches it up, opens it, slides a card out.

"This is you!" says Clay.

He holds his breath at the sight of his own image.

"Adam Chung," he reads. "Morales Street. Delgado Beach. That's where I live."

There's the apartment now. Stucco and diamond-shaped iron-work. The landlord's half-finished Studebaker permanently parked in the driveway, never to be resuscitated.

"I'm thirty-seven, organ donor, one hundred eighty pounds."

His voice trails off. He can sense Clay beginning to fidget. He realizes he's probably scaring the poor kid.

"Give me the bag, please," he says. Meaning the plastic bag by the cardboard.

Clay fetches it promptly. The bag rustles. Clay holds up the mirror. You mean this? he asks with a look.

He nods. Clay hands it to him.

He stares at himself. Paler, not smiling like his ID self. Hair longer, beard that draws his jawline to a scraggly point. Eyes gone smoky and square with fatigue. Adam.

"Thank you." He hands back the mirror lest he smash it.

"Was it because of them?" Clay produces another card from his wallet.

It is a photo of his wife, Margot, holding his baby daughter, June.

PART IV

THE DREAM HOUSE

FIFTY

"IF SHE'S BLACK," SAYS CLAY, "WHAT'S THAT MAKE YOUR BABY?"

This question, thinks Adam with a sigh. I remember this question.

Adam hates this question, and his eyes flash black.

"I don't know, a human being?" says Adam. "What's that make *you*?"

He immediately regrets the snap. But Clay doesn't wince or frown or anything. The boy stands unmoved.

"People ask me all the time, too," says Clay. "I don't know what to call me."

And he shrugs.

Again, Adam twitches to think what kind of home this kid is living in. He supposes he'll find out soon enough.

Be delicate, she used to say. Margot. *We have to remember to be delicate with each other.*

The boy's eyes shift to the floor, just the slightest hint of tenderness to them. In the end, after all, he is just a boy.

"What else of mine do you have?" says Adam with a sigh.

"Nothing," he says. "That's all you had. I swear."

"You shouldn't go through someone's pockets," says Adam.

"I thought you were dead," whines Clay.

"Don't mind if I do, let's pat down this dead person right here."

Clay turns to the ground for solace.

"Come on, man," says Adam. Grumbling.

Take a breath, said Margot. Be delicate. Imagine for a second.

Imagine, he thinks. Okay. He takes three deep breaths. Imagine it's dark. A strange figure appears out of nowhere to stand on a bridge. Imagine the boy's eyes growing large as this visitor disappears backward into the channel. Then thinking about it all night as he tried to sleep, and rushing out to investigate first thing the next day. The weather already growing warm as the boy stands over the body of a man who fell twenty feet and just stayed there all night in the same spot.

"I collect things," murmurs Clay. "Don't be mad." He says it with defeat.

"Hey," says Adam. "Next time do this." He holds two fingers to his neck to illustrate how to check for a pulse. "Or, you know, just ask. Are you alive, sir? Don't just start digging for treasure."

"I'm sorry," says Clay.

He'd looked dead. Jesus. Clay, creeped out big-time, probably didn't take the time to check if he was breathing. He wouldn't, if it'd been him. Adam pictured him snatching the wallet out of his pocket— quick as a fencing lunge—and dashing away.

Then, hours later, seeing the spot in the sand empty. A ghosty!

Adam exhales. He takes a fourth deep breath, exhales again through his nose. This feels familiar, he realizes. This intolerance for mistakes big and small. This temper. He always meant to be better about it.

Adam reaches an arm around the boy, who has gone totally emotionless, and tries jiggling him back to life. He forces a smile.

"I'm not mad," says Adam.

He jiggles and jiggles.

"You're my Man Friday," says Adam.

Clay looks up. "What's a manfriday?"

"It's okay you were scared. In fact, you know what? Thank you. You let me use your awesome shelter."

He sees Clay's eyes flicker with warmth.

"I would probably try to kill myself, too," Clay says.

———————

CLAY HAS OPENED A CAN AND NOW LIGHTS THE STOVE, CAREFULLY placing the spent match alongside the others. He places the can onto the flame. The flame is too large, and Adam shows Clay how to adjust it with the knob.

Margot. They were in a garden somewhere. Not a garden. There was a goat. Some kind of petting zoo. She wore a too-large sweater with black fringe at the sleeves to match the black of her loose curls evenly framing eyebrows that gave her a serious demeanor, even when laughing, and frequently made her the target of earnest conversation by strangers. She wore a simple button shirt, simple jeans. He stood admiring the way her pant legs tapered to her boots, an homage to her grunge days.

Mom jeans, he said.

She looked back at him. You take that back! she said.

Milf jeans, he said.

She pursed a smile, as if tasting sudden sweet, and acquiesced. Dilf shorts, she said.

Bracelets of hammered silver graced her thin wrists, which she held crossed to support baby June, all in a ball of pink. They had sworn against pink, and yet. The three of them sat on a big brown log with hay and an axe and a wooden goat in the background.

I have to say you folks are quite the ecumenical family, said the photographer.

Adam knew very well what that word meant even if he didn't exactly know what it meant, and he knew Margot did and didn't, too, and together they cringed at the camera with that shared resignation they'd cultivated for years.

Anyway it had been one of his favorite days, cringe and all. Life was like that.

"It was a car crash," says Adam finally. "I guess you could call it an accident. No. It was no accident."

Clay watches him talk.

"They were both in the car, the car got rear-ended. Some asshole prick going fast. It was a high-speed police chase."

Clay casts his eyes downward as he listens, as if in church. Not supposed to swear in church. Adam steadies himself.

"We had this big fight that day," says Adam.

She'd slammed the front door, leaving him alone in a world gone suddenly and absolutely still.

"She pulled over on this high flyover ramp. So high. She pulled over to the right for the sirens, because that's what you're *supposed to do*." He shakes his head. "Then this guy going ninety just sends the car up the side thing. The barrier. And it went like—"

Adam raises his hand, then slowly lets it fall to his thigh. Landing gently there. Just moments ago, Clay had done something similar.

Adam can only stare at his own hand lying motionless.

"Did they die instantly?" Clay whispers.

He nods.

"Could your baby talk yet?"

The tears come at that.

You know, said the crow, the crash was just the start.

Clay reaches in his pack for a paper towel and hands it to him. Adam sneezes and blows his nose and sneezes again and busily adjusts his blanket.

"Doesn't matter," says Adam. "Not anymore."

"I'm sorry your wife and baby died."

"World went to S-H-I-T anyway," says Adam. "They would've died like everyone else. Doesn't matter."

Adam begins rifling through his wallet. "Credit cards, rewards points." He laughs. "Gone." Cards spill onto the floor. "Your friends. Your dad. Gone, gone."

Clay begins to fiercely pick at a thread on his knee.

"Hey," says Adam, softening. "I take it back. They probably made it to an army base or something. Your dad's coming back." He sneezes again. He presses the paper towel to his nose and tries giving Clay his best hopeful look.

Adam remembers the blue toy figurine. He reaches into the cinder block and offers it. Clay cradles it in his small hands and examines every detail.

"You think we'll go to an army base?" says Clay.

"Sure."

"You too, right?"

Adam struggles to imagine this. "Not so sure about that."

"But you'll die here without supplies."

"You guys are braver than me. You and your mom."

Clay screws up his face like everything he's saying makes no sense, and the sincerity of his utter confusion breaks his heart a little.

"I think this is how I'm supposed to end," he tells Clay. "I think I'm okay with that."

"Okay," sings Clay, disappointed. Poor kid is probably used to disappointment.

Adam scrambles to cheer him up. He fits Clay's tiny shoulder into his palm. "For now this is our safe house, okay? We can map the channel. Figure out what makes it tick. Maybe even make some wind forecasts."

Clay seems to like this, and smiles. But the smile doesn't last.

"We're leaving in two days," Clay says. He rubs his action figure with a thumb.

Clay finally places the toy in his pack with great care, the way one would conceal a stolen item, quietly drawing the zipper shut one tooth at a time.

"Gotta go, bye," he says, his usual catchphrase now barely audible.

Then Clay hugs him. It is a real hug from a real boy.

He runs off splashing across the swelling riverbed into the rain.

FIFTY-ONE

THE POLICEMEN HAD LEFT THE APARTMENT, ALL RADIOS AND SHOES
and squeaking leather utility belts, and his phone rang. He lifted it to
his ear without saying anything.

You're there, said Byron. Do not move. I'm coming over.

The cops were just here.

Shit. Do not touch anything. No TV or radio or anything, no internet, definitely no internet.

Byron ended the call, leaving him standing there listening to
nothing. The sound of rain was everywhere now. It was even inside
the apartment. How did it do that?

The police officer helplessly raising her hands, out of words.

Adam glanced at his laptop. It felt like it was a mile away.

Definitely no internet, Byron had said.

But there before him was a remote control right within arm's
reach, so Adam did what you did with a remote and turned on the
television.

There appeared a talking cheeseburger and a sassy White woman
shaking her head, and then there was a blaring fanfare and a swoop-
ing news graphic and an aerial shot of an orange muscle car being
chased by police on a crowded wet freeway.

The car was approaching a flyover jammed solid with traffic. Two or three of the cars had pulled over to the right. He frowned at one of them. The white one. The turn signal blinking, a pinpoint beacon in a storm.

A voice spoke: *A high-speed chase across three cities ends in a spectacular tragedy, tonight at ten.* The video held for a moment, accompanied by a frenetic ostinato—crazed marimbas canting around booming kettledrums—before dissolving to soundless black.

Adam stood dumbfounded. Like he'd just glimpsed another world reflected in a windowpane as it swung shut.

The television now showed three contented older men traveling in a classic convertible down a pine forest road on their way to a fly fishing expedition. *Guys like you don't let a weak prostate slow you down.*

I used to get up to urinate four times a night, said one of the men.

––––––––––

ADAM JOLTS AWAKE. HE IS SWEATING.

Outside, rain continues to fall. What time is it? Just a second ago he'd been shivering. He sneezes and vulgar nasty mucus juices out from his nose. He gets up, wipes it on the slope outside, groans a big loud *fuck me* and in the next instant checks to see if any kids heard him swear, an old habit. Clay isn't there. He retreats again, adjusting the thin blanket curtain against the harsh outside air. Thing barely does shit.

Once, in a billowy hotel bed, Adam had been sick like this. A tiny bunker of a room with strange light switches and a bidet in the bathroom. Europe? He was with a woman. The woman was his wife. Her name was Margot. Margot sat at a little desk writing postcards. Margot drank wine. Margot sat in nothing but her underwear with one leg hiked up to let her chin rest upon her knee. It was a pose perfected over many nights of study at college.

She wrinkled her nose at him and smiled. Big sick baby, she said.

If I die, he said, I bequeath unto you all my stuff.

She laughed, took a sip. I might wander a little bit around the canals by myself, if that's okay.

Be careful, he said. She felt different here. She never walked outside at night alone. But this was Amsterdam and not Los Angeles, so maybe it'd be okay.

Be careful, she mimicked back. She reached for her glass but instead toppled it, spilling red.

ADAM HAS TO URINATE BUT HELL NO, NOT OUT IN THAT FREEZING COLD. He winces at the ceiling. He imagines Clay setting up this shelter. Sneaking things out over the course of a month. It is a good setup.

Another coughing fit. Christ. He can't sleep, can't stay awake. He imagines he's living under a highway overpass, low booms of cars pummeling away at a tiny fault in the concrete above. It isn't cars. It's his blood thudding in time.

He reaches for one of Clay's sand pattern drawings, finds the ballpoint pen, and adds in a crime-scene dead body outline. He laughs. There's me!

Cars above going boom-boom, boom-boom with their tires. Oh, how they used to drive every morning to work, and then back in the evening. Rivers of cars flowing everywhere. All dead and rusted shut now, full of dried-out commuter corpses waiting for someone to come burn them up already with a propane tank explosion. They died just as they lived! he says, laughing again. Stuck in traffic!

You are bad, says Margot.

Come kiss me.

She does, and his eyes flutter open.

It's safe here. Concrete three feet thick. Needs a goddamn front door, but otherwise Clay had managed a lot with a little.

"You managed a lot with a little," he tells Clay. The boy stands before him.

When did Clay get here?

"You need to get inside," says Clay. He's probably been staring at him for a while, judging from the deep concern on his face.

"I'm just going to scare the shit out of your mom. S-H-I-T, sorry."

"I mean my backup safe house."

Clay tugs at his arm to help him up and together they step out into the awesome gray downpour. The sand pattern is flooded over into a quivering pool that merges with all the other pools everywhere. Adam and Clay splash across to the other side of the channel through ankle-deep water. A corner of his blanket drags behind him and quickly grows heavy with wet.

"Leave it," says Clay, urging Adam on.

He does. The blanket sinks until it becomes flat with the surface.

Clay leads him up the bank and down the shoulder a ways until they reach the plywood barrier of ENTRANCE 1 (SEALED), and he pulls back on an edge of the wooden sheet until it allows an opening about eight inches across. Clay squeezes through and beckons from the other side, his wet hair plastered to his forehead.

"Come on," says Clay. "Adam!"

The sound of his own name startles him out of his feverish haze. He looks back at the channel. Rain everywhere. The dry, sunbaked riverbed from a few days earlier seems like a fiction. Now it's filling with water that flows with such elemental ease, as if to simply proclaim: I am a river, I was always a river, I will always be a river. Give me time and I'll climb the banks after you. I'll flood the houses if I want. I'll give passage to an old White man and his large wooden ark filled with animals if I want.

Adam laughs. "Bye, river," he says to the river. He squeezes through. Clay pulls the plywood shut behind them. The rain increases its chorus.

"This way," says Clay.

They duck through one skeletal house after another until they reach a small pyramid of cinder blocks, which they use to scale a low wall. Clay goes first, then Adam. He wants to collapse with each step.

He lies on top of the wall and just rolls himself over. If there's a pit of snakes on the other side, he'll just have to be okay with falling into a pit of snakes.

He falls instead onto perfect grass. Grass so dark as to be almost blue. He looks up.

A backyard?

My God. The lawn stretches unblemished forever before him. Polyhedric ivory vases of all sizes line the wall, each containing brilliant desert succulents. Patio furniture the color of beautiful pale beechwood sits flanked by steel torchrods thrust into clear vases of blue cubes before a crystal fire table, its flames unperturbed by the pelting droplets. A bowl of plastic mangoes brimming with water sits shivering nearby. Margarita glasses packed with fake ice. A colossal barbecue shining like a centurion.

Weatherproof speakers hang in the eaves and play low music barely audible in the thundering rain. *Tall and tan and young and lovely, the girl from Ipanema goes walking.*

Something whines to life in the corner and nearly scares Adam out of his beloved shoes with its sudden approach. A boxy green beetle moving on plastic yellow wheels. It begins mowing slow zigzags across the wet grass.

"Hi, Mo," says Clay. He strides across the concrete patio, slides open a glass door, and waits for Adam to come.

Adam stands transfixed. The rain soaks him through.

"Everything's on a master timer," says Clay. "Come in."

Adam enters. Clay slides the glass door shut and seals out the world behind him.

FIFTY-TWO

"WE CAN'T TURN ON THE LIGHTS," SAYS CLAY. "MOM MIGHT SEE 'EM. No one's allowed here."

Adam stands shivering. Or sweating, or both. There's a creamy leather couch sprawling across the giant room like a soft rectangular slab. An antique Balinese coffee table. Some books wrapped in a kind of silver parchment. Ceramic tubers painted crimson sit on a maze shelf shining with an opalescent veneer. A cascade of quartz pendants float above it all.

"You're dripping," says Clay. He fusses about. He takes his shoes off, pads away, and returns with a bathrobe.

"Put this on and come this way." He pads away again, down a hall.

Adam looks at his shoes. He stands in a pool of water on a glossy bamboo floor. My poor favorite shoes, he thinks. Adam Chung's favorite shoes.

He slowly undresses, leaving his clothes in a wet heap, and puts on the bathrobe. It's musty but dry and warm. He fishes the dripping brass key from his shoe, wipes it dry. Slips it into the pocket of the bathrobe, lest Clay find it and add it to whatever collection he is amassing.

He creeps down the hall. There's a black Chinese console table with a jade envelope dagger and pamphlets neatly fanned out: AR-ROYO PLATO VILLA ESTATES. He sees wall outlets and light switches and a climate control panel glowing green.

"Electricity?" he says.

The hallway floor teeters sideways and he braces himself against a wall for a moment.

A sputtering sound startles him. A shower.

Clay scoots in on fast little feet. "You should take a hot shower and get into bed," he barks, then vanishes again.

Adam shuffles onward, eventually discovering a marble bathroom. Potpourri sits in a long pewter canoe.

He drops his robe, shivering, and enters a glass cube filled with steam. The warm water softens his joints and melts his bones. He tips his head back and lets his mouth overflow. He imagines oil and soot and sand being loosened from his body, from his hair, ears, anus, fingernails, all of it being carried away down the chrome hexagon drain and along immortal plastic composite piping that will never rust or crack or leak. Simply carried to god knows where, perhaps in pipes embedded deep in the concrete banks of the river channel. Some defunct sewage processing center, some ruined beach. Away.

The power here is solar. Has to be. But where does the water come from?

He steps out of the shower stall, pink and renewed. He wraps himself back in the bathrobe, checks the key in the pocket with a touch, and peers down the hall.

"Bedtime for bedbugs," calls Clay from somewhere.

His eyes flicker. Bedtime indeed. He steps out of his robe and creeps into bed, briefly exposing his tender warm skin to the air. With effort he draws the covers up over his shivering body. He waits for the sheets to warm up.

Clay appears with a white cup filled with orange. "Drink this."

A glass touches his lips and the tang of citrus explodes across his tongue. Orange juice! How the hell did they find orange juice?

"You must have a freezer," Adam mumbles.

"Why do you keep saying the world is over?" says Clay.

He puts something else to Adam's mouth now: a small cup of syrup thick with alcohol and menthol and a puckering artificial grape taste. He gulps it down.

"What did you just give me?" says Adam.

"Is it over-over?"

"Maybe not entirely over-over," he mumbles. "But I don't know how much there's worth living for."

"You really think there's nothing out there?"

Something about the boy's voice forces him to open his eyes a slit. Clay is crying.

"Don't worry about what I said earlier," says Adam. "You're gonna see your dad again. There's gotta be people rebuilding somewhere. Everything's gonna be okay." He grazes Clay's face with weary fingers. "We always make the best of it."

Adam is drifting off now, sinking deep into the bed.

"Mom always says so," says Clay. "Even with the global financial meltdown and stuff."

"Probably riots then," he whispers. "Riots and unrest."

"What's unrest?"

Adam falls asleep.

FIFTY-THREE

THEN ADAM DIES.

No sound, no sensation but a soft warmth enveloping him. He reaches out an arm and feels nothing but endless, creamy bedsheets. This has to be that light at the end of the tunnel they always talked about: the glow of these perfect sheets. And the cozy white noise of rain falling just outside the window. He can feel her next to him.

"Sweetie," he says.

"You rest," says Margot. "I'll check on June."

"I'll do it."

"You rest." She slides away beneath an infinite billowing wave.

"Wait."

Adam sits up. He is in a bedroom, sparsely decorated with a cream dresser and ceramic pineapples bracketing a line of blanked-out books. He sees himself in an oval mirror antiqued with tarnish around the edges. He stares back at his reflection and his reflection stares back with astonishment to find a man just like him in this voluminous bed.

He slips out of the bed and examines the books. They contain pages cut out of old newspapers, all in Chinese, merely decorative.

There's a large orb made of cork in the corner, and on top of the orb sit his clothes, dry and stacked and folded. Atop the clothes sits his stupid, consolation-prize straight razor. He pads across the dense carpet and crushes the clothes to his face, inhaling the scent of laundry. Baby powder, that's the name of the scent. No one uses baby powder anymore. They hadn't with June.

He could really see June crawling around on carpet like this.

He takes another long shower. Good and long and probably too hot, but whatever. There is water and power here!

The shower has a mirror that somehow doesn't fog up, and he uses it to shave. Oily clumps of stubble dribble off his face. Later, in the bright full-length mirror of this splendid bathroom, he can see that his cheeks have hollowed out slightly. He's lost weight, at least since the last time he was able to examine his entire body at once, in the great Before. He was a little overweight back then. What he would give to be a little overweight again.

He dresses and heads down the hall.

"Clay?"

He enters the living room again, with its whale of a white couch and billion-foot-high ceiling. *Cathedral* ceiling. Pretty friggin' sweet.

On the adjoining kitchen bar sits a bowl of cereal and a mini jug of milk and a banana. He examines the items from all angles. They are real. He smells the milk—smells fine, fine enough for dehydrated or evaporated or whatever—and pours it in. He takes a tentative first spoonful, and then sucks the whole bowl down. Then he bites open the banana and consumes it in three quick bites. It's brown from having been frozen and thawed but is still creamy and sweet.

Thank you, Clay.

Adam gazes out through the sliding glass doors. The rain continues outside. The crystal fire table is dormant now, and the robotic mower rests in its docking station at the edge of the patio. Everything's on a master timer, he thinks. He finds a napkin and blows his nose. His fever has broken.

On the coffee table are magazines about design and photography and architecture. Indicators of most excellent taste and education.

Aspirational. Remember that word? The kitchen with its pasta maker and micro-zester and aluminum nest of plastic quince and espresso machine.

Espresso. Jesus.

He opens and closes cabinets, unable to slam them shut due to their built-in anti-slam mechanisms, searching among plates and cups and boxed food and cans of soup. Clay must've stocked this kitchen slowly over a period of weeks. He smiles, shakes his head: *This Clay kid!*

Eventually he finds a white demitasse. He places the cup on the machine's perforated steel tray and pushes a glowing button. There's a whirr, a rattle of beans, and then a chugging stream of coffee that fills the air with a redolent roasted warmth. He can barely wait for the drip to complete before taking a trembling first sip. Beautifully bitter.

Shelter, what shelter? he thinks. I'm spending my last days here. Cheers.

Sipping his coffee in his bathrobe, he explores the model home.

There's the console table and its pamphlets with doomed smiling future residents on their covers. He turns them over to hide the faces from view. On the back of each pamphlet is a business card bearing a blank for a name followed by YOUR SALES REPRESENTATIVE.

Generic business cards mean rapid sales staff turnover. Must've been a tough sell out here.

Adam examines the living room. The television's glossy monolith looms on a slate hearth.

Spectacular tragedy, tonight at ten.

He averts his eyes. This is the sort of thing he's been dreading about entering these houses. The sea of objects laden with memory, waiting to discharge their current at the slightest touch.

He takes some flat white stones from a gold basket and stacks them into a small tower and turns away. The cairn will remind him not to look in the direction of the screen. He decides he should cover the television with a sheet later. That and most of the other things in the house. Make everything blank, like the shelter.

He goes down the hall and is unnerved to discover a child's room. Foam floor tiles with goddamn ABCs and 123s in primary colors. There's a bunk bed, blue spaceship sheets on the bottom, pink horses on the top. There's a rocking horse and a play oven and a building set, all of it unused and shining. There is a book titled *Baby's First Colors*.

June never got to learning colors. He tries to imagine her as a toddler, then a young girl, and then even further, as a teenager and beyond.

Margot would hate this room all the way to hell, and she'd be right. Adam closes the door. He'd fill it with concrete and seal it off with a big red X if he could.

At the far end of the hall is the SALES OFFICE, labeled as such with a plastic business placard incongruent with the rest of the house. Another bowl, more fake fruit. A glass desk balanced on sweeping aluminum spindles holds a mesh cup of orange pencils and more blank business cards. There is a small television mounted on an articulating arm.

Not a television. A computer monitor.

His mind swims. So many hours, he remembers, hours and hours and hours spent in front of glowing computer monitors typing and watching videos and scrolling and talking in that weird way we used to, full of acronyms and tags and ats, all stuff that barely made sense then and certainly doesn't matter at all now.

Now it's just you and whoever's left to hear your voice.

A tiny white dot pulses on the corner of the monitor's bezel.

Adam wants to smash it.

He backs out into the hallway until he hits the opposite wall. The wall moves slightly upon contact.

It's not a wall. It is a door, locked somehow from the other side. Not quite locked, however: the knob turns. He can see a towel jammed underneath. He pushes harder. Some obstruction or something at the bottom.

He kneels, and with queasy relief notices the doorknob has no keyhole. This door is not the answer to his particular mystery. Probably a closet locked from within long ago by an accidental avalanche of supplies.

A sound interrupts his thoughts: the glass door sliding open, a brief hiss of rain, then the door sliding shut again.

Clay appears at the far end of the hall, a black ghost against the bright gray world outside. Adam can't make out his face.

"That door's been locked forever," says Clay.

FIFTY-FOUR

CLAY OPENS HIS PACK. IT'S STUFFED WITH ELECTRONICS.

"Wanna play a game on the big teevee?" says Clay.

Adam is drinking orange juice straight from the bottle. It makes him feel like a king. He sets it down.

Clay hands him a plastic snap-case with a bloody, muscled man wielding a shotgun on its cover. The shotgun has a chain saw for a barrel, and the man wears a baby mask with Xs for eyes. He stands before a smoking city in ruin, everything spattered with red. The game is called *The Last Drop of Blood*.

"Um, maybe later," says Adam, unsettled. "How about a get-to-know-you quiz?"

Clay puts the game away, not the least bit fazed. "Okay."

Intel time. Here we go.

"You tell me something, I tell you something, like ping-pong."

"Ping-pong, rally on."

He smiles at Clay, but Clay doesn't smile back. He looks a little lost.

"You leave tomorrow, right?" says Adam.

Clay looks down at his pack and zips it closed, tooth by tooth.

"Are you scared?" says Adam.

Clay pauses before giving the fakest answer ever: "No."

"You're gonna be fine," says Adam. "No matter what you find out there."

Clay closes the final tooth but holds on to the zipper.

"You're gonna be okay," says Adam.

"Can we play now?" says Clay.

Of course. Leave it to grown-ups to beat a horse dead flat into the ground.

"Sure thing!" hollers Adam. He gives Clay the biggest smile he can. "Get ready!"

And to Adam's unreasonable delight, Clay brightens a little. He hadn't realized how badly he wanted to cheer him up. Kids were hell when they got sad. He used to work his ass off to win smiles from his class on stagnant Monday mornings. For those forty-five minutes, he would do whatever it took.

"What time do you get out of bed in the morning?" says Adam.

"Seven a.m.," says Clay quickly. "My turn. Where do you live?"

Adam thinks for a moment. "Here, I guess."

Clay doesn't find this answer satisfying at all. "I mean before."

"You know I can't remember any of that," says Adam, although by now he does. He just can't bear to say the name of his old neighborhood out loud.

Clay senses the lie and furrows his miniature brow.

Adam moves on, quickly. "After you get up at seven a.m., do you A, draw, B, write, or C, play video games?"

Clay barely lets him finish the question. "Video games."

Clay waits and says nothing.

"Your turn, buddy," says Adam.

"Mom gets up an hour after that and I make her coffee and toaster tarts or something. Then she locks herself in the office to do her work. Then I go play in the backyard or go to my room to stay out of her hair."

"She works on her plan."

"Mhm."

Again Clay waits. He doesn't seem interested in taking his turn. He seems more in the mood to give out answers.

Window of opportunity, said Byron.

"What's one thing you've never told anyone?" says Adam.

This, Adam knows, is a wildly inappropriate question for an adult to be asking a child. But Clay is leaving tomorrow, and he has to know everything there is to know about this place that will become his last home.

Clay thinks. "I don't really play in the backyard," he murmurs, low. "I collect things. I have a pretty big collection. No one knows about that."

Clay collects what, besides rocks? Weapons? Food? Some totally unexpected resource, something that was once overlooked but is now worth killing over?

"Oh, I'd love to see it, buddy," says Adam.

"Okay," says Clay. But he doesn't move. He just goes on reciting his day. "Mom makes lunch in the afternoon, then we eat, then she goes back in her room, then I'm supposed to play. Then it's my homework."

He doesn't understand this. "Homework?"

"I use her old laptop. It's *so slow.*"

He stares at him. "Are you talking about a school?"

Clay nods. "It's never too early to start building your future."

But there isn't supposed to *be* a future. He's missing something. A network of survivors, communicating via—what? Some kind of analog peer-to-peer radio-based internet reminiscent of the old bulletin board days? He said his mom's laptop was so slow. Questions crowd in like bees.

Start with the first question, said Byron, and then work through them one by one. Take your time.

"So this school—" says Adam.

"I have a job," Clay says, as if reciting a monologue. "Everyone does. You have to stay responsible even when everything's gone to shit."

"Hey."

"In fact, it's even more important when everything's gone to shit."

"S-H-I-T, buddy."

"Mom says that all the time. Shit, shit, shit." Clay frowns at a bottle cap on the counter.

"I feel your pain," tries Adam. Secretly he's at a loss for words. The kid is clamming up. He wants to revive the ping-pong rally-on, but what can he say? *Everything's gonna be okay*, over and over again? Nothing is okay, and will never be for decades to come, if ever. All Adam can think of is to offer up some of his orange juice. Which is Clay's to begin with, but whatever.

Clay politely refuses. "Can I have your bottle cap?"

Dead, thinks Adam. The line of questioning is dead for now. He reminds himself to stay patient. He has the rest of today, then that's it.

He hands the cap to Clay.

Clay accepts it and immediately zips over to the kitchen. He opens the cabinet beneath the sink and kneels down out of sight.

Adam follows. Peers.

In the cabinet are little clear plastic tubs, each filled with a particular kind of object. One has rocks. another has dirt. Clay opens one filled with bottle caps.

"This one is Brad Shaw, this one is Brad's mom and dad. This one is Paige Saito. That's everyone who used to live here. I got caps from everyone before they finished moving out. They all had drinks because it was so hot."

He rinses Adam's cap clean, dries it, and puts it in the tub.

"Is that one me?" says Adam.

"It's me," says Clay. "I'm the one leaving, right, dummy? So now you watch the tub."

Clay hands it to Adam. Adam puts it into the tub. It is his job now.

Clay watches him carefully, with barely a trace of emotion as always. But Adam can see him snarl just for an instant with frustration, as he struggles with some storm inside his head.

Finally Clay just spits it out: "I think you should come with us."

"Oh, buddy," says Adam. "I'm gonna stay here."

"Don't you have friends?"

"I have to stay here."

"Where's your house?"

"I'd be no good out there," says Adam. "I suck at all that."

Clay stomps a foot. "You came from somewhere! Where?"

"Clay, you have your father to find. I don't have that. I have no place to go out there. It's not just me. Listen. It's thousands of people. Probably millions. I don't know how much your mom is telling you. Do you understand what I'm telling you?"

Adam holds the rattling tub with both hands. "You need to go where your mom thinks you need to go. I can't have anything to do with that. I have to stay here." He looks around at the fine house and all its fine details. "It's not a bad way to go."

He softens his face as best he can, but Clay is not comforted. He's irritated, in fact.

"No offense, but I wish you could please not say spooky stuff like that," says Clay, squinting.

"Like what?"

"Like the world is over. I thought you were doing pretend."

They stare at each other. There is some form of inevitability hurtling at Adam right now. The world can't simply be how it seems. It never is, after all. There is always another world right beneath.

Clay's eyes widen, as if to say *He doesn't know!* And he smiles with that giddy eagerness kids get when, say, performing a magic trick for a real audience for the very first time.

Clay grows brighter and brighter. He beams with anticipation at the secret he is about to unveil. He runs flailing to the living room, where he finds a slim black wand and draws an invisible lasso above his head with it. He strikes a flamenco pose, cocks a thumb.

The screen comes to life.

Two women in aprons slice apples. Clay changes poses, and the television changes to a man in a forest.

"Of these majestic trees are over a century old, and the local," and the image switches again.

A crowd of women scream as confetti drifts down onto their heads and a gleaming car rotates slowly on a stage, and another woman yells, "In time for the holidays you could be driving home in style with!" The image changes too quickly to make any sense.

"Everyone's still here," says Clay. Flip, flip, flip. "Everything's okay. See?"

"Terror with," Jet-Ski, couple kissing, football, "down and two," "tended warranty that," loud guitar, "APR financing with just," "In the Middle Eastern regi," girls singing, cartoon frog, "esus Christ soar," golf applause, "Eight zero one one zero five."

"Turn it off," says Adam.

"Ing up next on afternoon drama," motorcycles, bloody men boxing, a floating baby, a newscaster, two newscasters, a car on fire in the gorgeous afternoon sunlight.

"Turn it off!" yells Adam.

Clay looks like he's just gotten slapped. His joy melts away at once. His face returns to stone.

Clay turns the television off. The room sits in ringing silence. He places the skinny remote on the console table, next to the cairn Adam had made earlier.

"The model house has full cable," says Clay, and leaves.

PART V

THE SECRET PLACE

FIFTY-FIVE

PEOPLE STAYED TO CLEAN UP AFTER THE WAKE AT THE APARTMENT.
There'd been speeches and meaningful pop songs played to bowed
heads. Adam couldn't remember what songs or which mourners,
didn't want to. His parents weren't there because—right—they were
both dead. Margot's surviving father was too sick to attend, holed up
in a West Texas hospital fighting off some new virus known as H1N1,
which the nurse called *hiney*.

"I know she'd be so glad you all could make it," he announced,
and crumpled to the floor. Dozens of hands reached out to catch him.
The first, of course, was Byron. They all helped him to the biggest chair
he owned. Byron—who'd quickly taken on the role of host for the
wake—made sure everyone was topped off and snacked up. He worked
the line as people waited. Why were people waiting? They each took
turns approaching Adam in his big ugly chair and paid him more care
and attention than he'd ever received in his whole life.

That's why they called it a *receiving* line.

A receiving line also meant people were making their leave. Made
sense. He couldn't expect them to stay all night and through to the
next morning and the day after that and the day after that day.

But isn't that what Byron did?

In the silence after the last guest departed—record player playing for no one now—Byron clapped his hands and simply screamed as loud as he could.

You try it, he said.

Eh, said Adam.

Come on. I have to admit I don't really get *how in the world* you're not crying right now but you gotta get it out somehow.

I don't really cry, said Adam.

That's impossible. Do it.

Adam slouched deeper, shaded his eyes with a hand. Aaah.

Byron squatted in close. Come on, man, *raaaah!*

Adam sprang back: *Aaaah!*

That's good, said Byron. He handed him a pillow. Try it in this.

Byron had chosen a pillow at random. He couldn't have known about its significance, how it was one of those dumb compromises you make when you're newly married and learning how to outfit a house together, how outfitting a house carried the weight of permanence, so you better work it out carefully. Or how Margot loved plain white everything to an almost obsessive degree, how he wanted at least a little color, I mean we're not building an ice hotel here, so taupe it was, how about this taupe, okay?

Maybe this was how married people got boring so suddenly, with one nano-compromise after another until they lived in a thoroughly half-assed world. But if being married meant being boring, then being boring meant absolutely everything to him.

Taupe, the acme of mundanity, fuggit.

Single, wild-haired, wild-eyed Byron couldn't have known how or why something like taupe could cause the dam to crack, and Adam should've known a single pillow wouldn't be enough to contain the torrent no matter how hard he buried his face. But it turned out Byron chose right.

Let it out, man, said Byron. Good.

They stayed up watching a sport neither of them cared about. Adam had no appetite, so Byron had none, either. Adam did not want to get fucked up, so Byron packed away the bourbon and did not get fucked up, either. When Adam woke up the next morning in his bed, he knew it was Byron who'd carried him there.

He walked out of the forever damned bedroom—relieved to be away from its scents—and found Byron sitting before a plate of eggs and bacon and Irish coffee, heavy on the Irish. It looked inviting and nauseating at the same time.

Hey, said Byron. He waved a plate at him.

Hey, said Adam. He waved a hand in response: *No thanks.*

He knew Byron had the good sense not to ask him how he was doing. Nothing as ludicrous as that. Instead, Byron became Papa Byron.

You have to at least eat lunch, he said. You have until then.

It was so sweet and kind that Adam could only gently laugh. Okay, Dad.

I'm not gonna worry about you until then, warned Byron.

Okay.

He watched Byron eat. The man ate like a princess in camouflage.

What, said Byron.

Nothing, said Adam.

Byron aligned his fork and sipped his warm alcohol using both hands. You eat like a hyena in heat, Chung. Half your food winds up down your shirt.

They laughed. It felt so weird to laugh. Adam couldn't do it.

We had a big fight that day, he said.

Byron sucked a stuck crumb, swallowed it. I know, man.

We had a big fight and now I know—*now* I know—the purpose of the helicopters up there was to get me to wake up. Be *better.* Stop being an *asshole.* But I just got pissed off at them. I'm so stupid.

Byron exploded from his chair and gave him a hard squeeze for a long moment. You're not stupid, he said. You're not stupid. The world is stupid. You are not stupid. The world is stupid. You are very much not. You are not stupid.

Finally Byron faced him and said, Okay?

They took them away, said Adam, crying freely for the first time in his adult life. Why did they take them away from me?

Because they're stupid, said Byron. That's all. It's not fair, and they're all just stupid. They don't deserve a guy like you. No way.

On the counter, tea candles flickered around the framed photo of Margot and June in black and white. Byron must've replaced the candles with fresh ones. Adam was grateful. He could never do something like that.

The world does not deserve a person like you, never forget that, said Byron.

———————

FRIENDS WOULD COME TO VISIT IN THE DAYS FOLLOWING, ALWAYS AN-nounced by Byron in his butler-school-dropout style. They brought Adam food and flowers and drink to where he sat, out on his tiny balcony facing the junk lot. But after a while—a shockingly short while for Adam, who knew he was being unfair and unreasonable toward his well-wishers—the visits trickled down to nothing. It was just him and Byron.

Byron, as usual, said the unsayable thing Adam was already thinking.

Fuckin' friends in need, man.

Hey, said Adam.

Let 'em go, said Byron. I'm still here.

People have lives. They have schedules and stuff. It's okay. The world shambles on.

Well, I'll be here as long as you need me.

Okay.

Dude, said Byron. I don't mean any disrespect but it's kind of a little early, don't you think?

Adam stopped in midpour, capped the bottle. It's just this one for now.

Well, I'll have one if you're having one.

I know you're looking out for me, said Adam. I really appreciate that.

I mean it when I say as long as you need me, said Byron.

But even Byron had things to do, because Byron was human like everyone else. As his visits slowed down to once a week, Adam never said a thing. It was natural and to be expected. There was no single moment where you knew it was time to stop coming over. Things just ebbed, and ebbed, and ebbed.

In the shower, when he remembered to shower, Adam would draw an *M* in the glass, next to a *J*. The fog would come and he'd freshen up the letters again.

He'd stopped going to work. Two subs for the kiddos, Byron said over the phone. Whole school was down in the dumps. A few kids making inappropriate jokes but we understand it's coming from a place of grief. The suits were being cool, they said take as much time as you need.

Calls would end, and Adam would stare at the phone. He had messages waiting and feeds unread, little numbers racking up everywhere like debt.

He lived out on that grimy little balcony, playing a mindless gemstone puzzle game over and over again until he was too drunk to focus on the screen. He napped, got up to urinate, flushed the toilet down. Stretched a little. He microwaved food that arrived on his doorstep, sent by somebody. He got a disbursement from the life insurance company with surprising alacrity. They really saved their customer service chops for times like these.

Times like these.

And now, in one of the world's great ironies, he suddenly found himself with time and money, more than enough to hire movers and decorate a brand-new house inside and out if he wanted.

———

HE STARTED IN THE DIM PREDAWN HOURS OF EARLY MORNING, SETTING items out on his lawn in rough categories. Electronics. Appliances. Small furniture. To hell with it, large furniture, too. Cookware. Stupid unused golf clubs, stupid stationary bike.

Then the tough stuff. Baby furniture. Toys. Board books. A rocker horse with the price tag still attached. He threw away the breast pump parts and bottles.

There was the toy drum, with its triple yin-yang. Clothing and shoes and jewelry and tiny baby jumpers and tiny baby shoes, none of which he could stand to leave sitting exposed under the open sky. So he put it all into clear plastic trash bags and labeled each ASSORTED BABY THINGS $20.

There were half-empty bottles of cleaning supplies, a big jar of coins, a futuristic brass key.

He considered plunging the brass key to the bottom of the coin jar to become a cryptic prize for someone years in the future. Or throwing it away? Or melting it? As much as he hated the thing, as much sorrow as it gave him, he knew that getting rid of the key would amount to sacrilege—

(*Margot, dancing with the key in one hand, June in the other*)

—so he tucked it into his shoe, and in his shoe it stayed.

In this way, I can pretend you are still with me.

In this way, I can pretend I am keeping you safe.

The sun rose. A steady crowd moved in and out of the apartment building lawn, touching things with inquisitive index fingers as he watched from a student's chair, coffee and flip phone set on its L-shaped fold-out desk. One by one he called out to the sale hunters.

Five dollars.

Three dollars for the pair.

That one's free, enjoy.

The buyers sensed something wrong—prices were way too low—but the bargains made it easy to shrug off their worries. His apartment neighbors tiptoed by without touching a thing. Like: *There's that man who lost his wife and baby. Here are all his cursed possessions.*

He sold a laptop to an elderly woman for fifty dollars. It was Margot's. You'll have to delete everything yourself, he said. I don't remember the password. The elderly woman spoke almost no English and lavished him with gratitude.

I wish I could remember the password. I'm so sorry.

A hefty White man, typical of the Hard Bargainers he'd learned to spot and classify, pointed at the steel-faceted Moka pot Margot had had since college. The man was with his female clone of a wife, who wore the same race car T-shirt and cowboy belt and jeans as her husband. This one's a Italian original, he pointed out. *Eye-talian.*

Hey, Charlie! How much you willing to part with this for! said the man.

Adam blinked. *Charlie?*

Just for fuckery, Adam put on his best ching-chong-ling-long. For you, he said, wan tousand dolla. He sharpened the tilt of his gaze. And den I fuk you wife.

The man looked like he had just inhaled a passing sparrow.

Anyway, yeah that's a thousand bucks, said Adam. No, two thousand.

What the hell is wrong with you?

Get out of my sight, said Adam.

The shoppers froze, creating the oddest of sculpture gardens for a moment.

You're an asshole, said the man. What a mean, asshole way to treat people. His wife pulled him away with all her might like a dog walker walking a cow.

With the Hard Bargainers gone, the crowd began moving again.

An adolescent girl examined the Moka pot with wonder. She was most likely the granddaughter of the elderly woman who bought the laptop. She wore jeans and bright sneakers and a torn T-shirt with the name of a band on it, already American and growing more so each year she lived here. She spoke a quiet mix of English and Spanish.

That's five dollars, said Adam.

The girl approached, wary but excited. She laid a perfectly crisp bill on his desktop.

Thank you, she said.

What school do you go to?

Sorry?

What school do you go to? I'm a teacher.

East West High.

His phone buzzed. It was Byron. Come out tonight, man, his message said. You need it. This is not healthy.

Actually, he said, take the phone, too.

The girl's mouth fell open. But—you're still using it.

No, I'm done. Here.

He entered a secret code, D-padded to a big red DELETE ALL?, and hit the OK button. The phone erased itself. Then he ejected the SIM card and dropped it into a drain.

Her grandmother protested. He held out the device until she relented, and the girl finally accepted the phone as if she'd been chosen for some great task.

Do good in school, okay? he said.

It's *Do well*, said the girl without thinking.

That's the spirit, he said, pleased entirely. It felt so good to be pleased.

As she and her grandmother left they gave him one last look, still astounded by their luck this dewy morning keening with birdsong on infinite loop.

FIFTY-SIX

OVER DEAD LANDS RIDGE, HE WILL FIND PEOPLE. NOT DEAD PEOPLE, not zombies. Enough with that. He'll find normal people, driving around in circles, throwing things away to make room for new things, eating up and shitting out and eating right back up again. And why not?

Why not.

Dead Lands ridge has a real name on a real map somewhere. Probably even has hikers looking down right at the model house he is in. *Guess that housing tract wasn't too big to fail.*

Worlds don't end. They carry on. There is no such thing at all as the world ending.

No vandals clubbed people on the back of the head. He'd done that himself somehow.

He stands for a long time just staring at the big blank TV. He has no idea how to feel. Should he laugh? Or rage? Or cry? None of those make sense for this moment. He can barely even breathe.

He notices a large throw on the couch and uses it to cover the television for the most part. He reaches back behind the thing and yanks hard on a plug. A tiny green light dies.

He takes the remote control apart and stuffs it and its battery deep into the couch.

Clay's pack rests at the foot of the couch, forgotten. Adam

considers opening it for a moment, but thinks no. Kids need at least a few secrets of their own, no matter how silly.

He stares at the pack and is overcome with the urge to go door to door until he finds his mother.

Who the hell leaves her son to wander around an abandoned aqueduct? he wants to say. He shoots crows, did you know that? Do you have any idea at all what you have? He set up a whole shelter out there, and it basically saved my life. Did you know that? Do you really appreciate what Clay is capable of? What kind of mother are you?

Adam finds his clothes, changes out of his robe. Pushes the brass key into his shoe.

He walks down the hall, seeing everything anew. The pamphlets and business cards on the console. He takes a pen, clicks it, and writes ADAM CHUNG on the blank in neat capital letters.

Now he is suddenly a sales agent. Clay's mom probably won't even bat an eye. This strikes him as hilarious.

There's that thermostat on the wall, glowing green. He taps it once to increment the temperature. Something beneath the house stirs to accommodate his request. He taps to decrement, and the house falls silent once again.

He stares at the office computer on its glass surface. He could push a button, sure. Click the thingy a few times. The mouse.

He opens the door to the nursery and climbs up to the top bunk, the girl's bunk, and lies there. He can practically touch the white ceiling. It feels like being dead. My God, if he dies right here right now, no one will find him for years. He'll slowly become desiccate and black. He'll go right up when a wanderer eventually comes to burn the whole place down by accident. Then the wanderer will take his place, become kindling themselves, and all that fire leading to smoke leading to wood leading back to fire will form an endless cycle.

For now, though, what cozy company: a dozen stuffed animals, rabbits and pandas and bears and so on, all still with their tags on. All things June never got to really comprehend. After all, June had only just learned how to lie on her tummy and hold her head up without face-planting into her own drool. Her hair had just begun to find its bend.

Her node had gotten cut short, while other nodes just keep right on going in all those in-between worlds: the one where she learned to climb a bunk, or run away from boys at school. Write a proof, throw a clay vase, sing with her bestie on a road trip with the windows rolled down.

He never got to know his June.

He turns his head and scoffs. This room was put together by people who didn't know jack shit about kids. Where are the burp cloths and wadded-up diapers you're too tired to throw away properly? Where's the carbon monoxide monitor duct-taped to the wall? The empty plastic cups of wine drying out beside the glider?

This room is a kind of badly told story for people looking to start a family. Maybe it's good enough for them. That's forgivable; they didn't know any better. No one can know until they really *know* it for themselves.

Anyway, this room isn't anywhere near good enough for him.

He'll leave Arroyo Plato after Clay leaves.

He climbs down from the awful bed.

He goes out in the hallway to stand before the door with the towel jammed underneath. He pushes. The door doesn't budge. It's not locked like normal, though. Even locked doors move slightly when bumped. This door has been jammed solid.

He pushes the towel back with a finger but can see nothing through the dark gap. He kneels and can detect a smell—sour, like food left out. Grimacing, he curls a finger under the door and feels along its inner edge. It catches against something. A wooden rod. He shoves sideways until the rod dislodges and falls to the floor inside with a clank.

He stands, turns the doorknob, slowly swings it open. The smell is stronger now.

He turns on the light to reveal a bathroom with clear containers by the sink, filled with balls of wire and the gossamer leaves from the reeds at the river channel, the same ones he'd been measuring with his lines. A stack of cardboard sheets, too. The one on top has one of his wind charts from the shelter. His heart falls at the sight.

I shouldn't be here, he thinks. This is a secret place.

There is a shower curtain drawn shut, and it's this he feels most afraid of. This isn't for me to see, he thinks. I really should not be here.

He pushes the curtain aside and sees a tub filled with crows, like black leaves suspended in water.

Nearby is a cardboard sheet labeled CHANGE WATER written in Clay's small hand, and a list of dates and initials next to each.

A small cloud of red oozes from one of the crows. Its eye stares at him from beneath the surface.

I told you there was more, it says.

FIFTY-SEVEN

ADAM KNEELS BY THE TUB FOR A LONG WHILE. HE CAN'T TELL WHICH IS the one he'd seen Clay kill, but it's in here. All the birds he'd assumed were dragged away by kit foxes, they are in here.

If he'd had any idea of what he was talking about, he'd know what a kit fox looked like. But he can't tell a kit fox from any other kind of fox. He probably heard the words *kit* and *fox* at some point and liked how they sounded together, and his brain painted a little cartoon of what such a creature might look like. But in the end he doesn't know anything at all.

He can see Clay lying in his bed with that little face of his, gone completely blank. He shouldn't have snapped at him about the television. He is, as far as he knows, the kid's only friend.

The sight of the cardboard wind chart shatters his heart with a sudden zing of pain. His heavy-handed line next to Clay's thinner, almost painterly hand, telling the simple, meaningless story of the wind: one minute it's stronger, the next it's not. This reed bends this much, that one that much. All you can tell from the chart was that wind indeed exists, and tends to move things around.

If he had a magnet, he'd stick it on the fridge. He'd frame it if he could.

When Adam was little, he hid things, too. What with all the daily stupid questions and name-calling, even eggs thrown at his back from a passing truck, as if one boy could single-handedly steal all the jobs in America. Adam grew into that timeless immigrant kid cliché: never really belonging anywhere, and therefore never sure he actually had a solid, tangible existence.

That summer day, so long ago, when he stuck a garden hose in a tiny hole and had been delighted to see hundreds of ants pouring out of another. He fetched a jar and caught most of them. He went to bed that night with dozens of tiny white bites all over his ankles and wrists, but didn't care. He had his water jar, with its glistening bottom sediment of dead ants, kept safely sealed under his bed.

"I'm sorry I can't be there for you," says Adam.

He finds the metal lever for the bath drain and throws it with a *thunk*. The water level begins to sink. Adam watches the black mass shift and bristle as the draining water exposes wet feathers to the air, inch by inch. There is a sharp fermented edge to the smell now.

He waits for the last of the water to slurp down the drain. Then he throws the stopper switch back and opens the faucet to send cold water screaming into the tub.

The process reverses. The soggy heap of feathers inflates with the rising water, then begins to float. He fills it as far as he can. Clay had taped over the tub's overflow drain to give the dead birds a few more inches of water to occupy.

He stops the water and all is silent again.

He marks the CHANGE WATER chart. For the date, he writes a pair of question marks. Then he leaves his initials: AC.

He closes the shower curtain, refolds the towel to fit the width of the door threshold, and turns out the light. He guides the door shut and moves the rod back into place. Clay must've been doing this for weeks now. Months.

Clay has tied a string loop to the top of the rod to make it easier to wedge the door firmly using just one finger.

Clever kid.

FIFTY-EIGHT

ADAM REALIZES HE'S BEEN STARING AT THE OFFICE COMPUTER FOR what must've been ten minutes. He peels his eyes away and feels his way to the chair. He will sit and open the computer and let his muscle memory carry him the rest of the way.

But first, he decides he'll procrastinate. So many cabinets here to open and close, so much to see. Sticky notes and copy paper, mailing labels and envelopes and blank name tags with ARROYO PLATO stamped into the bronze plastic. Reams of never-completed housing contract forms jogged squarely into perfect stacks. A folder tray marked HOT LEADS sits empty.

One cabinet contains a heavy bangle of metal shingles. Brass keys, all identical to the one in his shoe. His heart surges as if passing a painful dollop of lava. This ring of keys is the point of origin for his own. Brass keys, never used. Didn't Hemingway write that?

They didn't even bother locking the cabinet full of keys. As if to say, pick any house you want. We give up.

Adam closes his eyes. He is in a neighborhood full of houses. He now knows his key opens one of them. He'll find out what's inside. Then he'll leave the key and shut the door behind him and walk away as best he can. That can be a plan to follow.

Adam opens his eyes. In another cabinet he finds a heavy crystal highball, a chrome ice bucket, and a large flask of whiskey. Tough sell indeed. The salespeople must have gotten to the point where they didn't bother faking it anymore.

He pads out to the kitchen with the bucket, sends ice cubes crashing into it with the refrigerator dispenser, and returns to the office desk to sit and pour himself a softly chiming glass.

He raises a toast: I salute you, doomed Arroyo Plato sales associates! Then he takes his first sip. It's been forever since he last drank, and he feels almost immediately buzzed.

He closes his eyes, takes a cliff-diver's breath.

He opens the computer.

There is no password, and he is instantly confronted by a photo of a two-faced kitten with one shared eyeball at the conjoining seam.

"Jesus Christ," he yelps. He is about to close the tab but then notices there are a dozen others open. He clicks each one to see. There is a kid's balloon game running in one. An article about crows in another. Another tab has an illustrated list of local desert flora and fauna. There is an actual picture of a kit fox. They are endangered.

He clicks more tabs. Video game reviews, cartoon figurines for sale, a car crash in which a compact car rear-ends a truck at high speed, severing the driver in two, blackened body surrounded by emergency workers in masks and vibrant purple nitrile gloves, entrails snaking away from a legless torso. *TRUE: Urban Myth of Micro Car Driver Cut in Half*

More tabs.

Parkour instructions. CGI rabbits with machine guns. A blond White woman taking a penis into her mouth and disgorging it again, and again, and again, forever. A White man's erection ejaculating a white blob of semen into black space, again and again, forever.

These are Clay's browser tabs. My God, he thinks, biting a knuckle. The kid is only eight. I would never give my son free rein on a computer. Hell no. I would protect him from all that and everything else.

But he's not your son, is he? You don't have a kid anymore. You don't have June. You don't have Margot. You barely have anything.

So what is it you do have?

Adam opens a new window and leaves the others undisturbed. It sits blank and waiting.

He takes another sip of the whiskey, then another, then one more for the sake of the last one. He sets the drink on the glass desk with a clang.

He begins typing: *high speed car chase rear end.*

Hundreds of results appear, all wrong.

flyover, he adds.

Flyover is the key word. Key, unlock, open.

The top result appears right away, waiting to be selected.

Spectacular Tragedy on Loop Expressway Flyover Brings Multi-City Chase to Tragic End (CONTAINS GRAPHIC MATERIAL). Watch Now >>

He takes another drink. If someone saw me now, he thinks, they'd think I was doing important work sitting at an impressive desk like this. Concentrating on the screen like I am.

He is in fact doing very important work. There is nothing more important he could be doing with this computer.

He clicks.

It is a local news channel site. Four attractive newscasters greet him, all with confident arms folded: the Channel Nine SmartNews Team. Next to them is a jittering box of text telling him to lose weight by freezing fat, accompanied by a banana with a red X through it. Another box to the right hawks edible fruit arrangements delivered right to your door for the holidays.

Click to Play beckons a large black rectangle. Innocuous words, easy words. *Click*, click my tongue, click my heels together in midair. *Play*, all work no play, play ball, gameplay. *Click*, and *play* will ensue.

He takes another sip, so long it burns. He tries to imagine what the face of God looks like. Some old White dude floating among the clouds with a bunch of plastic bags, sending the word *berries* echoing across the quilted hills.

Adam clicks.

A video begins. You could be saving hundreds of dollars in heating bills with this simple European home construction trick, but city permits won't allow it. Learn what you can do to start saving big now.

A White man appears, a Hard Bargainer. "I personally find the whole thing to be completely outrageous," he drawls. "That the city can keep homeowners like me from saving money? And the environment? It's just draconian."

He's puzzled. Is this the wrong video? The title is correct. Maybe it's a technical glitch? He notices a countdown in the corner.

ADVERTISEMENT

Your video will be available in three, two, one.

The video freezes, and a spinning flower appears. Finally he is presented with aerial footage of a highway traffic jam.

Two newscasters speak from behind a desk. A man and a woman. The woman does all the talking, with full lips that look wet.

"Police have a suspect in custody in critical condition tonight after a high-speed chase across three neighborhoods ended in a spectacular tragedy."

Now a photo of a young, severe White man with fencepost teeth. Everything on-screen is in constant motion, slowly shrinking or growing or sliding. The man's name shoots into view and slows, but never stops: David James. In the background, layers of translucent arcs in brilliant cobalt and aqua shift upon one another. Now and then a dazzling lens flare flashes.

"Twenty-four-year-old David James fled the police after a routine stop for a broken taillight, leading them across Downtown, Hancock, Playa Mesa, and finally to just outside Delgado Beach, where tragedy struck."

Back to the newscasters again.

"What you're about to witness may be shocking," the man says. "Viewers at home, please use your discretion."

Adam knows this phrase. It means that they are about to show something violent, and if you didn't want to see it you had but seconds to turn off your television. But no one ever did. He never did. Until.

What he is about to witness is the video he's watched many times over. He never meant to, but computers auto-played videos whether you wanted to watch them or not. What he is about to witness is already ingrained in his memory. He knows it by heart.

Now there is a small copper-colored car, the kind with one fender replaced with a mismatching one like one of the hack jobs from his father's shop. It speeds along local roads. Through a red light, narrowly missing cross traffic.

"The suspect, driving a metallic orange 1990 Matsuda 550LT, runs the red here, almost striking this white 2010 Athena MTK."

A circle appears to indicate the near collision. Matsuda vs. Athena. He remembers assuming the Athena driver was an older woman, White like her car, probably wealthy. Like most people he has a small taxonomy of personalities matched by car type, all of them derogatory: the weak, the overcompensating, the reckless, the boring. After this point in the video, he remembers now, the reporters stop using people names and use car names instead, like a shorthand.

The police car plods behind. Lights strobing. Another police car appears, then another.

"As more police joined the chase the Matsuda veered onto this highway on-ramp here, already clogged with rush-hour commuters."

A lime-green line, hand-drawn by someone at the television station, drags across the ramp to indicate its location.

"The Matsuda speeds along the shoulder to avoid the traffic and continues to do so, at one point just shoving its way through this gap between these cars and the retaining wall."

The little car ricochets its way through the disheveled queue and sheds a side mirror. It keeps going.

"At one point the Matsuda feints toward the exit but then jukes back to prolong the pursuit, just pushing past anything in its way."

The cars drive on and on. From this vantage point high in the air the chase is robbed of any sense of speed, and the vehicles seem to be creeping along at their usual pace. It all feels reasonable and undramatic.

A rectangle slides up from the bottom of the video to take advantage of the lull in the action. Are you paying too much for your car insurance? Find out now. There is an owl dressed as a professor. Take the Hoot Quote Challenge.

He tries to dismiss it, but mis-clicks and instead opens another window with a larger version of the owl. He bangs the window shut and returns to the video. There is an anger building inside him that feels familiar. He knows this rage.

It's all the *disrespect*.

"Then the Matsuda made this fateful turn onto the carpool ramp merging toward the southbound 56 interstate, where tragedy struck."

The video freezes for a moment. The green line appears again, slashing from the copper car to another car up ahead that has pulled over to the right, terminating in an X.

Margot. June.

"The Matsuda doesn't even notice the car obstructing its path up ahead. It's believed James was texting at this moment, possibly a farewell to his family."

"Police are withholding that information at this time," says the male newscaster.

"And that's when the unthinkable happened. Watch."

The Matsuda moves along, oblivious, along this line of cars waiting so high in the air. On this surreal arc of concrete suspended in the sky. The way the helicopter cameraman frames the shot places it out of reality. A colossal bridge in the heavens above a distant landscape obscured by rain.

The Matsuda strikes the car from behind, creating a scintillating cloud of debris. It shoves it up onto the retaining wall, where it teeters for just a moment. Then the car tips away out of sight.

"The Matsuda collides with this 2008 hunter-green Archer with enough force to throw it off the ramp and send it plummeting below, one hundred and four feet, or over seven stories."

Another green line illustrates the path of movement.

"Our local affiliate just happened to be there on the ground," growls the male newscaster, "to witness firsthand the tragic result."

"What you are about to see is highly disturbing," says the female voice.

A newscaster on the street appears, clutching an umbrella and a microphone outfitted with a bright orange wind bulb. She stands in a residential area with the monumental flyover ramp towering in the distance.

"All right," she says, preening her hair. "Jeff, where do you want me to stand?"

An arm appears in the frame, instructing her to move left.

"It is fureezing! Okay, Jeff, live in three. Two."

Behind her, the car comes spilling over the lip of the flyover and drifts downward with a kind of floating grace.

"Jesus!" says someone off-screen.

The car lands without a sound.

"One," says the newscaster, unaware.

In that instant the sound of the impact reaches them, like an enormous gate hurled shut. The newscaster whirls around, sees the flattened car lying upside down. She turns back to the camera, her composure gone, replaced by a cartoonlike pantomime of shock: eyes, nostrils, and mouth all perfect Os held solid for a full, pauseable, screenshottable moment.

This is the expression. He remembers now. This is the thing that added tragedy on top of tragedy.

The newscaster hurries toward the wreckage, followed by a tumbling camera.

Back to the warmth of the studio.

"The two victims were Morgo—Margon—Margot Margen," says the female newscaster.

"Margot Morgan," says the other.

"Margot Morgan, I'm sorry, thirty-five-year-old African American from Allman Heights, and June Chang Morgan, just ten months old. The two souls obviously perishing on impact."

Their faces float on the screen. Margot and June. The blue arcs shift in the background. A lens flare streaks by.

"Just heartbreaking." Her lips glisten.

"Absolutely. Now, police did find methamphetamine in James's car and will press charges of possession, and are also investigating a possible role in drug dealing. James remains in critical condition."

They set their papers down.

"Coming up next," says the male newscaster, "the Pullman football mascot and his uplifting surprise for children with leukemia."

A man in a mongoose costume does a cartwheel on a field before a line of cheerleaders.

FIFTY-NINE

THERE'S MORE TO IT, SINGS THE CROW FROM DOWN THE HALL, FROM the bottom of its watery mass grave. You know there is more.

"Shut it," says Adam. He drinks off the whiskey, pours another.

The video has been replaced with a tiled wall of choices. More high-speed chases, other newscaster fails, *You Might Also Enjoy.*

Adam remembers now how he'd spent so many hours just like this: sitting in front of a computer, thinking hard, drinking hard, breathing hard. How the incoherent rage had polluted his head thoroughly. *What a world! If it bleeds, it leads! Give them bread and circuses!*

Hers isn't the only high-speed-chase tragedy to choose from. There are hundreds of others to bookmark, add to a playlist, share with friends. Like. Flag. *You Might Also Enjoy.*

Adam scrolls down and reads the comments. Suddenly he is flung back into his dark apartment, unshaven and unwashed for five days. The only light the glow of his computer screen. Kitchen counter tumbling with takeout containers. Cardboard moving boxes everywhere exploding with the things he couldn't yet bear to throw away or sell. This was before the yard sale, right. It'd taken forever to go through everything, because it was almost impossible even to touch the objects with his bare fingertips. Indeed: he'd spent an hour seething at a clear dolphin filled with oil and blue water that tumbled a tiny viscous wave when tilted. It was from the honeymoon, tchotchke stores on a tropical island.

Weeks earlier, Adam had tracked down every version of the crash video he could find, urging people to take them down, tilting at windmills like that Spanish knight in that Spanish book. Except the windmills were people—thousands of them—and how mutable and slippery! How despicable!

Please remove this video, it's my wife and baby who died, Adam would write.

That's terrible. DM the OP, said one. DM stood for *direct message*, idiotic online jargon meaning *contact directly*, and OP stood for *original poster*. So he did. They never responded.

And why would they? The video garnered two million views that in turn garnered significant amounts of advertising money for the *original poster. Insane car crashes caught on camera* seemed to be a specialty of his. Or hers? It was hard for Adam to imagine a woman curating horror for money, but who in God's great smoldering post-Eden afterscape could know?

Sux sorry, said another comment.

If you're the husband then why are you watching your own wife and kid eating it, that's fucked up

I'm sorry but she shouldn't have pulled over wrong place wrong time god be with you

She did nothing wrong, he would argue. *The police even said so.*

Fuck tha police

She was black

Fake Video false Flag crisis Actors . . . ratings Hoax!!!!

Not fake, it was live on the news

4:33 car goes bye bye lol

Sending positive thoughts and prayers

4:50 laughing not laughing, going to hell in 3 2 boom

You are sick, Adam wrote and wrote. *This video needs to be taken down now.*

But his words were swept away like gutter leaves by the endlessly replenishing torrent of comments.

This what you get when you let them run free on the streets

Dude was white cracker ass racist

Take back our streets #onelesscar

More comments meant more instances of the same video, and why not? It was an effortless project to download the video, post it for yourself, and instantly start earning weed money at minimum.

A truncated version of the video had been published under the title *LIVE IN 3, 2 FAIL*. That clip showed up in a morbid montage of horrific car crashes titled *BEST OF BRUTAL HORROR CAR CRASHES*. Finally, there was an ultra-short version simply titled *THREE TWO FAIL*. It wasn't even a video anymore. It was an animated image, cut down to show just the plummeting car and the newscaster's reaction in an endless loop.

Three two fail became the catchphrase, he now recalls. Right.

The crash had gone what was known as *viral*. It had spread from host to host, with no way to stop the contagion.

––––––––

THE CRASH WOULD NEVER GO AWAY. OR THE COMMENTS. IT WAS NOW part of the permanent archive of the unending present. The moronic inferno gushed in place, broadening its shores wherever its sputum hit the hissing, recoiling sea. This wasn't about history or posterity. This was the total nullification of all light and color.

After a month of protesting every instance of the video he could find, Adam quit.

My dear Margot and June. You could kill them any time you wanted on demand.

Adam began wandering the darkest corners online. Why not. It was all there: beheadings in some third-world country, fresh close-ups of gunshot victims. Bodies ripped in two by terrorist bombs. A distracted texting woman cut in half by a malfunctioning elevator.

Two women in bikinis shitting into a cup, then eating the shit. That last one was so popular there were T-shirts for sale.

Something snagged and spun in his brain—a red string on a spool madly winding fatter and fatter—and he found he couldn't stop looking. He wanted to see how far it went.

A train plowed into a crowd of fleeing villagers. *Play!* Young women addicted to a brand-new drug that ate their flesh so badly you could see the bone and viscera within. *Subscribe!*

He just could not stop looking! And the computer happily provided its endless stream of horror all day and all night for multiple days and multiple nights.

When his phone would ring—always Byron calling—he would cover the buzzing device with a pillow and continue browsing. Such an anodyne word, *browsing.* Just *browsing,* thanks!

He browsed and browsed. A man standing on a windy bridge, sniped in the head, collapsing into his own gushing blood. Skip ad in five, four, three two fail.

This was the junk canon Margot and June had been inducted into.

Adam soon drank constantly. A van full of explosives, he thought. Just like that White guy in Oklahoma. Except I'll pull up to the video tech company itself.

Perhaps realizing how wrong that thought was, he changed his mind. Maybe simpler-slash-better to just livestream himself blowing his brains out. Tag it correctly for the search engines. A kind of farewell video.

But he knew the video wouldn't amount to even the tiniest speck of shit, because as quickly as it appeared it would fade away as the infinite feed slotted in the next thing to scroll past. There was no beating the feed. The feed would checkmate him every time. It didn't care if he was happy or sad or alive or dead.

Nature is not a whore, Margot said one time, two wines in. She swayed against the fridge sipping from a jam jar from her childhood as they waited for microwave popcorn. She's not a harsh mistress. She's not even a she.

The popcorn began to stir.

If a baby deer dies in the forest, she said, you can mourn or not mourn. Doesn't matter. The rats will get to her, and the birds and insects will finish off the smaller bits. And in a few days, nothing. In the meantime, nature will just keep on making more baby deer. I'm rambling.

And you swear you're not being cynical? he said.

Margot kicked at him and missed. I'm not! she said. That's you saying that.

That you're cynical.

I don't think I'm cynical.

So are you or are you not? he said.

Both, said Margot. Get it?

Grr.

The deer dying has nothing to do with cynicism or hope. It's beyond your neat little dichotomies.

Adam drank off his glass and idly thumbed the arch of her foot resting atop his thigh. Moral relativism something something.

That's all I'm saying, she said. Oh my god that feels good.

You can't rule out evil, though. You got serial killers and dictators and blablabla. You know there's no other explanation for that except evil.

Margot switched feet, and he obliged with another amateur massage. I mean, call it evil if it makes you feel better, she said. Now you have an excuse to be all cynical about everything. But how long can you stay cynical, practically speaking?

Adam worked his thumb and thought about that for a good long moment—a life without hope, a bitter life, a life without joy—and conceded her question with a *huh*.

Cynicism is a trapdoor left wide open, said Margot. Hope is the lock that keeps it shut. Now here's the key, asshole, don't mess this up!

They laughed then, and he spilled the perfect amount of wine for it to be funny and not any kind of real mess.

Are you quoting something? he said finally.

She beamed. I just made it up.

You need to drink more, he said. And more often.

He dropped her foot, stood, pulled her in for a jammy sweet kiss. The popcorn applauded with its rat-a-tat.

FINALLY ONE DAY HE WAS READING A WEBSITE IN THE BLACK-AND-white light of dusk. It had been what—weeks? Months?

It was a gossip site, celebrities and pop culture and trends. It was a relief to be reading normal things again, without that urge to check if the crash video was still there. He knew it was, existing alongside all the other horrors in the world he could do nothing about.

All around Adam the apartment sat empty. The yard sale was a few days ago. His phone was now in the possession of that bright and kind young girl. Adam now had plenty of bare hardwood floor to lie flat on and stare up at the blank ceiling. He'd vacuumed it, swabbed to a shine. The whole place looked like no one lived there. It somehow made things easier. He didn't question why, and the whiskey kept him that way.

Oh look here now, it says his college football team blew a routine field goal and lost what should've been an easy championship.

This, my friends, is how you choke proper, said one commenter.

Your fail is our win kthxbye, said another.

They posted an animated image showing the disastrous kick that sent the ball veering wide of the goalposts, and the coach's stunned reaction face. The thing about animated images was that they had neither play nor pause button; they ran whether you wanted them or not. So when the image cut to a newscaster in residential area with a monumental flyover ramp towering in the distance, Adam could only watch in mid-sip. The car fell to the ground, the newscaster whipped around, and the famous caption appeared: *THREE TWO FAIL.*

An apt comparison, he found himself thinking, in that instant before conscious objection could stir. The coach's face paralleled the newscaster's face with perfect comic timing.

Adam laughed, just the shortest little whistle through wet teeth.

Then he folded his laptop screen back onto itself, snapping the computer in two at the hinge. He flung it down the hall.

He grabbed his keys and his bottle of whiskey and crashed out the front door.

He went for a drive.

SIXTY

ADAM CLOSES HIS BROWSER WINDOWS. HE'S CAREFUL TO LEAVE CLAY'S browser windows open. He shuts the leasing office computer and leaves the room and shuffles into the nursery, bumping the doorjamb on his way in. He climbs into the bunk bed again. He likes it up here. It's just safer. Adam knows that doesn't make any sense, but still.

Margot, my sweetheart. Lurching forward, then watching with baffled terror as the horizon turned all the way around. And June, totally helpless to know what any of this was or why. And then: nothing.

There is no evil and there is no good. There are just things that happen, and after that there is nothing.

He replays that last night as best he can, not omitting any details. It had been late. The city was quiet. He drove carefully, just like a drunk would. When he reached the highway he rolled down the windows and sang screaming with the stereo into the frigid wind.

Before now I was always searching, he yelled. Before now I was always gone. Before the radio broke down. Before long.

He sped north and the landscape became lower and more suburban until eventually there was nothing but black hills against an indigo sky. He drove without seeing another car for fifteen minutes at a time. Then twenty, then thirty. Still, he had a ways to go. Desert insects spun into his headlights like snow.

Finally: glowing billboards sailed into view in the nightscape. They were badly shredded, peeled at the corners, sagging entirely off the frame like curtains.

An elderly couple strolled with golf clubs shining. RESORT STYLE LIVING.

A family splashed each other in a pool. MAKE YOUR STARTER HOME YOUR DREAM HOME.

A grand Spanish-style suburban tract home stood before a stone fountain. ARROYO PLATO VILLA ESTATES HOMES STARTING AT $400,000. The number had been slashed and replaced with $250,000. This was an astonishingly low amount, even for the time. A house in the city would cost four times as much and be markedly shittier.

He and Margot had forty thousand dollars in savings. With the double payments of life insurance money, all-alone-Adam now had more than twice that. But he was loath to touch any of it. He could hardly bear to spend it on stuff like whiskey or food delivery or rent.

They passed through this same spot on a road trip one time forever ago, when the billboards were intact enough to make their silent sales pitch to no one out in the middle of the vast nothing.

Adam drove. No helicopters out here in the desert, he'd said.

No friends, either, said Margot. Her feet were up on the dash. Her belly was showing by this point, and seeing it drew a surge of desire from him. Who knew a pregnant belly could be so sexy? He got why dudes of old made fertility statues. How could you not?

Big huge house, Adam countered. Central vacuuming?

Big huge commute? said Margot.

I thought we wanted the space?

I mean, sure, said Margot, but this is a skosh extreme.

Then let's live extreeeeme, he growled.

Margot hiccuped a few giggles. What on earth are we gonna do with that much house?

They traveled farther and farther into the sunny blankness. Sky. Hill. Road. Sign. WATCH DOWNHILL SPEED. Them, the lone travelers.

Margot gazed at the beige landscape and waved a languid hand. Eh, I'd probably like it here despite myself, she said. I bet the schools are all brand-new and super fantastic to work at. I bet I'll feel totally different once June comes.

Hi, June, he said. He cupped Margot's chin with his free hand and glanced at her, at her belly. Hi, my darlings.

HE'D MISSED THE OFF-RAMP IN THE DARK. HE PULLED OVER, KILLED the engine, and grapevined his legs to keep his balance. In the pure darkness he could make out a road off the highway leading into some low hills.

Hateful car, said Adam, then grabbed his bottle and began walking.

He stumbled along the desert floor, stepping around scrub bushes that were spiny and round like giant urchins. Everything around him as dark as the deep sea, so simply underwater with darkness that light could only barely reach him. He looked up. A brilliant cloud of stars glittered from horizon to horizon. The moon a fine pale arc drawn in one delicate stroke. Once his eyes adjusted, the whole landscape suddenly seemed to glow white.

He climbed up to the road and walked along its shoulder for a while. No cars came or went. He moved to the road's center and walked along the yellow line as if it were a balance beam. Whole road to himself, yeehaa. At one point he unzipped and urinated right in the open, drawing a ragged circle like a blitzed sprinkler.

I claim this part of the road, he cackled. Margot would never believe this behavior. She would kill him if she saw him right now.

An hour later he passed through the gap in the hills and stood before a long, straight approach leading into a windy basin surrounded by taller hills. Way in the distance? A single orange streetlamp winking on and off. A candle struggling to stay lit. That's where I'll go, he thought. He took a swig of the whiskey, which was

Very Good Shit. Glen-Something. Glen-Go-Fuck-Yourself. He capped the bottle and swaggered on.

He passed between two stone portal columns, each marked AR-ROYO PLATO. Around the portal was nothing. It looked like aliens dropped them here a thousand years ago, snickered, and took off again.

They were like a joke, because: where were the houses?

Adam continued toward the light. It held its glow steady for him.

He began seeing the skeletal forms of half-built house frames emerging from all sides. Clean, perfect asphalt covered in points by crescents of snowy white sand drifts. Front yards of packed dirt. Bundles of forgotten lumber.

There was a story about a ship discovered drifting at sea. When rescuers discovered it, they boarded to find fresh cups of coffee and music playing on a stereo and a complete meal of pot roast and peas and potatoes, all still hot and steaming and waiting to be eaten by passengers who were no longer there.

There was a dread to that story he found thrilling. He felt the same dread, only this time it was the unfun kind. Anyone could be hiding out here. The orange beacon might reveal nothing. He could get murdered and no one would know for months, even years, as the desert climate turned him into blackened leftovers like the corpse he would later find in the ghost condo. He wouldn't care so much about the dying as compared to the pain of getting killed by a perfect stranger. The dying was nothing.

For now, Adam gave himself a mission: *Just get to the orange light. Then you'll know why you came here tonight.*

As he neared, he could see that the streetlamp kept watch over four completed houses in the distance, brand-new in construction and flawless but for their dirt yards out front. No porch lights burned and no TVs flickered, but at least there was the lamp. Flags and banners came increasingly into view around him, all worn gossamer thin by the desert wind. FUTURE COMMUNITY POOL. FUTURE K-8 SCHOOL.

FULLY ACCREDITED. SHOPS AND RESTAURANTS AT THE PRIMAVERA PLAZA. DINE, RELAX, CONNECT.

None of it built yet. Or, as it turned out, ever.

He reached the four completed houses and hoisted his bottle high. I honor thee for thine steadfast courage in the face of being forsaken in this desolate place. Gold stars all around! He laughed, and the sound was stolen by the underwater wind and carried away.

We totally could've lived here. Get in first while prices were low. Once it filled up with families and children and shoppers he could brag that he'd been here back when there were only four houses.

It'd of course be just him in a house all alone.

There goes that guy, the people would whisper. He's Three Two Fail.

He took another swig. Plenty left in the bottle. Awesome.

He shuffled his way past the dark houses and into an unfinished lot. In the dirt backyard a tall sand drift had accumulated against the back wall. He took a running start and climbed it, recalling an old Japanese film he had seen once about a man trapped in a sand pit with a strange woman, and the climactic scene when he clambers to the surface for the first time in months. He forgot how it ended. Did the man escape?

Right—he chose to stay. In the end the dude chose to stay.

Adam wouldn't've stayed if it was him. Would he?

A vast river channel came into view. Beyond it, a charred wasteland ending in a glowing ridge of tall, jagged hills.

He dropped down beyond the wall. There was a bridge spanning the dry channel. He stood in the middle and let the wind billow his shirt.

The channel was a magnificent sight. White and flawless and luminescent in the dark deep. A perfect massive bend of concrete carved right into the surface of the planet. Built all at once in a single frenzy of ambition, then abandoned once everything crashed. Once the defaults grew and the numbers became irrefutable.

No people would ever gather here. There'd never be a river. The water dried up a long time ago if there was even any water to begin with. He imagined the dim ghosts of creatures adrift in its fantasy current.

This was the perfect place to do it.

He took one last sip of whiskey. Thank you, whiskey. He set it down. Stood, patted his pocket, found his wallet: good. They'd find it after his body had shriveled up. They'd begin putting the pieces together. Holy crap, they would realize. He's that guy. But this time, he'd finally no longer be that guy because he'd no longer *be* at all. He'd have finally made his escape.

Thank you, little streetlight.

He turned around, closed his eyes. He let the wind swell one last time. Then he tipped back and fell into nothingness.

SIXTY-ONE

ADAM WAKES TO A GUNSHOT. HE SITS UP AND LISTENS.

He hears it again. Not a gunshot. A car door, slamming. Shit—Clay!

Today is Clay's last day here! He leaps from the bunk and hurries out to the front door. He turns the steel handle three degrees, then turns it back. He can't just appear out of nowhere. Clay's mother would spook. He can't just go out there and babble about how *Your son saved my life as I lay starving in your son's secret bivouac by the river.*

Another car door slams. Shit.

Adam gets an idea. He scrambles back to the office, takes the business card from his pocket, and slides it into a clear PVC tag holder that he affixes to his chest. He checks himself in a cabinet inside door mirror. His shave is holding up.

He dashes back to the front door and takes a stage breath. There is a basket full of crimson umbrellas, all labeled ARROYO PLATO. Pretty convincing prop. He takes one, exhales to purge the nerves, and steps out into the morning air.

Two houses down, he sees a compact White woman struggling in the misty rain with two rolling suitcases, one lime green, the other a strawberry red, gay colors, emblazoned with funny English: THE NEW

TRAVEL LIFE BY MATSUZAKA on one, GLOBAL LET'S GO SINCE 1998 on the other.

"Clay!" she yells. She wears a tight shirt with rainbow bears on it, oddly juvenile, and tight jeans. Tight everything on her stocky body, and all of it seemingly left over from her high school days. Small green bow-tie pins rest on flat brown hair that frames her round face in a bob.

She sees him approaching and immediately draws her luggage closer to her, which makes sense.

"Whoa," she says. She openly bears a look of suspicion.

So this is Clay's mom. Not quite the rugged frontierswoman he'd imagined. But then he'd imagined a lot of things, right, crazy Adam? What else will turn out to be just another one of your figments?

"Can I help you?" she says, her voice rising.

He's been staring. "I'm so sorry," says Adam quickly. "I didn't think anyone would be here. Just spaced out, ha ha."

This seems to put her more at ease. "I didn't think anyone was there, either." She glances over his shoulder at the model home. Then she squints at his name tag through the rain. "Hi, Adam."

"Adam Chung. Just started working here. Hi . . . ?"

"Winnie."

"Nice to meet you," says Adam in his best cheery retail voice. "Let me help with that. Hold this."

He hands her the umbrella and hoists each suitcase into the back of her minivan. They are shockingly heavy; he feigns ease as he lifts them. The trunk is already packed solid. Crushed cardboard boxes, garbage bags stuffed with clothes. A box with half-finished potato chip bags and cartons of juice. A plastic laundry basket full of books with titles like *Earn Your Dental Hygienist Degree Online* and *Palomino College Course Guide*.

"I just get here," says Adam, "and you're just leaving!" He adds a laugh, and is relieved to receive a chuckle back from her.

"I'd ask you to do something about our lawns," she says, "But it dunreally matter now. Of course it decides to rain the week we leave, right? Clay!" She has a slight drawl. She jingles her car keys in one hand. On the ring is a brass rectangle he already knows is named REVERE.

"Are you folks leaving for good?"

"I mean yes and no," she sighs, and tugs at her shirt. Her eyes cloud as they trip up onto the distant horizon. Maybe she is a frontierswoman, and Adam just doesn't know enough to tell.

He leans to hold the umbrella over her. To his surprise, she takes a sidestep closer. Like a lot of Asian guys, he's been called *nonthreatening* before, and he senses it now. Fortunately?

Adam catches himself smirking and fixes his face back to a regular smile.

"Underwater, underwater, underwater," she laments, pointing at each of the houses. Then she points at her own. "Underwater. If I'm gonna be underwater anyway I might as well be with my family and not stuck in this postapocalyptic hellhole. No offense."

He's heard the word *underwater* before. It doesn't mean submerged; it's some kind of financial term. He could look it up, but that would mean opening up the cursed laptop. So Adam instead imagines houses crusted with coral at the bottom of the sea.

"Where is that Clay," she mutters.

"Your husband?" he asks, leading her.

"My son. My husband is in Osaka. He's Japanese?" She says it like he might somehow know the guy. Maybe Adam isn't nonthreatening after all, but is instead a familiar face like her husband's viewed through her eyes. Adam is used to seeing himself through other people's eyes.

Clay emerges from the house and now stares at Adam. What does he see?

"Hey there, buddy," says Adam. He feels ridiculous pretending not to know him, but what else can he do? The boy gazes at him for a long second and understands the charade.

"Hi," says Clay.

"Clay honey, did you remember to unplug everything?" says Winnie.

Clay shrugs. He glances at Adam's name tag. His eyes betray a flash of familiarity for a moment before reverting to their default state.

"Clay, come on, for chrissake," she says, and stomps into the house. "I'm not gonna bleed money because you can't remember one simple thing."

They stand alone now, Adam and Clay. He knows there isn't long before she comes back. He struggles to find words to say. But then Clay speaks first.

"I came back to the model house for my backpack while you were asleep." He pauses. "Thanks for changing the water." He pulls his hoodie over his head with a sudden motion, to hide.

Adam fights the urge to hug the kid. He can tell Clay knows the tub isn't normal. Clay knows something is wrong with himself, and he seems to want to apologize for his behavior. Adam understands this. He wants to apologize for his behavior, too.

"You're welcome," says Adam.

"Are you gonna keep taking care of them?"

"I can't stay here."

Clay looks like he expected this answer. "Okay."

"Hey," says Adam.

"Hay is for horses," says Clay.

"I wanna say thank you, too," says Adam.

Clay grows uncomfortable. "For what?"

"What do you mean, for what?" says Adam. "You saved my dumb ass."

Clay glares at the ground. *Did I?*

"Anyway," says Adam. "Thanks."

Clay doesn't seem to hear, distracted as he is by some thought. He casts Adam a hopeful look that he then strings to the car handle. "You could just come with us. We can all fit."

"Dude," says Adam, and can only make a helpless gesture beyond that.

In the silence, Clay cups both hands together and raises them to his lips to produce a low woody whistle that sounds just like *Who-woo? Who?*

You're a magical creature, Clay.

Winnie returns.

"Okay all right okay!" she says.

"Have fun in Osaka," Adam says.

"Oh, we're not going to Osaka," laughs Winnie. "Although with everything how it is, maybe we should, ha? We're just over to Rancho Paloma at my sister's. Clay honey, you are absolutely soaking wet." She beckons Clay over by scooping the air with downturned fingers, an Asian gesture.

The three of them stand in a tight cluster under the red umbrella as the rain suddenly pounds down indiscriminately on everything everywhere.

"How long are you two gone for?" says Adam.

"Just till my husband gets back. A few months."

"He's never coming back," says Clay.

"Uh-uh," snaps his mother. "You take that back right now."

Clay says nothing. Winnie sighs. She looks accustomed to defeat. She switches tack.

"We'll get to Angela's and then you can play with the twins and in the pool when it stops raining, nkay? We're gonna have so much fun, we're gonna make the best of it the best we can like we talked about, nkay? Clay!"

Clay says nothing.

"Please get in," she huffs. She turns to Adam, flips a mode selector back to a polite smile. "He's just shy."

Clay—who looks at nothing, because he is very good at looking at nothing—enters the van and slams the door shut without so much as a *see ya.*

But: Adam can see him peering back in the side-view mirror. Opening and closing his small hand slowly. Bye, bye. Bye, bye. Those dark eyes of his still waiting to be deciphered. Not by Adam, alas, but damn, hopefully by somebody sometime soon.

"Can I ask you something?" says Adam to Winnie.

"Sure."

"What happened to the whole subdivision across the river?"

"Theydin tell you? Wow, ha ha, no, I'm sorry I don't mean to laugh, but!" The woman is positively giddy to be leaving. "It was a brush fire! I mean, *first* there's the whole financial meltdown, *then* all the investors pull out, *then* a fire hits. The flames were scary huge. The river was the only thing that kept us from burning up with it, like a firebreak?"

Adam imagines being in the shelter while curtains of fire roared overhead. He glances at the van's side mirror. Clay has stopped waving and now just stares ahead.

"That was like six months ago. We knew for sure then that we weren't getting any more neighbors. I'm just a little embarrassed to be the last one to turn out the light."

"Well, I appreciate it," says Adam, just for something to say. He can't think of anything else, and it seems neither can she. The rain crescendoes to fill the gap.

"So, Adam Chung, what do they have you all doing out here?"

"Not much," he says. "Just watching over the merchandise."

She levels her eyes and laughs a single *ha*. "You should consider getting another job." She opens her van door. "Anyway, thank you for your help. Besta luck!"

The van starts and eases away. Adam waves at Clay. Clay presses his palm to the glass. It bleeds white there. Then Clay retreats back into his hoodie and the van accelerates down the street and out of sight.

SIXTY-TWO

ADAM STANDS IN THE RED GLOW OF THE UMBRELLA DRUMMING WITH rain, truly alone now. Impulsive thoughts run through his head. He could scream obscenities as loud as he can, walk around freezing naked. Break into all the houses and rummage through the junk of dreams too bulky or useless to carry.

So there has been some kind of financial meltdown. Something in the incomprehensible machine jammed the pipes and stopped the flow of money downward from the great golden cistern on high. He's always taken great pride in not knowing jack-diddly about these kinds of things and keeping it that way. Dismissing all of finance as the abstract playground of the rich. But here in this brand-new ghost town, he stands amazed: How could the workaday drudgery of a bank office on the other side of the country have led to this?

Is there even a real answer to that kind of question? Would it even matter? What's done is done, cannot be undone, the world shambles on. It's not like humanity will learn a single thing from it.

How long can you stay cynical, practically speaking? Margot had once said.

Maybe he'll just stay here until he dies, after all. Create new routines. Wake up, fix an espresso while there is still espresso to fix, sweep the sand from the backyard. Measure drift patterns once things dry out. Pour a whiskey from the infinite whiskey cabinet and watch Mo zigzag across the only lawn for miles.

Change the water.

Black feathers, in water.

It is time to leave.

He walks down the street and through a half-built lot to the spot in the plywood wall that bends back easily. He steps through the gap and emerges onto the river channel shoulder and blinks at what he sees.

The river is full.

Must be four feet deep now. He watches the fast-moving brown water gushing from the three drains at the terminus in the far distance, my god. To think how rain can gather into a flood like this. Big enough to hold a boat.

A mattress floats by, followed by a huge Styrofoam crag. All of the flotsam he first found under the bridge must be miles away by now. Hopefully along with it sails the body of the old man, that bastard.

He takes that back. What's done is done.

Amazingly, his array of clear strings holds up against the torrent. They radiate from the shelter and vanish into the fast-moving flood.

He crosses the channel using the bridge. How about another leap in? he thinks. See where this new river takes you?

He steps down the slope of the opposite bank to the shelter. The blanket, heavy now with moisture, sways in the gusty chill. He closes the umbrella in a shower of droplets, removes his name tag, and enters.

Everything is as he left it. A few of the cardboard sheets with wind data remain. A few cans. The matchbox and camping stove. The cinder block anchoring the clear strings has not moved from its spot, he notes with pride.

He finds the U.S. SHELBY CO. can opener, opens a can with a kiss. He strikes a match, lights the stove, places the spent match next to the line of others.

The discs move up and down and he begins a new chart, using wavy lines to indicate the flowing river. He eats, rinses the can with water, and drinks the remainder. He'll have to sit out in the pouring rain to fetch faucet water, if he wants water that way. But now he has the umbrella, he thinks slyly.

He has no idea what he is doing right now. Also, he has no idea what to do next.

Is that why he's come back into the shelter?

He steps outside the shelter to urinate, watching the stream vanish into the wet concrete. He doesn't have to pour water down. Man, the river has to be five feet deep now. A trip to the gauge at the terminus would confirm that.

So off he goes, umbrella in hand. He counts out the familiar number of paces. It's a comfort to know how many it takes. As Adam walks, the rain fills the basin with an arena of sound, all the way from the droplets pelting the umbrella right above him to the soft white noise sweeping the far hills.

He reaches the trio of pipes. The gauge is very much in use again now: four feet plus. Incredible. Water pours smoothly out of the giant drains with endless vitality. But this is the desert, and he knows once the rain stops the whole thing will revert back to its hot, dry state in a matter of days. That'd be something to track.

Is that what we're going to do, then? Find thing after thing to track?

Adam travels back to the model home and goes straight to the bathroom.

He drains the tub and puts the sour dripping carcasses into a garbage bag and clears everything out. He takes Clay's containers and goes to place them in the trash bins in the side alley of the model house. It's obvious they haven't been emptied in years. He imagines Clay's mom letting her trash pile up in someone else's yard—no trucks to collect it—while she worked on her escape plan.

Adam then digs a hole in an unfinished backyard some distance away and buries the bag of crows within. He drags mildewy paver stones over the mound and stomps to flatten them.

Back in the model home's leasing office, he closes all the open browser windows on the computer and scrubs the history. He notices a spreadsheet, opens it, and sees his name there: *CHUNG*. Next to the name is an address:

7 YUCCA

He closes the spreadsheet and shuts down the computer for good. "Seven Yucca," he says with wonder. "Seven Yucca."

He goes around the house, wiping every surface he can with puffs soaked in alcohol. There can be no evidence of either him or Clay.

The garage contains six identical white bicycles, all bearing the Arroyo Plato logo. Charming machines done in an old-fashioned style, with fenders and streamlined heads and tail lamps. Orange safety pennants flying from their seat tubes. Each has a large wire basket in the front and panniers in the back.

Adam emerges gliding from the silently opening garage, loaded up with creature comforts: a thermos of coffee, a pillow, a towel, breakfast bars, and so on. Once back at the shelter, he rests the bicycle under the bridge to keep it dry.

He still doesn't have any kind of plan, but he knows one thing for sure: unlike the man in that book trapped among the dunes, he won't stay here forever.

He remembers things easily now. The way Margot looked in the morning, puffy-eyed and cranky. Seeing June resting on her naked breast. The particular smell of her neck.

He remembers the agony of realizing the world couldn't be expected to care about their absence—that that was an unreasonable request for one person to make. This is okay. If he'd been asked to care about the fate of every member of humanity he'd turn away, too.

He takes the day of the crash and rewinds it in his mind to the moment he uttered those horrible words to her. *Leave me the fuck alone.*

"I apologize," he says to the shelter ceiling. "I wish I'd been better. I should've been better."

Then there is Byron, telling him none of this was his fault. It's hard to believe him, but Adam knows he has to get there somehow.

The funeral took place on a boat off the coast. The dozen or so mourners struggled to keep their balance on the rocking deck. Two urns plunged into the water, one demi-sized. The busy chop of the ocean bore no scar of their entry. The priest made crooning sounds as Adam's heart crushed down to nothing.

Here come more memories, flowing easier and easier.

The day of the yard sale had been sweltering. After he'd sold everything, he put every framed photo in the house into a steel ammo box he'd bought from an army surplus store. A drop of sweat dripped off his nose and into the box just before he locked it shut. He and Margot and June smiled on and on in the darkness. I knew you. I loved you. Our love mattered. No one could ever deny that.

With the apartment finally emptied, he would move on to emptying his accounts next: email, social networks, everything.

That big heavy ammo box, he knew, would remain unopened forever if he never went back to the apartment. Even if the landlord threw out his things after months of unpaid rent, that box would make its way into a trash truck, tumble into a landfill, and rest there until the end of humankind.

He imagines similar boxes in the four abandoned houses of Arroyo Plato, waiting for their owners to return and open them and have their contents once again be gazed upon under the light of the sun.

He had not put the futuristic brass house key in the ammo box. He kept that single artifact on him for a particular reason, and now he finally knows why.

He'll go back home soon. He'll find a new job. Something different and more solitary, because he can't bear the thought of teaching again and struggling to connect with all those energetic souls. He'll just fail them.

And speaking of failing people, he'll find Byron and apologize. God knows what Byron has been doing this whole time.

For now, he marks the movements of the shifting cardboard discs, along with the date and the word FINAL.

SIXTY-THREE

MORNING. ADAM STRETCHES—STIFF FROM THE COLD OF THE STORM—
and pins the curtain open to reveal a world already bathing in the
brilliant orange glow of morning. The sky an unbroken bolt of blue.
The rain just another memory to eventually forget.

Beneath him, a brand-new river laps at the banks as it travels.
The water has pushed away all the dirt and debris and flows clear. He
could bathe in it if he wants, before it recedes back into the nothing it
really was.

For now, breakfast: canned chicken soup and a breakfast bar. He
eats and watches the transparent wavelets dance and sparkle.

"Ahoy," cries someone.

Adam looks up. A bearded White man in a large, sophisticated-
looking canoe floats toward him in the distance. He wears a wide hat
and keeps the canoe on course by dipping long paddles in the water
now and then.

Adam knows doodly-squid about seafaring protocol, so he just
kind of waves back.

The man edges his canoe up to the bank and rests it there, half in
and half out of the water.

"You live here?" It's a jovial question.

"Not really," says Adam.

"You Chinese?"

"Sure," says Adam with a shrug. "What are you?"

"I'm just standard-issue White," he laughs. "I'm supposed to be Scottish French, but you know." He makes a farting sound and laughs some more. *"Ni hao."*

"Bonjour," says Adam.

"You got a good setup here," says the canoe man. "Clear views to the east where the fire came through. I don't think anyone lives over on that side if I'm not mistaken."

"It's abandoned."

"Although I thought I saw another building or something burning just a few days back."

"Probably abandoned, too," says Adam.

"Well, with this administration it's no wonder. Kinda stuff's happening all over 'cause of the Fed tinkering with things that never needed tinkering to begin with."

"Sure," says Adam.

"You got the right idea to sit tight here. No one ever goes through this neck of the woods." He grows paternal and even kind. "You got all your supplies ready? Got your guns and gold?"

"Yes?"

"Fiat money ain't worth the paper without a government. Plus we got global warming now. I'll give them that one." He glances at the river, perhaps at his long journey ahead. "You're in good shape."

"Can I ask where you're going?"

"Absolutely," he hollers. "I shot the tunnels back there. Scariest thing I ever did, but man was it a ride. This is a custom sea kayak of my very own. I have in here with me seventy-two thousand calories of durable rations in waterproof containers, plus a water purifier below deck. I am also equipped with a digital camera and solar chargers. Nice little loadout of weaponry, too. I'm taking this to Hawaii, my friend. They got uninhabited islands there. That's gonna be my setup."

You are comprehensively insane, thinks Adam. "Cool."

The man pushes off with his paddle and begins to drift away. "Stay sharp."

Adam watches him drift away. Within moments he becomes entangled in the clear lines in the water. He swears with disgust, as if caught in a sticky spider's web. He unfolds a knife, slashes about, and continues down the river.

The unmoored lines sink away and the cardboard discs, now connected to nothing, stop. Adam can only laugh. The true purpose of his apparatus has finally been fulfilled. The true purpose was to irritate the living shit out of that old guy, and they'd performed beautifully.

SIXTY-FOUR

SEA KAYAK TO HAWAII. DANG. ALTHOUGH ADAM GUESSES CRAZIER things've been done by those with enough delusion to match their will. There was that sixteen-year-old kid who sailed around the world, what's-his-name. Or that old guy who lives on that deserted Australian island, with only a dog as his company. Dog Friday? Adam laughs at these mini-memories that are not really memories, but rather optional trivia that never quite sticks and requires constant lookups in order to be fully recalled. Maybe before computers people had the ability to retain that kind of bullhonky. Maybe there was simply less bullhonky to keep track of back then.

Well, that world is long gone.

He pulls the blanket down from its pegs, leaving the shelter exposed. He folds it in half four times.

The seat cushion comes next, along with the bubble wrap. He sets those in a corner.

The cans, camping stove, clear string, and matches he lines up next to the other stuff. He sweeps the line of spent matches into his hand and casts those into the river. The vinyl banner, with its smiling faces hawking Arroyo Plato, stays in the dark where it is. Let the next guy unroll it if he wants.

He jogs the remaining sheets of cardboard and sets them back.

When he does, he notices the last one is covered with dot games. The one where player one draws a line on a dot grid, then player two draws a line, and so on, with the goal being to complete more squares than the other. Dot game? Pigs in a box?

He can't recall the name, and is fine with it.

Each completed square has been labeled by the players. There is *CLAY*. There is also a *BEN*. And a *NAIA*, and a *DAMON*, too. A little cluster of cartoon faces saying things like *chicken sticks* and *miss flower loves pizza*, each drawn by different kids. There is a moonscape with tiny spaceships taking off and landing in the midst of a space war thick with dot-dot-dot laser fire. A giant rabbit stands casting spells; a fleet of hot dogs scream *WAH HA HA*.

Adam imagines Clay's little friends swimming far away from their underwater homes one by one, and decides to keep the cardboard sheet in the basket for posterity along with the rest of his supplies there. Travel supplies, he calls them, because he'll be traveling today.

He unties the clear strings from the cinder block and lets them slink into the river. Then he heaves the cinder block to the side of the shoulder road. He leaves the metal bucket.

He sits at the faucet refilling his water containers. He could fill them with purified water from the model home's refrigerator, sure. But the ritual is quite nice. When they are topped off he closes the spigot with his wine tool, not too tight. He gives the faucet a little kick.

"Hateful creature," he says.

He brings the wine tool back up to the shelter, tells it *thanks*, and leaves it for the next guy.

But come on. There won't be a next guy.

And if there is, doesn't that mean something bad will have to happen to bring them to this place?

Sure. But still: doesn't all this stuff sitting here look so nice? It looks cozy, even. Like the next guy is already here inhabiting the space.

Let's leave them be.

Adam walks away from the shelter. The rooftops of the empty

houses peek above the cinder-block wall across the river. A crow lands on one.

"Caw," says the crow.

Adam gets on the bike and begins pedaling. Only one last thing left to do.

IT FEELS GOOD TO MOVE.

Adam glides down empty streets washed by rain and wind and now dried to black by the sun. The mint-condition bike silent and clean beneath him as he takes a turn with eyes locked onto a street sign thrust into raw earth where a sidewalk will never be.

"Seven Yucca," he says.

Around him are houses that can barely be called houses. Just frames of wood gone gray over the months. He imagines them back on day one. How fresh and bright yellow they must have been. Bursting with that lumbery smell—the fragrance of resin and burn as they were trimmed with the short screams of flashing circular saws.

But now, a stack of sheet plywood all warped beyond repair, edges flaky as baklava squares scaled up to gargantuan proportions. A nearby pile of concrete bags has melted together into one solid mass.

There it is: YUCCA ST.

"One," says Adam, pedaling steadily. "Two, three, four, five, six."

He comes to a stop, dismounts. Kicks the kickstand.

"Seven."

The house is nothing but a slab. Lumber hadn't even reached their plot. All there is are little metal mounting points still filled with yesterday's rainwater. Wires grow out of each, creating leafless, lifeless plants of your most basic artificial colors, white and red and green and black.

He climbs the porch steps. He's seen ruins where all that's left are steps leading up to an empty platform. This is like that, but in miniature.

He takes off his shoes and lines them up where the front door would have been. He removes the brass key, holds it forth. Then he steps into the home and walks, passing right through its invisible walls. Through its plumbing and wiring. All its veins and nerves and bowels.

This might've been her room, perhaps. That might have been ours. Short concrete beams rise a few inches from the surface, but even they can't adequately describe the kind of life that could have been lived there.

The beams draw themselves into the rough shape of a plus symbol near the center of the foundation, and so he chooses that as the spot. He kneels, lays down the brass key, lays a tear on top of that. He feels his mouth tighten down flat. To think, one day the money ran out and the builders had no choice but to abandon everything where it stood. It would always be better in Margot's imagination. Always be beautiful and just right.

Already his tear is evaporating under the desert sun.

"What are we gonna do," he says, "with this much goddamn house?"

PART VI

THE OCEAN

SIXTY-FIVE

THE CROSS BREEZE HOOTING LOW IN HIS EARS, THE TIRES HAPPILY crunching up the dirt road, the crisp *tic tic tic* of the hub as it pauses when he stops pedaling to coast—what had once been a tedious foot slog passes in mere minutes. Before he knows it, Adam is at the cairns far from the houses.

He stops, dismounts, and sits to drink some water from his Arroyo Plato bottle. Dozens of the rock piles still stand among the spilled remains of those that had tumbled into what now is a clear and deep river. The cairns are crafted with intent, each with a base stone shaped like a wedge to let it sit solidly upon the canted surface.

Adam stands, shuffles down the slope, and shoves a cairn over with his foot. The rocks tumble and plop with fat splashes. The crumbly sound of warm stone rolling on warm concrete is too satisfying not to kick over another. One by one he sends them down. I am the supernatural force that topples the stones. Just me. God wouldn't bother.

The carcass of the crow must be far downstream by now. Wherever this thing empties out. Or maybe it got stuck in the reeds? Anyway, the only way to be sure would be to wait for the river to shrink down to a figment again: a bone-dry fiction of a river.

Adam kicks over the last remaining stone tower and moves on.

HE BIKES FOR MILES IN SILENCE. THE CHANNEL STRAIGHTENS AND heads toward a gap between opposite sets of hills that turn out to be a pass.

He pedals and watches the pass draw closer and closer.

At one point he decides to freestyle a little and rides the bicycle on the angled slope of the channel. He turns, catches the wheel at a funny perpendicular, and would've somersaulted had he not put down a foot on the up slope—the correct side—enabling him to climb huffing to the level shoulder again. That would've been truly dumb, out here miles away from help. Like award-winning dumb.

Still, though, he can't stop smiling.

I'm having fun, he realizes.

All the platitudes are true. All that schmaltzy shit he used to dismiss with a cynic's chuff: *Live for today, it's the simple pleasures, you can't take it with you*, the stuff of throw pillows. But it's true, isn't it? Your job, your car, your house, all your crap doesn't look all that special sitting unattended under a blinding sun. It could be mistaken for someone else's stuff, even.

Things get worse when you drive that car to, say, an expensive mountain meditation retreat only to find dozens of assholes already there. How did they get there before you? Are you somehow late? Where'd they get those clothes, those shoes? Is there any place on earth you can ever be truly alone in? Will a different car get me there?

No wonder there is so much rage. The flailing tantrums of morons against the meaningless quests demanded by an indifferent universe.

No.

Stop calling them morons. They're not full of rage. They're *frustrated. Fusstrated*, Clay would say.

The road dips below a narrow service bridge. In the darkness underneath there is no sign of life, neither broken beer bottle nor used condom.

He emerges into the light again and keeps pedaling along the shimmering river. He reaches the gap in the hills, and as he passes through he sees white buildings of the city arranged in a sprawling grid before him, a vast microchip made of chalk.

SIXTY-SIX

THE DIRT PATH SLAMS UP INTO HIS TIRES AND BECOMES GLASS-SMOOTH concrete. A road appears to his right. Then a telephone pole, and a short line of parked cars before a squat, dismal warehouse. Even a few trees now. The slopes of the river channel have fallen and narrowed to create a simple square trough, not nearly as grand as the old channel.

The river path bisects a massive business park. Towers of brown and brass and amber reflect hot parallelograms of light. Adam dives into the shadow beneath a series of immense overpasses that each must accommodate ten-lane roads up above. A single keystone of daylight in the distance leads him through this sudden cavernous night. He whoops. Not for fun—he's afraid of who else might be down here. He thinks he smells urine. He whoops again. His voice ricochets back and away.

He stops in a slash of brilliant white falling from above. Like a spotlight it illuminates a padlocked gate standing amid a cloud of sparkling dust motes.

He dismounts, drinks some water. Something rumbles overhead. A truck. The rumbling crescendoes and decrescendoes just as fast, leaving only the echoing, burbling river.

The gate has been tied shut with a chain and only allows for a tantalizing, narrow gap neither he nor the bike can fit through. The gate guards nothing. It is a truly stupid gate. When he kicks it, it springs right back. That's how loose it is, like a stupid metal trampoline standing on edge. Just beyond it the path continues unobstructed.

To his right is a wall, and to his left is a sheer drop into the lightless water moving below. The edge of the gate extends some ten feet over the river channel and is crowned with spiky ironwork to discourage anyone misguided enough to climb laterally, dangling themselves over the channel and risking death. Or worse, like broken legs or paralysis. Pick whichever.

The only goddamn piece-o-shit way is up and over.

"I hate you," says Adam to the gate, and thinks.

The burbling increases in volume to match his ponderations. He lifts the bicycle. Jesus, it is not light. But he notices the back rack has a hooklike protrusion, one that matches the fence's wire gauge nicely, and nods to himself.

THEY CHASED EACH OTHER, HIS GIRLS. JUNE WOBBLED THROUGH THE water arches without touching a drop; Margot stooped to follow and got zapped with cold wet in a diagonal line across her back.

I'm giving up on shoes, cried Margot. She took hers and June's off, tossed them over.

It's a fountain! cried Adam with a laugh. Who needs shoes?

My god, June had been walking for almost two weeks by then. It changed everything.

They'd driven two hours for the butterfly pavilion, but then they ran across this fountain along the way to the entrance—and it was full of toddlers toddling about.

It's like they're drunk, said Adam. We're born drunk, and then we sober up, and when we're old we get drunk again because fuck it.

Watch your language! said Margot.

She can't understand!

I said bitch, watch your motherfucking language! said Margot with a smile. And shit!

Shit, said June.

Margot reflexively hit Adam. You started it.

Don't hit like Mama, said Adam to June, in his high singsong dad voice.

You wanna go play with the big babies? said Margot, in her high singsong mom voice.

They'd arrived late, because apparently now they were to arrive late to everything, but whatever. Look how hilarious these toddlers were, careening through arch after arch, sometimes flopping their butts right down onto a gushing nozzle! They only stopped their bumbling stumbling to stare at one another in that dumbfounded kid way.

Did you make a new friend, June bug? sang Margot. Say hi!

Adam didn't know that in five minutes the whole water park would shut off, but that didn't matter. What mattered was they'd been lucky enough to catch this moment before it evaporated into nothing. Sure, there were hundreds of other moments happening all over the park they would never be a part of. They'd caught *this* one, and it was a very, very good one, precisely because they were in it.

Adam snapped picture after picture with his brand-new, needlessly complicated camera, and they all came out blurry.

What the hell, said Adam.

Are you on shutter priority? said a voice. He looked up to see a fellow dad: cargo shorts, boonie hat, corporate tee. Camera, too. His was bigger, more expensive looking. The guy was Black. He pointed and asked,

Are those two yours?

Yep, said Adam.

Beautiful, said the dad.

In saying this, Adam knew the dad was very kindly giving him permission to point at an Asian woman in purple farmer's overalls with her weebly-wobbly mixed kid and ask,

Are those two yours?

It's like you knew, said the dad.

Then Adam did something he never did with strangers before, which was offer up a fist bump. Before June, he'd generally been ignorant of people and family. But now he knew there was a world of parents all speaking in shorthand, because that's what happened to people who all walked the same hot coals barefoot and survived to reach the other end.

But with these two parents, Adam sensed an even stronger shorthand. He wanted to ask how it'd been for them. Did they get a lot of crap? A little? Were their parents cool with everything? He typically saw more Black guys with Asian girls and almost never the other way around like him and Margot, but still. He was tickled by a ridiculous urge to give them his email address, invite them over, and become lifelong friends over the course of one loud lunch.

He turned the knob of his camera to S. Like this?

Correct, said the dad. With all this solid shade I'd keep it around one five-hundredth of a second. They're small but they move fast!

One five-hundredth, said Adam, fumbling with stoner grace. Controls are so tiny.

Right? said the dad. You get used to it. I teach photography.

He held out a business card, hesitated, then wrote on the back with a pen he kept on a lanyard like the big dorky dad he was.

That's my cell. We could do a playdate or something.

Adam studied the card for the right and proper amount of time before pocketing it. Awesome, he said.

The dad nodded at Adam's camera. Take a shot.

Adam did, and it came out perfect. Three seconds later, the fountains shut off.

Butterflies, let's go, bellowed the dad.

We're headed there, too, said Adam.

So they gathered their stuff and hip-slung their babies and hustled forth.

I'm Elias, said the dad.

I'm Ella, said the mom. This is Lily.

Ella and Elias, Margot and Adam, said Margot. Hi, Lily!

At the crystal dome entrance of the butterfly pavilion, a worker was bending down to lock the door.

No, please, cried Adam, and ran ahead. He rapped on the glass.

We just had our last timed entry, sir, said the woman. She was White, older, maybe in her sixties, a volunteer retiree in a bright teal knit polo.

Come on, said Adam. Please. It took us two hours to get here.

The woman gave Adam's wet clothes a wry look. Did you get stuck in the fountain?

Margot and the new couple approached.

Whoop, here's more of 'em, said the woman.

Normally Adam would stop to anatomize the words *here's more of 'em* for traces of racism, but he decided now was not the time. He was in the sudden grip of a strange, slightly ridiculous sense of responsibility, as if coming here were all his idea—indeed, as if he had invited Ella and Elias, as if it were his fault they'd all gotten waylaid by the irresistible water fountain. He knew this feeling made no kind of sense, and yet it drove him.

Come on, please, he said, his breath a tiny fog. Did you ever have kids? I know that's a personal question.

The woman pinned her eyebrows up with mild surprise. Yes, and I have grandkids now.

What's she saying? said Margot behind him.

Adam pressed on in a low murmur. You must be so proud.

The woman smiled as she began to transport herself away. Three girls and a little baby boy. She glanced at June and Lily. About the same age as those two.

About their age, huh? said Adam, sensing victory. Same as your beautiful adorable amazing poochie woochie grandkids?

The woman rolled her eyes: *Not fair.* Then she sighed, and Adam knew he'd won.

The woman heaved the glass open. It's your lucky day, folks.

You're the best, said Adam.

I know, said the woman.

Nice job, Dad, said Elias. He switched to a long white lens like something off the space shuttle, and narrowed his gaze at the spectrum of multicolored targets surrounding him. Ella gasped at a monarch butterfly clinging to her fingertip, then gave it a name.

Queenie, she said.

Daddy did it, sang Margot. She held up June's little hand. High five, daddy, yay.

Then she gave a grown-up kiss just for him. Best daddy ever. Who'da thought.

I hadn't, said Adam.

The four of them chased the babies while frantically catching small slices of joy for themselves, the way parents did—*stolen moments!*—and even though in just three days' time Adam would never see any of them again, that didn't matter yet. Not yet.

IN THE ECHOING DANK DARK, ADAM STUDIES THE BIKE'S BASKET AND notices it has a release mechanism. Thank God. He hooks the basket of supplies in his arm and climbs the fence easily enough. He drops to the other side, leaves the basket a safe distance down the path, and climbs back over.

Now the hard part.

He hoists the bike as high as he can and hooks it from its rear rack onto the chain fence. He lets it hang and find its center of gravity. Okay. Then he climbs a bit and, with one free hand, lifts the bike and rehooks it a few links upward.

This is going to take forever.

He takes a breath, unhooks the bike, hefts it up six or so inches, and hooks it on again. His left arm already sore. He'll have to switch soon.

Unhook, hoist, rehook, pause to take a breath. He exhales and slips, and the bike goes crashing down with him. One wheel hangs over the edge of the water channel and revolves slowly, as if wounded.

Adam's *gaddangit* reverberates throughout. He squats, searches for a drink of water. But his bottles are on the other side of the fence.

Hateful fence!

This is like a crappy little bonus ending to the grand puzzle. Here are the choices now: leave the bike and continue on foot, or—dumbass—head to the surface and call a cab home. Like what a normal person would do. There's even a utility ladder right over there, heading up and out through a tube of light.

Adam looks at the bike and the words printed on its frame. AR-ROYO PLATO VILLA ESTATES. He can leave it right here as it lies.

Seems like an indignity, though. Maybe shove it into the water? Its fall cushioned by water cradling it gently to rest at the bottom? The flow will soon dwindle to a trickle to reveal this perfectly good bike logged with water, water that will rust its joints over time.

How much time? Years of lying still undiscovered? Years of flash floods from sudden desert rains upstream followed by long dry spells, metal parts disintegrating a little more each time. The last bit of paint finally flaking off. The decal lettering sailing free into the water.

He is startled to find a tear in his eyelid. He wipes it away with exasperation. I mean just get it done already. Whatever it takes.

He drags the bike away from the edge and begins again.

He will take his time. He climbs, lifts the bike, and hooks it. Then he rests, back down on the ground if he has to, while the bike hangs perilously above him. He switches arms and climbs and keeps a sharp eye on the hook as it passes over the chain links.

The hardest part is flipping the bicycle over the top. The only way he can think to do it is to sit atop the fence, straddle it with the top pipe jammed into his crotch, and try to brace himself as best he can with legs akimbo.

He can't do this part slowly. He has to pull hard.

He counts: three, two, one! He swings the bike over. The momentum is more than he realizes, and the bike goes crashing down. He follows after, landing hard on his hip.

"Fuck me," he cries. "Fuck me fuck me fuck me."

He begins laughing quietly to himself. If he had been watching himself from afar, observing his doppelgänger engaged in this bone-headed spectacle, he would have thought: Check out this guy here. Little bit of slapstick way down here in the shadows.

His hip is probably bruised now. But the bike is fine. The thing is a tank.

He is past the gate. He will see how far the path goes, and follow it all the way to the end.

SIXTY-SEVEN

ADAM PEDALS ON, OUT OF THE DARKNESS AND BACK INTO THE SUN.
The concrete path climbs and becomes a miniature two-lane road on black asphalt, painted with official stencil: LANE BIKE. He reads it backward. BIKE LANE. The lane runs along the rear edges of people's backyards, and he can see all that is hidden in them. Children's toys, lawn mowers, bags of soil. Even a beautiful shrine to a god all made from junk glued together and spray-painted gold.

Graffiti now blankets the walls of the channel below, all of it bright and fresh and vibrant as if teenaged crews had just finished spraying the final touches on their exploding logotypes moments before the water came flooding in.

He dips under another bridge and is surrounded by towering support columns plastered with street art. A set of giant eyes watches him with all the black-and-white drama a copy machine toner can muster. A little heavy-handed, but still cool.

Ha. What the hell does he know about cool?

He knows nothing, he knows everything. Maybe it's all the same.

These bridge netherworlds are places that never got sun and will never completely dry out. They are places where—look—someone has parked a caravan of shopping carts bursting with plastic bags across the channel. A colorful string of laundry flaps in the wind like prayer flags. A leathery bearded man emerges from a stained camping tent to douse his head with water from a plastic jug. His eyes follow Adam as he does this. The water pours down his chest and spills onto the puffy winter coat he has tied around his waist. He doesn't seem to notice or care that it's getting wet. On each limb is tied a small white plastic bag.

Of all the humans on Earth, it's the old man. *The* old man.

They both stare, each thinking the other is a phantom. Fucker has the entire underside of the bridge to himself, and a whole city to scavenge from. Adam notices he's divided each concrete niche by function: a bedroom, a kitchenette, a study, even. Fuckin' fucker has conquered a small corner of the universe. He is goddamn self-sufficient.

Adam stands frozen in midpedal. The old man stands dripping with water.

One complaint to the cops and this little dominion could get dashed to bits. To think, they had once wrestled each other to the ground, man-to-man.

"Nice setup," calls Adam.

The old man wipes his face, blinks at him with sudden lucidity. "Berries." Then he becomes wild again.

Adam pedals up and out and back onto the sunny bike path. He knows exactly where he is: Hancock, just southeast of the 56 highway. The bicycle makes quiet chirping sounds as it moves. A line of pelicans drifts slow and heavy across the path. A jogger passes, music whispering from his headphones. Someone shouts, "On your left!" and a peloton of triathletes sails by.

Adam can smell the ocean.

The houses give way to open wetlands, and the channel widens again to its original sloped form to accommodate growing numbers of reed thickets and ghostly white fish streaking along its bottom. Then the flat concrete banks break apart and become a tumble of rocks stained with lichen and barnacles and occasional black crabs glistening with movement. And the waves of the water seem to flow in the opposite direction now. Like the river has changed its mind and decided to travel back inland. In the distance he sees a flock of seagulls, each lissome and white, with wings hooked like boomerangs.

A group of children pick their way across the rocky riverbank. They wear identical teal shirts, some kind of field trip. The kids are collecting stones to build little towers. Cairns. Hundreds of cairns line the river, old and new. Adam feels a pang of guilt for knocking over the ones back at Arroyo Plato. But hey: there are plenty of rocks to go around. He doesn't get what cairns mean, but as long as there are rocks and people, there will be the impulse to build little stacks.

Three children pose for a photo before their creation. They are just so sweet.

Clay, Clay, Clay. I hope you make new friends.

Adam continues on. The water deepens in color and depth, becoming a green that fades to a true Pacific blue as it travels up ahead toward the distance and empties out into a sparkling marina filled with the serene white triangles of boats. He can see a shopping area right on the water with hundreds of diners at open-air tables. Cyclists zip by everywhere now.

The bike path merges with another path, and then another, and then he finds himself among children, parents, elderly couples. Teenagers. A woman with a dog in her bike basket and a freakin' glass of wine in her handlebar cup holder.

Everyone at ease, as if living is the simplest thing in the world to do.

He reaches the edge of the sandy beach, dismounts, stretches. Beautiful day, everyone around him in beautiful motion. Adam isn't really sure what to do with himself, aside from gawking at all the people around him, so he instead focuses on the horizon.

And there, he sees a large kayak beached at the end of the jetty and a man sitting beside it on the rocks. Mr. Sea Kayak Hard Bargainer. He is smoking a cigarette.

"You're never going to Hawaii," says Adam.

"What?" says the man, against the breeze.

Adam turns his back to him and savors the sun on his face.

"Who's never going to Hawaii?" says another voice.

Adam looks over to see a woman in a smart charcoal pantsuit with an access badge clipped to a lapel, all business. She takes an earnest bite out of an ice cream bar, as if it were her last.

"Just talking to myself," says Adam.

She takes another bite and inspects the horizon and says, "I do that, too."

"Sorry," says Adam. "But where did you get ice cream?"

She keeps her gaze steady and points with her frozen treat. Over there.

"Thank you. Have a great day."

"I'm trying to, believe me," she says.

He walks to the snack truck and points at the picture of the vanilla bar coated with the chocolate shell. He opens his wallet to pay the vendor, and there are Margot and June, smiling forever.

He returns to the water's edge and takes a bite of the ice cream and swears he can see the curve of the ocean horizon. Gotta be all in his head. There's no way he could perceive that at sea level. Or is there? He takes another bite, entranced. A pelican glides into view, dips its beak into the water, and banks inland. It'd caught a fish in midflight without losing an ounce of speed.

Man, he can eat ice cream forever.

His leg buzzes. How can that be? He has no phone.

Still, he felt something.

He knows it's Byron calling.

―――――――――

ADAM KNOWS THE WAY BY HEART.

Once the silver bike path gives way to the shit-grime reality of the city streets, the bike ride becomes a thousand times less pleasant.

Cars growl up close and speed off out of spite. A pickle-nosed driver actually screams at him to get out of the road, and when he moves onto the sidewalk a yoga hag screams at him to get off that. He can't win.

But Adam doesn't give two shits, two grapes, two of anything else. He's been moving along at a fine pace, and already has reached the entrance of Byron's neighborhood. The corner with the palm tree stump someone has painted white, meaning turn right. The waxy red no-parking curb, which must be hopped, before heading straight down the surprisingly clean alley—a shortcut—lined with hulking plastic trash bins of black for trash, green for yard waste, blue for recycling. Little rectangles of orange flutter everywhere. On every pole standing, in fact.

Adam squints. Flyers?

He slows to a stop and sees his own face looking back at him.

MISSING! ADAM CHUNG

LAST SEEN DEC 12, 2010, DELGADO BEACH AREA

ASIAN AMERICAN MALE, BLACK T-SHIRT, JEANS, RED SNEAKERS, 5FT 9IN, 180LBS, AGE 37

PLEASE CONTACT BYRON AT

Adam reads the flyer again and again, with shame and panic and fear increasing each time. Finally he grips the handlebars and jackhammers the bike up and down again and again, bouncing things clear out of the basket.

"Fuck! Fuck! Fuck!"

He stands and cranks down on the pedal so hard he thinks he might break the chain. He takes on speed.

"I am a fuckin' dickskin fuckin' asshole," he mutters to himself. His self does not disagree. "Let's go, come on."

Byron's house sits amid odd little canals and bridges, some forgotten themed development from the thirties his grandmother bought into long ago. It has swans and retirees. One of them shakes a fist at him now.

"No bikes!"

Adam implores the heavens. *If you're dying for attention, man, I swear just ride a freakin' bike around town.*

"Emergency," cries Adam. He speeds past and rumbles across a narrow wooden overpass.

He turns onto the walkway—but not quickly enough, because his front wheel clonks into the sandy margin and just kind of gives up. The whole bike slides out from under him.

Forget the bike. Adam gets to his feet and sprints now, eyes fixed on the landmark of Byron's ludicrous forty-foot-tall hexagonal beam radio antenna—normally an eyesore but simply majestic today as its spidery thin metal catches the light of the setting sun.

He finds the front door, raises a fist to knock, freezes.

I'm sorry I made you worry.

I'm sorry I didn't come to you first.

I'm sorry I was so stupid.

The door opens.

Byron drops an entire glass of Tequila Sunrise, his favorite. "What the fuck."

"Shit," said Adam.

"It's plastic, it's fine," says Byron. "What the fuck, man! What the fuck! What the fuck!"

"I'm sorry," says Adam before getting his lungs crushed.

"You're alive, what the fuck," says Byron into his neck. He releases him and yells across the canal at the retiree. "He's alive!"

"That your best friend?" says the retiree.

"He's okay!" hollers Byron.

"Well, that's wonderful," says the retiree.

Byron shakes Adam's head and begins squeezing all its features.

"You look *sunburnt*. You look *skinny*." Only then does he remember to be angry. He releases him, aims a finger. "I was worried for weeks, you fuckin' dickskin—"

"—fuckin' asshole," Adam finishes. "I'm sorry. I'm sorry like you wouldn't believe."

"Set that aside for a sec," says Byron. "Tell me, *right now*, what happened to you."

"I'm a bad friend," says Adam. "I don't deserve a friend like you. I don't deserve anyone."

Byron shifts his weight, double-burdened as he is with rising anger now competing with rising concern. "Dude."

Adam swallows. No amount of swallowing can stop the tears. Clutching his hair in both fists only squeezes them out worse.

"They got taken from me, they're gone, so I figured why not," says Adam.

Byron clasps his fists and kisses a knuckle hard almost in prayer. He is barely audible. "Why not what."

Adam feels his entire body malfunction. His breathing, his phlegm, tears, heart, knees, all of it in quivering error.

"Why not me, too," says Adam.

His meaning hangs in the air, desperate for Byron to take it in.

Byron of course does. It makes him melt nearly to death.

"Come here," says Byron. Crying, too. "Come inside. Okay? Sit down."

Guided by Byron's hand, Adam floats across the threshold and slowly down onto the couch. Byron sits across. He wedges his face dry between the meat of his thumbs. He says nothing, because he doesn't have to. He just waits for Adam to begin.

But where to begin?

Begin at the end, Adam guesses. Then loop it back around again until things make some kind of sense.

"Who-oo, who? Who?" coos a bird outside.

Adam can only laugh. "Great horned owl followed me here."

Byron sniffles. "That's not an owl. That's a mourning dove."

"A mourning dove."

"They mate for life," says Byron. "We covered this at some point."

Adam cocks his head. "But I could've sworn you said it was a great horned owl."

"I must've got it wrong," says Byron, and splits in two with tears.

Adam doesn't know the exact reason yet, but he knows he will in good time. For now, all he knows is that Byron needs his friend. He needs him badly. Adam holds Byron as long as is necessary, repeating himself as many times as is necessary:

"I'm sorry, I'm sorry."

Finally Byron grows quiet. He sits up straight, beats both his knees. He lets out all the breath in his lungs. "Don't be sorry. None of this shit is your fault. That's what I keep trying to tell you."

"I know," says Adam. "So now I know, okay?"

Byron crumples his eyebrows with sorrow. *You don't yet, but I would never expect that of you.*

"I promise I'm okay," says Adam. He can't sit any longer and shoots to his feet. "Let me make you another drink."

Byron nods up at him. "Make two?"

Adam does. Everything in the kitchen is in the same places as usual. He brings the glasses over, and Byron leads him to the canal-side bench to watch the sunset, as had been his original plan before Adam came running up.

So now they resume Byron's original plan, together this time. "Much better together," says Byron.

Adam tries his absolute best to explain everything, but he seems to take forever. And Byron seems okay with that. Byron tells him it might take days or weeks or years to really explain it all. For now, this is a great start.

They haven't entirely missed the sunset. Beyond the canal's inlet and the empty sand beyond, they are able to catch the sun's final moments as it ends its turn, unobstructed but for twin brackets of distant palm trees framing its descent. All the way up until the moment it melts into the hard ocean of slate. A fiery lozenge dissolving at the edge of the world, bathing everything in golden light.

ACKNOWLEDGMENTS

This started out as a NaNoWriMo book. That stands for National Novel Writing Month, where writers around the world challenge themselves to put fifty thousand words down on paper in the month of November. If you haven't done it before, and you're curious to know what it's like to run a marathon inside your head, I highly recommend it.

Endless gratitude for my editor, Mark Tavani, who helped me unearth things buried in my own story that I hadn't even realized were there. He's either psychic or secretly running neurological tests on me in my sleep.

Jodi Reamer is the best agent a writer could dream of working with. Berries.

Thanks to the fabulous team at Penguin Putnam, including Ivan Held, Sally Kim, Ashley McClay, Alexis Welby, as well as Tricja Okuniewska, Katie Grinch, Nicole Biton, Elora Weil, and Sydney Cohen. Thanks also to Eric Fuentecilla for his beautifully evocative cover design.

Penny is a big baby dot-com, so shaddap.

My wife, Nicola, was the one who basically forced me to participate in NaNoWriMo to create what would be my first novel ever. For the entire month she single-parented our one-year-old while I spent days and nights holed up in the bedroom, writing. She was relentless in her encouragement and belief in the story. This book would not exist without her.

The first draft was finished in 2013, a year after our daughter was born and Nicola and I found ourselves effectively quarantined in the house to protect and care for the new baby. The final draft was completed in 2020, as we found ourselves literally quarantined to protect ourselves from a virus.

In a way, this book is about protection—the lengths we will go to keep loved ones safe, what happens when our efforts are not enough, and how we can possibly move on afterward. I'm writing this in 2021, during a time still plagued by isolation and uncertainty. I sincerely hope that by 2022, when this book will have hit the shelves, we'll finally be able to emerge and take in the vistas.